THIS IS THE PART WHERE YOU LAUGH

PETER BROWN HOFFMEISTER

WITHDRAWN

Alfred A. Knopf
New York

TO
ADRIANN RANTA
IRENE
26

IN THE MOUTH OF THE CROCODILE

WHEN IT'S GOOD AND DARK, I drag the two duffel bags to the edge of the lake. Out in front of me, smallmouth bass come alive on the surface of the water, and I wish I'd brought my fishing pole. But it's good I didn't—I don't want to draw attention to myself.

One of the bags twitches.

Down the east side, there's a series of wooden docks, all the same length, like gray piano keys jutting out into the lake. There's no one out on any of the docks now. I double-check each one. Make sure I'm alone.

I slide the first caiman out of its bag, the rubber bands and duct tape still in place. The caiman doesn't fight, so I start taking off the tape layers. When I get down to the big rubber bands around its mouth, I lean my forearm on its upper jaw the way the man showed me when I bought them. Then I take the final rubber bands off and jump out of the way.

The caiman opens its mouth and hisses, but it doesn't move.

"Go," I yell. "Get in the water."

It doesn't go anywhere.

I say, "Get."

But it stays where it is and hisses at me.

I back away. Take the other duffel bag up the shore a bit, far enough to give myself a little room but still close enough to see the first caiman's outline.

When I open the second duffel bag, I find that the caiman has wriggled free of most of its duct tape and rubber bands. It's clacking its jaws and thrashing around in the bag like it's trying to do a 360.

It whips its tail, and I say, "Whoa," and zip the bag closed again, feeling lucky that I didn't reach my hand in first. I step back and wait for the caiman to calm down.

After a minute, the bag goes still. I step forward, unzip it all the way, and jump back. The caiman fights and turns—flips the bag over before sliding through the opening and sidewinding toward me up the bank. The last piece of duct tape is still stuck to one of its back legs, keeping it off balance, a hitch in its step, but it's coming at me anyway.

I sprint backward, duck under a branch, trip on a root, and fall on my face in the dirt. I scramble to my feet and grab a stick, spin around to defend myself, but the caiman's not there. Not where I can see it.

I don't know much about caimans other than what I read online after I saw the ad, but I do know that they love to hunt and can run 30 miles per hour. That quickness worries me. And their jaws.

I creep back toward the water, toward the bank, holding my stick, hoping I'll see the caimans before they see me. But it's dark now and I can't tell what's a log or a clump of grass, or a small crocodile. I creep forward. Now I'm close to the lake and I can't see the first caiman, let alone the second. The duffel bags are out in front of me somewhere and the two caimans are there too, and I'm holding the stick and turning back and forth slowly, peering into the darkness all around me.

I planned on leaving no evidence, no sign that I was ever here, but I don't want to get attacked either, and it's dark now, and the reptiles are on either side of me.

I listen. Wait. Hunch down and look. But it's too dark.

I back up, watching my footing, and keep backing up, scanning for shapes in the dark. I turn at the big tree, and I'm closer to the road now, and the streetlight comes on, a yellow slant over my shoulder.

When I get to my bike, I grip the handlebars and take one last look at the lake.

That's for you, Grandma, I think, *for your last summer here.*

Because fuck cancer.

FOR MY GRANDMA

BECAUSE FUCK LIVING IN A manufactured double-wide in a trailer park after working hard her whole life as a teacher for not enough money, being disrespected by students and principals and school districts. Fuck being here in this trailer park and waiting to die.

Fuck cancer.

Because this will give her more entertainment than sitting in her room. This will give everyone along the lake some entertainment, something they need, something to talk about.

RETRIBUTION

I PEDAL THE DIRT PATH back to the pavement at the streetlight—
my empty trailer bouncing over the ruts—thinking about when
I saw the ad for the caimans posted outside the bathrooms at
the Chevron gas station, duct-taped to the wall. It read:

EXOTIC SOUTH AMERICAN CROCODILES
Growing Too Fast. Over Four Feet. Must Sell. Cheap.

And reading that was like when I change gears on my bike
and they grind for a second and it feels like the chain's going
to bind up and break, but then it slips into the right place and
suddenly I'm in a good gear and there isn't even a noise and
I'm pedaling along the road like I'm flying.

I cruise down the street to the backside of the park where I can
push through the gap in the hedge. But before I go home, I stop

at Mr. Tyler's single-wide, stash my bike and trailer under two huge rhododendrons, and sneak up to his porch.

The warm stink is awful. I hold my breath and look to see if anyone's around. Check up and down the street. Wait and listen as I crouch at the top of his front steps. The green plastic turf on his porch—shining in the light of the streetlamp—looks like layers of shaved wax.

I haven't pissed in hours, my bladder full. I whip it out and start pissing on the railings, across the front of the porch, take a step and splash some of it on the rocking chair, and as I'm finishing, turn and let the last few drops dribble down the front steps.

No one sees me, and I hop off the porch and jog back to my bike.

JEoPARDY! AND AP LIT

THAT NIGHT, BEFORE I GO to my tent, I check on my grandma. She's in bed watching *Jeopardy!*, talking to the TV. I sit next to her as she says, "What is heliocentrism?"

One of the contestants says, "What is heliocentrism?"

Then the host says, "That is correct."

I say, "Hey, Grandma, how are you feeling?"

My hand's next to her on the bedspread. She pats my fingers. "I'm doing well," she says. "Quite well."

"Really?"

She smiles at me and squeezes my hand. "I think so. As well as can be expected."

The contestant on the show picks another square and the host reads the answer. Grandma says, "Who is Henry the Eighth?"

The contestant says, "Who is Henry the Eighth?"

I say, "Is this a rerun or do you always just know the answers?"

Grandma smiles at me. "I was a high school teacher for 36 years, sweetie."

"And that's how you learned everything?"

"Well, my first school was a small school and I had to teach five different subjects while I was there, so I learned a lot along with the students." She squeezes my hand again.

I say, "Did you like teaching?"

"Yes," she says. "Definitely."

"Then tell me a story." I've always liked her stories, it doesn't matter what they're about. When Grandma and I used to go out in the canoe together, she'd tell me stories the whole time.

"Okay," she says. "Let me see. . . ." She drums her fingers on the back of my hand. I can tell she's thinking because she doesn't answer the next *Jeopardy!* clue.

"Okay," she says. "This one's from one of my last years of teaching." She shifts her shoulders. Resettles on her pillow. "I was teaching AP literature to a class of 35 students. There was this one boy, sort of like you, looked like you, had a serious face all the time like you, but he was always falling asleep in class. He was a bright enough boy, but I couldn't keep him awake when I lectured. So one day, while he was asleep, I walked right up to him and leaned in close to his face and blew on his nose. When that woke him up, I said, 'I almost kissed you. One more second, and I would have.'"

"You said that?"

"Yes. And you should have seen his face. I was almost 70 years old by then, all wrinkly and shrunken down, and he just about jumped out of his chair when he saw my face so close to his. I told him I couldn't wait for another chance to kiss him, that I would take that very next chance to plant a big wet one on his lips."

"Grandma." I shake my head. "He never fell asleep again, did he?"

"No," she says. "He almost did so many times, but then he'd sort of startle awake, and I'd see him check to see where I was in the room. Everyone else would see that too. His classmates would watch him, especially if he seemed tired. It became a sort of fun side story in that class, something that thickened the plot."

"He was probably terrified."

"He was a really nice kid. I just wanted to pull his leg a little." Grandma shifts again on her pillow, makes a small noise in her throat like she's trying to swallow something sharp.

"Are you okay?" I say. "Are you hurting a lot?"

"A little. But I'm okay." She closes her eyes.

"Do you need a pill?"

"No," she says. "I don't like the pills."

"Are you sure? You might need one."

"No thanks. I just need some sleep."

I kiss her forehead and stand up. "I'll let you rest."

When I'm at the door, she says, "Travis, you know I love you?"

I look back and she has her eyes closed, her head tilted to the side.

My eyes get itchy and I open my mouth, but I can feel how creaky my voice is going to sound, so I don't say anything.

Somehow Grandma knows I'm still in the doorway. "You sleep well tonight," she says. "36 nights in a row?"

"Yeah. Good memory."

She smiles, her eyes still closed. "Goodnight, sweetie."

"Goodnight, Grandma."

Coming down the hall, I hear her say, "What is photosynthesis?" just before the TV contestant says, "What is photosynthesis?"

When I enter the living room, I see a light, a spark, out on the back porch. I stop and watch. There's the spark again, then a flame above a pipe, and I see my grandpa's face lit by that small light. Grandpa inhales, holds his smoke, and exhales. He's standing sideways, not looking in the house but down at the pipe in his hands. He sparks the lighter and puffs again. Turns and looks out at the lake. I stare at his dark outline.

There's a paperweight on the table, smooth and round and heavy, with ZION NATIONAL PARK chiseled into it. I think about throwing it through the plate glass, watching the glass shards explode onto my grandpa. I pick it up, hold it in my hand. Then I set it down. Turn around. Go back to the bathroom and brush my teeth, wait, lean against the wall, wait until I hear my grandpa come into the house and walk past me, down the hall to his bedroom.

Then I leave the bathroom, go through the living room and out onto the back porch, through the thick marijuana smoke hanging under the eaves.

Down at my tent, Creature's left a page of his writing on my sleeping bag.

The Pervert's Guide to Russian Princesses
Princess #3 (Second Draft)

Princess Nina Georgievna, your face long enough to travel by car, your memories of your father like the color indigo at the break of midnight, executed Romanovs in 1919.

You tell me to come forward. You do not look at me as I walk around you. You hold up one finger, spin it in the air, and I keep walking.

Royal. You make your hand flat and I stop.

This is what I must do:

Lean in. A bottle of pure Mexican vanilla in your purse, I smell the scent behind your ears.

Stand behind you and peel the dress off of your shoulders. Run a finger down the ticked line of your spine.

Use my thumbs to rub the knots in your trapezius muscles.

Make up stories about your father being alive and well, hiding in Northern Europe, in Sweden, in an apartment in Stockholm.

Tilt your head back and suck softly on your neck as your breathing gets heavy.

Let you take my hand and guide it down the loosened front of your undergarments where there never was a bra.

Turn you around. Get down on my knees as you hike up your hem, the lace sliding to the tops of your thighs.

SWIMMING IN CIRCLES

SUNDAY EVENING. I WALK ALONG the shoreline north, toward where I released the caimans, making my way slowly through the bigger blackberry growths, ducking under vines, and stepping through the tall grass where it's grown over the trail.

I spook a gopher snake, five feet long and bulging with a rat. The snake slides out in front of me on the narrow trail, the rodent dragging along in the middle of its body, and I smile and walk behind it until it cuts a hard left into the heaviest of the blackberry thickets and I can't see it anymore.

At the small beach where I released the caimans, I find only two rubber bands and a piece of duct tape. No duffel bags. I look around, but they're nowhere. Someone must have taken them. I pick up the rubber bands and the duct tape and put them in my pocket.

Searching the shore, I expect small animals ripped apart and hundreds of crocodile footprints. But there are no tracks, no clues. I crouch down where the mud meets the round rock, but I don't see anything. I check in the bushes, the reeds at the lake's edge, and under the willows. I crawl beneath the blackberry overhang and start to worry. What if the caimans died right off? What if that first night was too cold even though it's summer?

I look up and see a girl walk out onto one of the docks in front of me, a few docks down. I've never seen this girl before, a teenage girl, thin, athletic-looking. Tall. Straight dark hair. I watch her walk to the end of the dock, bend down, and put one of her hands in the water. She's on her knees.

It's shadowy where I am, underneath the blackberry bushes in the late evening, but I scoot back anyway, deeper into the darkness. I watch the girl and wait to see what she'll do.

I want her to take off her shirt, to strip down to a bikini or a bra or something like in a movie, but she doesn't. She sees something on the water and leans forward. Hesitates at the end of the dock, then splats into the lake face-first, like a dive but from her knees, fully clothed, landing on her face, not smooth at all. She comes up to the surface right after, swims out and circles around.

I scoot forward, trying to see what she's doing.

She circles some more, reaches and turns. Swims a few strokes and reaches again. I can't see what she's reaching for. I stand to get a better view, a blackberry vine catching in my hair. I pull the vine to the side and step forward, almost out of the shadows.

The girl lurches, brings her hands together like she's catching a handful of water. She swims back to the dock, holds on to the wooden edge with one hand, and puts something in a bag with the other hand. Then she pulls herself out of the water, her clothes clinging to her skin. She stands up, and I wish it were lighter out, a little earlier in the evening, so I could see her better.

The girl grabs her bag, walks up the dock to the stairs on the hillside, jogs those steps, and disappears into her backyard.

I wait. Hope she'll return. But she doesn't. I watch the empty dock as it gets darker.

I walk back along the gravel path to the end of the blackberry overhangs, where the dirt trail is wider. There are three old trailers at the north end of the park, then the mobile homes, six in a row along the west shore before my grandparents'.

POET ONE AND TWO

MONDAY MORNING. THE ALARM ON my watch beeps and I push the button to turn it off. 6:15. I'm tired but I roll to my knees, unzip my tent door, and crawl out. Reach back for my socks and shoes, and put them on. Then I grab my basketball and dribble over to Creature's house, sit on his porch steps, and try not to think about sleep. Instead, I focus on my summer goals:

1. Build a better-than-50%-shooting-percentage midrange game.
2. Handle the ball more securely, work on dribble skills, especially on my left.
3. Get a lot stronger (do push-ups and pull-ups).

Creature arrives a few minutes later. He takes his paper-route bag off his shoulder. Slings it down next to me.

"Okay," I say. "Let's do this?"

"Travis, baby, I'm tired." Creature leans and stretches his

hamstrings. "Let's just sleep for a while. We can work out later."

"No. Damian Lillard was the first person to show up at the gym every day in college. We gotta be like that."

Creature rubs his eyes. "Sleep for two hours, then go at 8:30?"

I try to palm my basketball, but it slips. I keep trying.

Creature says, "Or we could just work out at night?"

"Creat, you're not even playing AAU this summer. You have to be more disciplined."

"But I'm a poet," he says, "and poet two-guards are miraculous."

"I can't remember. What did that announcer say at the Vegas tourney?"

"He called me the Cutthroat Creature on the Court."

"Right. So 'cutthroat' means you'd slit a throat to dominate. And summer workouts are like slowly slitting everyone else's throats. You'd be the only one living." I smile at Creature. Happy with myself. I don't usually say things so poetically.

"Whatever," he says.

I spread my hand wider on my basketball. I can almost palm it now, but it slips again.

"Here," Creature says, and takes the ball. "Dig your thumb in like this." He palms my ball right-handed, then left. Then hands it back to me. "Have you started that book I left for you?"

"The *Drown* one?"

"Yeah. The story collection."

"I don't know if—"

"No." He snaps his fingers and points at me. "You want me

to do workouts in the early morning? Then you have to develop your mind in return. Who's the teacher now, baby?"

I shake my head.

He says, "A great point guard is a baller *and* a thinker. A literary genius. A Method Man on the court."

I spin my ball in my hands. "You be the team's poet, and I'll get my hands dirty. Dive on the floor. Make hustle plays. We're good that way."

"No," Creature says. "No, no, no. We've got to both be poets. We need a backcourt full of literary thinking if we're going to run the pick-and-roll. You know what I'm saying?"

"You sound like my grandma."

"Then your grandma has good taste. She likes real literature. And anyway, that book I gave you is written by Edwidge Danticat. She's sick." Creature holds out his fist for me to tap it.

"Fine," I say, "I'll read the book. But that means you have to come train with me right now."

Creature comes back out of his house wearing shorts, carrying his basketball and two Rice Krispies Treats. He hands me one of the treats. "Breakfast of champions?"

I tear open the blue cellophane and eat as we start dribbling down the road.

I say, "All left-handed on the way there."

Creature says, "I was already dribbling left."

We step through the bushes and hop the wall, cross the little bridge to Ayres Road. When we get to the north end of the lake, Creature picks up his dribble. Stares at the water.

I pick up my dribble too. Think about the caimans. Wonder if they're eating yet. Wonder if they're building a nest or hiding out somewhere. Then I think about the girl, the girl in her wet clothes, how athletic she looked. I wish again that she'd taken her shirt off, that I could've seen a little more of her, or that I was closer to her dock when she was out there.

Creature says, "I'm never going to understand it."

"What?" I say. I'm still thinking about the girl.

He points to the west side of the lake, then the east. "How can half of this lake be for rich people and half of it be for trailer-park trash?"

"To be accurate," I say, "it's mostly elderly trailer-park trash."

"Right. Elderly trash. Whatever. Half's for rich and half's for people in trailers and mobile homes, single-wides and double-wides." Creature has his basketball resting on his hip, and he rolls it up and palms it. Holds it out in front of him. Then he says, "Disparities of wealth and power in America, and right here, an example of disparate living situations."

"Damn." I shake my head. "What did you score on the verbal part of the SATs, Creat?"

"790, baby. I missed two analogies, or as I like to think of it, I found different analogous connections."

I dribble through my legs. "What was your math score on that?"

"Let's not talk about math." Creature hocks a loogie and spits it onto the cement. "Math is for followers, for sheep, for people who are obsessed with right and wrong, with black and white. And since I'm not naturally inclined to racism, I don't enjoy mathematics." He smiles.

I go around my back with my basketball a couple of times. Roll my neck. Say, "Did you even score 500 on that math section?"

18

"Not even close." Creature laughs. "Thankfully, I didn't need that to qualify D-1, since it combines with reading to make your overall score."

I dribble low, drop my knee to double-dribble off my shin, AND1-style, and jam my thumb on the ball. "Ooh." I shake my thumb out. Flex my hand.

Creature says, "You can tell a man by his hands, right?" He spreads his fingers, the brown skin on the backs of his knuckles laced with light-colored scars. "See all of these?" he says. "Pride, that's all. Good pride in games. Bad pride at parties."

I say, "Well, there are a lot of dickheads out there."

"Maybe true. But also maybe we fight too much? Maybe some of those dickheads aren't worth the scars on the backs of our knuckles?" Creature holds his ball up above his head, pressing it like he's grabbed a rebound in traffic. "Keep your elbows out. Sharp as broken bottles." He drops the ball and starts his dribble again.

I dribble with him. "I got Mr. Tyler's porch again last night."

Creature laughs. "You think he knows what's causing that bad smell?"

"I don't know what he's thinking."

"Well, we better keep it up," Creature says. "I actually hold my piss sometimes just to let him have it. It's like a special gift from me to him."

"Yeah, last night it felt like I pissed a gallon when I finally let it go. I even got his rocking chair."

"Nice," Creature says. "Mr. Tyler deserves a healthy gallon of our love."

I'm alone when I play.

That's how it was at the court behind the motel where we

moved when I was eight, and that's how it is now. I'm alone. Even in games, it's like no one else is on the court with me. I ran into a moving screen once in a game in sixth grade, an obvious offensive foul, and it surprised me because until that moment I was playing the game by myself. I didn't see the other players until I ran into one of them. The man I was guarding wasn't even a whole person in front of me, he was just hips and the ball, and that's all I saw when I guarded him. I ran into his teammate on that screen, and my eyes flashed open, or I guess my eyes opened wider than they were before. Then I saw people everywhere, but just for a second.

They went away again as soon as I got to the free-throw stripe on the next possession. I toed the line, dribbled twice, spun the ball in my hand, brought it up, and exhaled. That's how it is for me. When the ball is in my hands, it doesn't matter. Nothing.

My hands are loose.

I don't need to steal anything.

I don't need to hit anything.

Nothing matters except whether or not I can make that play. Can I split the double team to get the ball across in under 10? Can I head-fake in the paint to catch the big on the intermediate? Can I dime the no-look bounce pass on the pick-and-slip?

I have teammates and I'm a true point. I love to pass, so this might not make sense to anyone, me being alone out there. It probably doesn't. I guess other basketball players don't think like that. Maybe, or maybe not. I've never heard anyone talk about the game the way it seems to me. But when my game's going, that's how it feels. What happens when that ball leaves my hands is no longer real. Once that ball's gone and I cut to the open space or I set a pick on the weak side, all I'm doing is moving through the labyrinth.

Creature slows every once in a while to run dribbles behind his back, always left to left, over the top, through his legs, and back to his left with a spin. I don't spin or do crossovers or anything fancy, just work not to lose my dribble and keep my head up.

Creature says, "You're gonna be the top point guard in the league this winter."

"If they let me play again."

"Forget about that. They'll let you play. Our team needs your playmaking and hustle."

"Maybe."

"Don't worry about that, baby. They'll forget about that little thing."

"That little thing?"

"Okay, that big thing," he says. "And maybe they won't forget about it, but they'll get past it, you know? I'll talk to Coach. I'm a senior leader now. I'll say that you're our best sophomore, and—the truth—you're our second-best player."

We jog and dribble down Gilham to the crossing at the skate park. There are double rims there, and we practice dribbling out of phantom traps, running behind our backs to cross center court, then right and left layins. We take turns.

When it's shooting time, we don't talk. That's my rule. I say, "A shooter has to cancel everything out. No talking. No whining. No excuses. Kobe Bryant made 2,000 shots per day when he was building his shot. *Made* 2,000. So *taking* 500 is the least we can do."

Creature doesn't like the no-talking rule, but he shrugs. "I guess you're my point guard."

We go to opposite rims and do our work.

After shooting, we meet in the middle to finish with push-ups. Cut-downs. Creature beats me on every set.

By the time I get to four, I'm struggling to do a single push-up. My shoulders are twitchy and my chest is burning.

Creature's already finished. He says, "You're looking a little shaky there, baby. Come on now."

I do the last few push-ups one at a time, resting on my knees between each one, and when I'm finished, the fronts of my shoulders are locked up. I say, "It feels like someone's driven nails into them." I shake out my arms while I sip water at the drinking fountain.

Creature says, "Pull-ups tomorrow, right?"

ANTIFREEZE

TEN YEARS AGO, MAYBE, WHEN I was about six, I wasn't angry yet, just little, and I kept stealing the tubes because I kept finding them. I hid them underneath the mattress that I shared with my mom in our motel room on 7th Street out in West Eugene.

My mom would look for them, and she wasn't happy about it because she thought she'd lost them. She threw our stuff around the room, our duffel bag, the backpack with my toys in it, the towels. She slid our one-burner hot plate to the side, rifled through her purse, looked behind that one big picture she had of a green field edged with white-barked trees. She picked up the lamp and checked underneath. Slammed it down and the lightbulb broke. She said, "Where the . . ." Then she saw me watching her and she said, "I'm sorry. I'm just really . . . I'm sorry."

I didn't give the tubes to her. Not even when I saw her like that, angry and desperate. She didn't know I had them, and I didn't want her to know because I liked having them. I knew they were important even before I knew what they were, before I saw her use one, and I guess I wanted to have something that she loved that much.

Then I saw her use one and it wasn't what I expected. She thought I was asleep and she sat back against the wall and laid everything out like she was a doctor on a TV show. She looked like she was about to do a surgery. My head was on the pillow and I squinted to watch each step as she did it, how she went through the whole process, and then I knew what the tubes were, what I'd been collecting. Sort of.

I didn't know why her eyes closed while she did it, or why her mouth opened and stayed open afterward, or why she breathed like she did.

Then she'd stop breathing those big loud breaths, but her mouth would stay open and her head would roll around on her shoulders like the wires that held it on her neck were connected too loose, like her head might fall off if she stood up quick.

Sometimes, when I knew she was passed out, and that she'd be passed out for a while, I'd take my collection of tubes from where I kept them hidden between the mattress and the box spring. I'd lay them all out, put the sharp ends one way like compass needles pointing north. Or I'd make a little tipi out of all of them, crisscrossing the needles at the top, pretending that someone lived inside that tipi.

It was always the future in my game, when people lived in all-plastic houses, and the man who lived under my tubes was the man named Zeus who lived behind the motel Dumpster. Zeus wore a purple tutu and begged for money, but always threw the pennies back at anyone who gave them to him. He kept the silver change. I never gave him anything, and sometimes he grabbed my arm and held me there and flipped up his tutu, and I hated when my mom asked me to take out the garbage because I worried that Zeus might grab me. In my game, when I built a shelter with my tubes, the tubes would always collapse, and Zeus would be crushed inside. Sometimes I'd have Zeus screaming and dying slowly, or sometimes he'd die without screaming, and he'd just gasp and gasp for air and I'd wait for him to get quiet. My mom had told me how to call 911, but I never called 911, not in one of my games and not for real, not even if Zeus held my wrist, not even if my mom was passed out and I was worried she might not wake up.

One night, my mom fell asleep right after she used a tube, and her head went loose and she slumped against the wall. I got up from bed and walked over to her. She still had the big rubber band around her bicep, the tube hanging from her forearm. So I pulled it out. Then I undid her rubber band and sat down on the floor next to her. I set the tube down in front of me and tied the rubber band around my left arm, using my teeth at one end like I'd seen my mom do. Then I picked up the tube.

I pumped my fist and held the tube in my right hand, waited for the vein to rise on my left forearm. Then I set the sharp end of the needle there, on top of the vein. When I pushed it, it didn't go in right away because I was scared and I didn't push it hard enough. I was worried about how much the needle might hurt, but then I pushed harder and the skin came up into a small mound, and the needle slid into that mound. I felt the prick of it and I didn't like the feeling, but I did it anyway, and I pushed the needle to the end.

Then I waited.

Having the tube there didn't feel like anything and I didn't breathe hard. I knew I'd skipped some steps in the ceremony, but that didn't matter to me because it didn't hurt too much to have it there in my arm, and I wasn't sure I wanted to breathe like my mom did anyway. That breathing she did always made my stomach feel tight, like just before I threw up.

I was next to my mom on the floor, and that was good. The tube and the rubber band were just like she did them, and I leaned against her body and I felt her body rising and falling with her breathing as she slept there. My breathing became her breathing, the same rhythm, and I fell asleep leaning against her.

I woke up to her shaking me.

She screamed, "What the fuck did you do?" Then she slapped me. It was worse than when Zeus caught my wrist. Worse than when he flipped up his tutu.

My mom pulled the tube out of my arm, quick, and threw it against the wall, and I hoped for some reason that it wouldn't break. I thought to myself, even in that moment, that I could find it later and put it with the others as long as she didn't break it.

She dug her fingernails into my shoulders and shook me, shook me four or five times, and she was crying, and her mouth was twisted like she was one of those witches from the Disney movies, and I looked at her teeth where the brown and yellow lines outlined each individual tooth. I tried to pull away from her, but her hands were too strong and she yelled, "What the hell is wrong with you? I'm not joking. Tell me."

I said, "I just . . ." But I didn't say anything else, and I wished I hadn't fallen asleep. I wished she wasn't screaming like that. I wasn't sorry that I'd stuck the tube in my arm because it hadn't really hurt, and I'd wanted to know how it felt for a long time. But I was sorry I'd gotten caught.

My mom stopped shaking me and hugged me instead. She started rocking and hugging me, and she was crying now, and she hugged me so tight that I had to turn my head to the side to get a breath in. Her body odor was like cooked onions at Taco Bell. She was sobbing and her voice sounded wet, garbled, and she said, "I'm quitting. Don't you even think for one second that I'm not quitting because I am." Her body shivered and she sobbed some more. "I'm done, you know? I'm done right now. Right here. I'm done."

That's what she said, but she was never done.

PABLO NERUDA

MIDDLE OF THE DAY. WE'RE at my grandparents' house. Creature says, "I found a new princess."

"You what?"

"Super hot, baby. From the 14th century. Her name's Saint Anna of Kashin."

"You found a hot 14th-century princess?"

"Gorgeous." Creature winks at me. "At least that's how she looks in the oil painting. She has a halo of gold around her head. It's like a smear of metal. Can you imagine making out with someone who has a halo of gold around her head?"

I say, "You know there's a small chance that she might not've had that halo of gold in real life."

Creature spins his basketball on his index finger, taps it with his left hand, and keeps the ball spinning. "I believe in halos. You believe what you want to believe, and I'll believe what I want, all right?"

I try to spin my ball on my index finger, but I don't have

that trick down yet. The ball keeps falling off one way or the other.

Creature says, "And I'm putting this girl in the guidebook for sure. She's a great addition. Did you read those pages I wrote the other day?"

"Yeah."

"And what'd you think?"

"It's weird, man."

"So?" he says.

"So the book's weird. And it's written different from how you talk too."

"I know, baby." Creature raises an eyebrow. "That's the magic of the guidebook. It brings out the literary man in me. The Pablo Neruda: *Body of a woman, white hills, white thighs, you look like a world, lying in surrender.*"

"Creat, I think you might be messed up in the head."

"You think?" Creature pivots around an invisible defender, then dribbles through his legs. He says, "I know what I like, and that's all. Basketball and books. Nothing else." He pulls up for a jump shot but doesn't let the ball go. He says, "Hey, you want to play under the bridge?"

"Sure, if there's a game."

"Should be," he says. "I'll catch you later, then?"

"Yep, and good luck with that Russian halo girl."

"Oh, don't even worry about that. She's mine already."

WALK OUT SLOW

LITTLE THINGS MOSTLY. THAT'S ALL. And I don't even know why. I like the feeling of it, I guess, that moment when I have it in my hand and I slide it into my pocket. Like there are guitar strings inside of me and the lowest string is vibrating that one deep sound.

Doesn't matter what it is, a candy bar, a key chain, a Christmas ornament. It doesn't have to be expensive. I don't care about that. Sometimes after I walk out and I don't get caught, I throw whatever it is in the bushes. I usually feel bad about it later, feel like something's wrong with me, but the next time I'm in a store, I get that urge again, and I start to ask myself, *What if I just walked out? What if I just put this in my pocket? Or even better, what if I held it in my hand and walked out so smooth and so slow that no one even noticed?*

THIS IS WHAT WE HOLD

SOMETIMES, WHEN I CLOSE MY eyes, I see your hands: puffy, wind-burned, pink-cracked, yellow seeping at the edges of the cracks. Too much outdoor living, outdoor cooking, outdoor sleeping in urban filth. Too little hand-washing.

Those same small hands I've always known, needle-scraped, nettle-scraped, black gunk under the fingernails, over-grown fingernails, broken fingernails with thick edges, nails jagging up and down like a hedge trimmed by a drunk.

I look at my hands. Think about what's fair and unfair. Wonder if I deserve the hands that I have: 2-in-1-oil-marked hands and imperfect, but clean enough. No infections. No pain. Nothing to worry about when I pull them out of my pockets, make food, or grip a basketball.

I wonder if we're given our hands, if the hands we'll have in our adult lives are there from our births, waiting for us, waiting for our futures. Or if our hands are a choice? A series of choices? And if so, are your hands a choice?

This is what I ask: Would anyone choose your hands?

GREEN

My GRANDPA'S IN THE STUDY, rooting around in a drawer. I can't hear if my grandma's up.

I say, "Hey," but Grandpa doesn't hear me. He probably doesn't have his hearing aids in yet. I walk past him into the kitchen.

I crack an egg into a cup and slug it down. Then I think about how many grams of protein I need to get bigger, to be as strong as Creature, so I crack another egg and drink that too. Then I pour some Cap'n Crunch in the cup, add milk, and get out a spoon.

My grandpa comes in and sits down across from me. He's putting his hearing aid in his right ear. He says, "How many nights in a row now?"

I swallow a bite of cereal. "Today's June 28th, so 38 nights so far."

He nods. "And what's your goal?"

"100 straight." I don't know why I do these things, but I always have. I make little goals for myself, little challenges. And when I think of something, I have to do it.

"Camping out 100 nights, huh?" Grandpa puts his other hearing aid in. "I never did something like that."

I take another bite. Talk with my mouth full. "Me either, until now."

Grandpa smiles. The morning version of him. Opposite of the night version. He picks up the paper and reads the City/Region section while I eat the rest of my cereal. I say, "Is Grandma up yet?"

"No. She had a rough night."

"Did she throw up a lot?" I go back to the cupboard for more Cap'n Crunch, add another egg, mix the yolk and cereal with the tip of my spoon, and picture the pounds spreading across my muscles.

Grandpa must not have heard me. I didn't realize that he'd been reading my lips before. He sometimes puts his hearing aids in but forgets to turn them on. I lean under the cupboard so he can see my mouth. "Did she throw up a lot?"

"Throw up? Yes," he says. "She threw up until, maybe . . . two a.m.?"

I push my cereal down into the milk with my spoon. Slurp a little. Go back to the table.

Grandpa says, "How many lawns are you mowing today?"

"Three."

"On the far side?"

"Always," I say. "No one over here can afford to pay."

Grandpa nods his head. He folds the newspaper and flips

it. "Did you see that someone moved into that Sullivan house last week?"

"Yep." I take another bite of cereal.

"Are you going to offer to do their lawn too?"

I take a bite and think about the girl on the dock. Say, "I probably should."

EDGING

FROM MY TENT, IT'S ONLY 300 yards to the back lawns of the nice homes across the lake, but since there's no direct access from our trailer park to the Gilham neighborhood, I have to bike half a mile on Green Acres, then half a mile up Gilham to get to the big houses on the far side.

My Schwinn is a steel frame, strong enough to pull the mini-trailer loaded with the lawn mower, weed whacker, trimmer, gas can, oil can, hand clippers, and debris buckets strapped down with bungee cords.

I don't knock on the door at my first house. I just start weed-whacking. The owners and I already have an agreement set up, so I do my work whether or not they're home. I know they'll pay me later, and they'll pay me well too. Good tippers. So I weed-whack, edge, then mow over the top.

Before I go to my second job, though, I stop at the house that the Sullivans used to own. I knock once and wait. No one comes. I consider leaving, but there's a car in the driveway, so I knock again.

I'm about to leave when the door swings open. It's the girl. She's my age, give or take a year, tall, near my height, 5'9". Real pretty but with a scar on her face, under her eye, a big scar, maybe two inches across then down another inch, like an L turned on its side.

She's staring at her phone, and she doesn't look up when she opens the door, just says, "Yeah?"

I hesitate.

She has tan skin with straight black hair pulled up the way soccer players do with the double Nike headbands, and she's one of those girls that cuts the collars out of her T-shirts. One side of her wide-open collar is off her shoulder, her pink bra strap crossing her collarbone into her shirt, and I follow that line down and look at her breasts. I try not to linger on them too long, but I check them out, and they're nice too. Then I look back up at her face, high cheekbones and that scar.

I can't see her eyes since she's still looking at her phone screen.

She says, "Do you need something?"

I feel scroungy in my stained work shirt, and I wish I'd showered that morning after playing basketball. The carpet on the stairs behind the girl is white. The entryway floor is polished hardwood. Even the porch I'm standing on is clean and swept. I wonder if I'm dropping grass cuttings on the porch right now, wonder if I should sweep the porch if I earn the job.

I say, "Is your mom or dad home?"

"No," she says. She's scrolling the touch screen with her finger, running through Facebook or something. She has a brace on her right knee. Strong legs. Thin ankles.

I say, "Will you give them this flyer for me?" I hold out the paper that my grandma and I typed up together.

The girl takes the flyer and I see her look at my hands, then stop and take another look. She glances up at my face before going back to her phone. She says, "I'll give it to them." She turns and catches the door with her heel. Pivots to shut it.

I take a step back so the door doesn't hit me in the face, and it's good I do, because when that door closes, it slams so hard it sounds like something breaks inside the house.

I smile.

I don't know why, but I've never minded when a pretty girl is a little rude at first. I like that edge. It reminds me of basketball, how you have to scrap a bit if you want to win.

I think about the girl as I work the next two yards, go through what I know about her: that scar, that pink bra strap, the way she swam in her clothes, her breasts, her legs, her knee brace, that quick cut of her green eyes.

LOSING

SATURDAY. I GO DOWN TO the middle school to see if anyone's playing on the outdoor courts, but the courts are empty. I dribble and shoot, do three sets of jump lunges and calf plyometrics to help build my vertical, and picture dunking while I do the sets.

Lots of guys who are 5'9" can dunk—and some guys, Nate Robinson for example, can throw down at that height—so it's annoying that I still can't. I'm close, and that's good. I can grab the rim now, and if I go up hard, I can slide the ball across the top of the rim. But mostly I get rim-checked on the front edge. Part of my problem is that I can't quite palm the ball, so I promise myself I'll do grip strength on my Gripmaster before I go to sleep.

On the way home from the school, I see a sign tacked to three consecutive telephone poles. I stop and dribble in place while I read the sign. It says:

LOST DOG
MINIATURE TERRIER—NAMED MILO
LAST SEEN NEAR AYRES LAKE
CALL (541) 521-3574

I guess I should feel bad, because I'm pretty sure I know what happened to that dog, but I don't. People lose dogs all the time, and usually to nothing as exciting as South American crocodiles. I lost a dog once, and it was messed up, and I was really sad for a while, but then I thought about it and realized that losing is all there is in life sometimes. Sometimes we just lose and lose and lose and there's nothing we can do about it, so I guess I'd rather be eaten by a crocodile than get dog leukemia or have old-age dog hip problems or some shit like that. At least this dog got to go out fighting for his life.

FISHING

I WALK DOWN TO THE lake and look at the water. It's greener lately. More algae. I haven't seen or heard anything since I released the caimans, and I'm just guessing they ate that dog, but I'm pretty sure. I read online that they need warm water and warm weather year-round, that they don't live this far north even in captivity, so I know that they might not survive for too long. But it's hot now, hot every day, and they have a chance to do well, at least for the summer, and this summer's all I need: a couple of evenings in the boat with Grandma, a few stories, something for Grandma to hear about, something interesting for her neighbors to tell her this last year.

We keep a canoe locked up near my tent. I undo the combination lock, take the chain off, flip the canoe over, pull fistfuls of clump grass to wipe out the spiderwebs. Then I go up to the porch to grab paddles, tackle, and my fishing pole from the trunk by the back door. Grandpa left half a bag of Doritos out on the picnic table next to his pipe, and I grab the chips too.

I strip off my shirt and throw it in the bottom of the canoe before dragging the boat to the water. I don't want to sweat through my shirt right before dark, before the day cools off.

I slide the bow of the canoe into the water, then the rest of the hull, weighting the stern on the shore rocks. I put my left foot in and kick off, easing over the shelf into the deep. That's my favorite moment of canoeing, the moment when the boat is floating for the first time and the whole thing rocks back and forth to find its center of balance. I like to wait and see how far the canoe will drift in a line, where the wind is blowing, and what'll happen if I don't paddle. It reminds me of that feeling I'd get when I was a kid and my mom was passed out and it was nighttime, and I knew she wasn't waking up for a long time. I'd sneak out of the motel room, down the hall to the stairwell, and out the front lobby. Then I'd walk down 7th Street, past the women in short skirts and fishnet stockings, the men drinking 40s out of paper bags. I knew some of them, and sometimes they'd wave at me or give me a look like I wasn't supposed to be out after dark.

I'd go in the 7-Eleven and wait until the clerk wasn't watching me. I'd walk up and down those aisles until I could slide something in my pocket and walk to the door without anyone seeing me. Then I'd be back out on the street, cruising along in the dark, more traffic at night, with the smells of car exhaust, motor oil, Subway, and Taco Bell mixing together in the night's air.

This evening, the lake is still, no wind, and the canoe cuts straight and slow across the deep. I paddle out to the center, looking across to the east side, to the long lawns behind the big houses, the wooden gazebos, and the plank-board docks that run 50 feet out into the water. Five of them have small sailboats tied to their moorings, but nobody else is out on the lake with me.

I eat handfuls of Doritos and wash them down with water.

I tie a rubber worm on and jig for smallmouth. Every once in a while, I paddle and watch the tip shiver with the weight of the canoe's movement. I paddle north, where the algae fields aren't as thick, where everything stays less boggy. It's an hour before I catch a fish, and the bass I do catch isn't big. It fights hard, but it's medium-smallish when I bring it in. I pull the hook with needle-nose pliers, hit the fish on the gunnel, and throw it in the bottom of the canoe to fillet and eat when I get back home. Breaded, that fish might make half of a meal.

I paddle back to the middle of the lake and jig some more, this time shipping the paddle, bobbing the rod in my hands, letting the canoe move with the wind. It's late evening now and the wind picks up, running north and west. The canoe pushes with the wind, and I hope for one of the rare bigmouth that feed in the open spaces late in the evening. I cast out into the hole between algae fields, jig and reel, and cast again.

I'm watching the tip of my rod, focused on the last eyelet, waiting for that hit on the rubber worm when the stern of the canoe clunks against something solid and the boat tips and I overcorrect and slip and fall into the bottom. I lie there for a second and hear someone laughing at me. When I sit up, I see it's the girl. She still has her soccer-player headbands on and her phone in her hand. She says, "You actually just about went in."

"Yeah," I say. "I was letting the canoe drift." I lean and grab the side of the dock. Hold myself there. "I was jigging for bass."

"Bass?" she says.

"Yeah." I pull myself onto the dock and stand up. "Bass." I hold out my hands. My hands are dirty and reek of fish.

The girl tilts her head. Makes a face. "I don't like bass."

"No?"

"No, I actually hate them."

"Why?"

She shrugs. Doesn't explain.

We stand there. She looks at her phone.

I say, "I'm Travis."

She's still looking at her phone. "Natalie," she says. She squints, looking at something on her screen, and the scar under her eye shivers.

With her looking down like that, I can check her out some more. So I do. She's strong, good shoulders, good quads. I can tell she works out. Plays a sport. And she still has that loose, cutout T-shirt on. I like that. Right now I can see the lacy top of one side of her pink bra. If the shirt was a little looser I could see the rest.

She adjusts her collar. "Are you staring at my fucking breasts?"

"No."

She turns off her phone. Looks right at me. "You weren't staring at them?"

"I don't know. Maybe?"

Natalie looks me up and down. I don't have my shirt on, and I look at my stomach and see a green line going across below my ribs, a mark from the dry algae on the bottom of the canoe. I must have smeared it on myself when I flipped the canoe over before I put it in the water. I rub at it with the tips of my fingers but it just smears wider.

Natalie giggles.

I want to ask her why she swam in her clothes the other night, why she was swimming in circles. But I don't. Instead, I say, "Do you want to go out in the canoe with me?"

"No," she says. She looks at her house, then back at me. She's facing the last rays of sunlight and I see that her eyes have flecks of yellow and orange in the green, like shards of campfire.

"Are you sure?"

"Yeah," she says. "I really have to go." She looks at something on her phone. Presses a few buttons with her thumbs. "I should go now."

"Okay."

"And you should probably paddle back. I don't think my stepdad would like you boating up to his dock and just—" She stops talking. She's looking behind me.

I turn around. My canoe's drifted away. The wind must have shifted, and it pulled the canoe out 30 or 40 feet from the dock. "I better . . ." I look at Natalie, back at the canoe. I take two steps and dive in, breaststroking under the water to try and reach the canoe in one effort, hoping to impress her. I come up, turn the canoe around, sidestroke it back to the dock. But when I get there and pull myself out of the water, Natalie's already walking away, almost to the shore.

I say, "See you later?"

She puts her hand up and waves, but doesn't look back. I watch her walk to the stone steps at the start of the hill, watch her jog up the cut steps on the hillside, the muscles in her legs flexing, her butt tightening with each step. She gets to the top of the steps and passes the two stone lions at the back end of the yard. Then I can't see her anymore.

I shiver.

I don't feel like fishing now. I get back in my canoe and paddle across the lake, beach the canoe on the gravel, and drag it up by my tent. I pull out my gear and the one bass, then flip the canoe, slide my gear and the paddles underneath, and go up to the house to cook the fish. I cook it in Krusteaz pancake mix and butter the way I learned to cook fish at the wilderness experience for troubled teens. I eat the bass with a few Ritz crackers and a glass of whole milk, and after I finish eating and washing my dishes, I walk back down to my tent.

Creature's left another page.

The Pervert's Guide to Russian Princesses
Princess #11 (First Draft)

Oh, Anna of Kashin, I want to flip your 14th-century royal robes over your head and smell your stomach and the deep creases underneath your breasts. I've heard you only bathe once a month, and your skin holds a heavy odor. Please, don't ever bathe again. I want more of your scent.

As a young woman, you were taught the strict virtues of humility and obedience, but I don't need you to be obedient to me. You can do what you want with me, anything, and I'll help you too. I'll take your wig off and pick the lice from your scalp.

You were married by nine, and survived a fire in the year 1295, when you were 10 years old. Maybe the halo in all of the paintings is the glowing remnant of that fire, and when I kiss you, my lips glow too, as if the halo is uranium, our love a cancer spreading through our bodies.

I will call you by your name of silence, the name you chose for yourself: Evfrosiniya. I will whisper that name in your ear as we hide together in a wardrobe. The Mongol hordes who tortured your sons will not find us. We'll be naked, with fur coats hanging above us. I'll pull one down and cover our bodies in fur. You'll scooch back into me, your bare back pressed to my chest, and I'll smell once more the oil on your skin as I hold you cradled against me.

THE MATRIX

I WAS IN A DRUGSTORE last year, and I saw these little blue birds made of glass, and I had to take one. I picked it up and looked on the bottom and it was marked $39.99. Only three inches tall and it was worth $40. I couldn't believe it. So I stuck it in my pocket.

An employee walked up and said, "Excuse me, young man, but could you please empty out your pockets?" He was kind of tall and thin. Maybe 10 years older than me.

We were near the door, by the front displays, and I hesitated. I wish I hadn't. I should've kept walking and made him make the difficult decision to stop me physically, but I froze and he put his hand on my shoulder and gave me that smile that really isn't a smile.

When people put their hands on me, it makes my jaw tighten like someone's ratcheting a bolt on the side of my face. I can feel all of my teeth pressing together, top and bottom, getting tighter and tighter, and some of my teeth don't seem to fit right. I didn't like the way this man was looking at me, and I tried to calm myself down and breathe, staring at two longer hairs just under his eye that he missed while shaving. I tried not to hit him.

When I did make a move, it wasn't a punch. It was more of a shove, two-handed. I popped him with two open hands and he was jolted off his feet.

He fell into a perfume display—no, *through* a perfume display—and the table broke and the bottles popped up into the air like in that movie *The Matrix*. I swear I could see the bottles just sparkling and hanging there for a second before they fell and exploded on the linoleum floor. The man tried to stand up, but the table had split in half and the tablecloth was folded around him, so standing only made things worse. He slipped again and went down hard, and then I noticed that there were other people all around us, none of them doing anything but just standing and staring at him and at me, and then I realized that I'd better run. So I did. I ran.

OF MONSTERS AND MEN

GRANDPA SAYS, "SOMETHING'S OUT THERE."

"Where?" I say.

"In the lake." He points with his cereal spoon.

I look where he's pointing. Make a serious face. "What kind of a something?"

He taps his spoon on the table. Says, "The lake monster kind."

I smile when he says that. "A lake monster?"

"You don't believe me?" He points his spoon at me.

I pour a bowl of Cap'n Crunch and grab a dry handful. Eat the yellow pieces out of my hand. "No. I don't believe in lake monsters."

Grandpa says, "It's not just me that thinks so. Our neighbor Rosa Nash came over last night and said she saw something weird too. She says something came up out of the water and ate a goose the other evening."

I pour milk over my cereal. Take a big bite. "A goose?"

"A huge goose. One of those big, fat white ones. She said the monster drug it, the goose, screaming and squawking to its death."

"All right," I say, "and you saw this monster eat a goose too?"

"No, I didn't. But I saw it eat something else. I saw the monster take down a blue heron in the shallows near the boggy end. I was walking the south-side trail the other morning, and I looked out at this perfect blue heron standing there in a foot of water when all of a sudden something ripped it off its feet." Grandpa claps his hands together. "And I'm not talking about any kind of fish or bird either, because this thing took the heron out into deep water and dragged it down just like Rosa Nash described with the goose. All I saw was a flash of the monster's tail."

"The monster has a tail now?"

"You go ahead and laugh," Grandpa says, "but this thing has a big monster tail." He takes a bite of cereal and chews. I can hear him breathing through his nose as he eats, chewing so hard it sounds like someone raking through gravel.

I say, "It could be a northern pike or something. I've caught some big fish out there."

"No," Grandpa says, "fish don't have monster tails." He takes another big bite of cereal and stares at me as he chews. He swallows and says, "I think you know the difference between a monster and a pike, right?"

I say, "Come on, Grandpa, a monster?" I drink my milk and stand up to clear my bowl.

He follows me into the kitchen. "One more thing: I'm not sure if it's safe for you to sleep out there anymore."

"In my tent?"

"Well, if there's a monster in the lake, I'm not sure it's a good idea to be sleeping right on the shore."

"I made a promise to myself: 100 nights straight. No matter what. And 'no matter what' means no matter what. Monsters included." I smile when I say "monsters."

Grandpa clunks his bowl down into the sink. "This is not a joke, Travis. I'll talk to your grandma about it."

I fill my cereal bowl with water from the tap and watch the milky cloud swirl in the bottom. Then I drink the white water. I say, "I'm gonna shoot some hoops now."

OSPREY'S HUNT

WHILE I SHOOT, I START to think about things, so after 100 makes, I go back inside and leave my basketball by the front door. In the guest room, I lift the throw pillow, unzip it, and pull out my jar. I put the jar in the bottom of my backpack next to my water bottle. Yell, "Grandpa, I'll be back."

Grandpa's watching MLB TV when I walk by. He doesn't say anything.

I bike down Coburg to the 126 overpass. Check the cages there. The dugouts. Walk back on each of the deer paths through the ivy. Find a man sleeping with a cardboard sign on his chest that says,

WAR VET—MONEY OR FOOD?
ANYTHING HELPS

He doesn't wake up as I step past him. I find an empty tent where the trail stops, the tent door next to a pile of garbage:

fast-food containers, half a T-shirt with a brown smear on it, a bike tire, two wine bottles, a green Coleman propane tank.

I bike past the Kendall Auto Group, over the Ferry Street Bridge. The wraparound. The gravel riverbank. There's a blue plastic tarp covering someone sleeping. Or not sleeping. There's no movement. No breathing. I sneak up and pull back the corner of the tarp. It's two big backpacks lying end to end, the size of a person but not a person. I put the tarp back in place. Fold the edges underneath a backpack.

I push my bike along the river path through Skinner's Butte Park. See a man carving a walking stick with a sheath knife, ornamenting the wood. He says, "See this tribal shit here, man?"

"Yeah," I say, "that's good." Then I keep going. Keep searching for her. I do this sometimes. Sometimes I just think about it, in the middle of something, and I want to find her right then, I can't even explain why.

I bike up the slope at the bridge before the rose gardens. Find three people sleeping at the chain-link. All of them too young, in their early thirties or something like that.

I lean my bike against my thigh. Swing my backpack off my shoulders. Get out my water bottle and take a drink. Stare at the river. There are riffles before the bridge, shallows across the water to the north bank, the deepest section only two feet. It's hot and I think about swimming, but no one swims right here for whatever reason.

I look upriver and down. There are too many places to look, too many places to hide. I put my water bottle back in the bottom of the pack and slide it on, tightening the straps.

I wonder if she's using a lot. I'm sure she's using some, but it's hard to know how much. There have to be times when she doesn't, when she runs out of money, or she feels guilty, or she tries to quit. Sometimes, when I was little, she'd talk about quitting. She'd say it like she was talking about building a dream house. She'd draw in the air in front of her, and I'd always wonder what she was drawing since it didn't match up to what she was saying. I'd watch her hands wave around, her fingers draw lines in the air, lines across and lines down, and she'd say, "I wouldn't even need it anymore. I wouldn't even think about it."

One time, when I was 10, she got methadone and quit for three weeks. She seemed okay, her hands a little shaky, but still okay. Then one night she locked herself in the bathroom and she didn't come out. It got quiet, real quiet, and I had that feeling again where everything tightens up, my shoulders too high, the muscles in my neck clenching, and I knocked on the bathroom door but she didn't answer me.

"Mom?" I said. "Are you okay?"

Then she wasn't using methadone anymore, and some days she didn't come home at all.

I'm thinking about that time and staring over my shoulder at the bridge, but I'm not really staring at anything. I can hear the cars clunking the metal splits, and the low sound of all those cars' motors running together.

I get on my bike and start pedaling back.

XBOX VS. DVDS

I SHOOT 200 SHOTS IN the driveway on the backboard that Grandpa and I hung when I was 13. I remember how happy I was that Grandpa was willing to put it up with me. He found the set on Craigslist for $45, and we spent a Saturday afternoon measuring and remeasuring, making sure the rim was at 10 feet exactly, sliding the backboard up and down over and over until we were sure and we could draw a mark on the siding. Then we spent 20 minutes making sure everything was level—the rim level in both directions, and the bottom of the backboard level straight across. We kept tilting it and checking, tilting it some more, and Grandpa tapped wood shims in at the bottom, and we kept checking because we wanted it to be perfect. Then we bolted it down with lag screws.

As we worked, I kept telling him, "Thank you. Thank you so much, Grandpa."

And he kept saying, "It's fine. Really. Don't worry about it."

That was before Grandma was sick, before everything was

different, before things weren't as good between him and me. That was before he started taking whatever Grandma got from the pharmacy.

I stand in front of the backboard and shoot 100 right-handed shots, then 100 left-handed shots. I start close and move out, the way I always do.

Then I walk over to Creature's house and knock on his front door. It seems like no one's there, but I keep knocking anyway since I can never really tell. His mom always keeps the blinds down and the house dark. She sleeps about 15 hours a day, eats weird food, and has this thing about exercise videos when she's not sleeping. Last time I was over there she kicked us off the Xbox so she could do one of her exercise DVDs.

So we gave up the TV then and Creature's mom got into a really tight outfit and started doing Tae Bo. She's always in good shape from doing those videos, and she's young too. She was maybe 16 when she had Creature, so I think she's still sort of in her prime physically, even if she's kind of crazy. Anyway, we were eating some cereal at the table and she was exercising right there in front of us, and it was hard not to watch her, so I just kept watching.

Creature reached across the table and smacked me on the side of my head. "What the hell are you looking at?"

I put my head down and took a quick bite.

Creature said, "This is ridiculous. Can you watch any more of this?"

"No," I said, but his mom was getting sweaty now and her clothes were so tight, and she really wasn't that old. As long as I forgot that she was Creature's mom, I could watch her all day long.

BABY DADDY

I knock on Creature's front door again.

The door opens a crack and his mom's face appears in the line of light. She looks like she just woke up. "Travis?"

"Oh hey, Mrs. M., is Creature . . . I mean . . . is Malik here?"

"No," she says, and combs her hair with her fingers. Smiles at me.

"Do you know where he is?"

"He's over hanging out with that Jill girl again."

"Oh."

"Yeah," she says, "I think you and I feel the same about that." Creature's mom licks her fingers, flattens her hair in the front. "I told him not to go over there anymore, but he doesn't listen to me." She slides the last few strands of hair behind her ears. Takes a deep breath and opens the door wider. "Wanna come in?" She's in a Lycra suit with a low V-neck. She plays with the collar a little, kind of peeling it back. Purses her lips.

I don't know how to feel when she acts like this. I don't know if she's actually flirting with me or just being friendly, and also, she's Creature's mom.

"Uh," I say, "I better go try to find Malik over at Jill's."

"Okay," she says, and stops playing with her collar. "If he's there, talk some sense into him?"

"I'll try," I say, then I hop off the porch.

I dribble crossovers all the way to Jill's house and I'm sweating by the time I get there. Jill's house is a blue mobile home at the end of the second loop, a quarter mile from Malik's. Her porch is covered in old Astroturf, patchy and thin, and the plastic railing that goes around the front is missing six of its dowels.

When I knock on her door, I hear music playing inside but nobody answers. I knock again. Her porch faces south and it's hot standing on that patchy Astroturf. I wait for a minute, then knock again, and jog back down the steps. I start to dribble in the direction of home, but I sort of begin to play a game in my head and get trapped in a full-court press by invisible defenders trying to keep me from crossing midcourt. I cut right, go behind my back, and sprint 30 feet. Then I pretend to take an inbounds going the other direction and break the press that way too. After that, it's sort of back and forth for a while. I'm sweating and dribbling hard against the defenders in my head when Creature comes out of the house.

He's sweating too. He says, "Whoa, T, that guy was all over you." He points at the air behind me. "And that guy's a monster." Creature smiles.

I pick up my dribble. "Come on, man. What are you doing at Jill's again? I thought you said you weren't coming back here anymore."

Creature leans down to tie his shoelaces. He doesn't even have his ball with him.

I say, "Did you forget something?"

"Oh, damn," he says. "My basketball."

He jogs back up the steps and knocks on the door. Jill opens it and kisses him long and slow. I don't like to see that. Then she hands him his basketball and pushes on his face.

He steps back and says, "You can't push me away. I'll see you again soon."

"Soon, baby." She winks at him.

Creature and I dribble down the street without talking.

When we get close to his house, Creature says, "I know what you're thinking."

"Yeah?"

"Yeah," he says, "that I'm 18 and she's 24."

I shrug. "I was really wondering how NBA guards can drive straight, go up right, switch to left, and still lay it in soft."

Creature says, "She already has two kids, and I know that." He dribbles right, right to right, then left to left, then changes to crossovers and jukes. "But," he says, "those kids have nothing to do with me."

"They could," I say. "You could be the next baby daddy." I smile at him.

He points at me. "No, no, no," he says. "That's never going to happen."

I dribble through my legs, turn, and dribble through my legs again. "How'd you meet her anyway? How'd all of this start?"

He says, "I didn't tell you?"

I shake my head.

"Oh, it was weird. She's at the end of my newspaper route one morning. She's just sitting on the porch looking hella fly."

"Just sitting on her porch early in the morning?"

"Yep, six o'clock. Just about when I finish my route and go home. It was like she knew I was coming. She was wearing this coat that didn't really cover her dress and this dress that didn't really cover her body."

"At six in the morning?"

"Oh baby, I mean it looked like she'd just put it on for me right then," he says. "Not that I was complaining. Nobody else in this park looks super fine at six in the morning. Mostly I get to see old guys in stained boxers or women all hunched over with their dentures out."

"Huh," I say.

"Don't 'huh' me. You'd have done the exact same thing in my position. She looked super fine with her messy mascara and her slinky lingerie under that tiny dress, and her kids were with their daddy that weekend, so there was nobody else home. There was nothing I could do about it."

"Nothing?"

"Well, you know, I'm a man." Creature palms his ball and stretches out his arms wide on both sides like that old Michael Jordan poster I used to have on my wall.

I do a quick crossover. " 'Nothing' because you're a man?"

Creature copies my crossover move but does it a little lower and a little smoother. Sometimes I feel like I'm oatmeal and he's Cream of Wheat.

"Trust me," he says, "if you saw Jill in lingerie, you'd be going back *twice* a day. No doubt. Maybe three times."

For some reason, right then I think of Creature's mom in

her workout gear. I dribble in place and get sort of carried away for a second, but then I stop myself and shake my head.

We're back at my house then, and we shoot for a while in the driveway.

I clang a miss off the side of the rim, and Creature retrieves the ball. "Do you want to play under the bridge with me tomorrow tonight? There's a big pickup game going on. Lots of older players, small-college players, a few guys down from Portland."

"Yeah," I say. "Let's do that."

We walk over by the porch to drink water out of the hose.

Creature says, "How's your grandma?"

I shake my head.

"That bad, huh?"

"I can tell it's getting real bad. She won't talk about it, but I know."

Creature bends down and reties his shoelaces. He says, "Have you asked her directly? Have you said, 'Grandma, what's really going on?'"

"No. I don't know why."

"Talk to her, then. See what's up."

"Okay." I palm my basketball against my wrist, run into the driveway, and try to dunk, but I get rim-checked, same as always.

YELLOW WIG

GRANDMA DOESN'T HAVE THE TV on. The room's nearly dark, one night-light plugged into the wall on her side of the bed. She looks asleep so I start to turn around, but she says, "Come on in, sweetie. I was just resting."

I go and sit on the side of her bed. "Hey, Grandma. How are you?"

"Good, sweetie, good."

I feel the thick veins on the back of her hand. In the light, they're bright blue, but now I can't see the color. I say, "How are you really doing?" I say it like Creature told me to. I want her to tell me the truth. And she can hear it in my voice.

"Oh, you know . . . ," she says.

I put my hand on her head then, where her hair is brittle, where it feels like strands of nylon.

Grandma sighs.

I say, "Are you gonna lose your hair again?"

"Yes," she says.

"So it's bad again?" I just want her to tell me. I just want the truth.

"Who knows?" she says. "I'm not even sure the doctors do."

I rub her scalp with the ends of my fingers and she closes her eyes. I had a dream recently that she was my kid. It was a weird dream because she was old and I was young, just like in real life, but she was my kid anyway, and she was sick, and I was always sitting by her bed. In the dream, she called me Dad and I nodded every time she said that, but when I woke up I was sweating and I had to get up and walk around to clear my head.

I say, "What did the doctors tell you?"

"Not much, sweetie, not much."

I wait for her to say more, but she doesn't.

"Grandma, would you tell me if it was real bad? Would you?"

She pats my hand. "You're a sweet boy, and it's not your job to worry about me."

I think about her being bald again, that strange yellow wig she wore two years ago, the one that reminded me of Mc-Donald's French fries. I don't know why. I say, "But I'll worry about you anyway."

"I know, sweetie. I know." She reaches up and touches my shoulder. "Are you still doing all of those push-ups and pull-ups this summer?"

"Yeah."

"Good," she says. "This is going to be a great year for you."

When she says that, I remember the news cameras. I remember how they were there on the court, how I looked over when I was sitting on the bench after I got ejected and the game finally resumed. All three cameras were pointed at me. I say, "I hope so. We all know last year wasn't a good year."

Grandma smiles. "Hopefully, that's all over now. Hopefully, those coaches will let that be in the past."

Just then, down the hall, the crowd cheers in the baseball game that Grandpa's watching, and we hear Grandpa say, "Oh yes. Oh yes. Run, you son-of-a-bitch! Yes!"

Grandma smiles.

The game gets quiet again and Grandpa mutters something but I can't hear what it is.

Grandma says, "I heard that there might be some sort of monster in the lake."

"Did Grandpa tell you that?"

She closes her eyes. "Everyone's talking about it."

That makes me happy. I tried to downplay it with Grandpa so he'd be even more sure, so he'd stick with his opinion. But Grandma is generally more reserved. She has to be encouraged to believe in something. "Could be something big," I say. "I guess people are saying that. So maybe we should go out and look for it tomorrow evening when the light's good. I could paddle for us and you could try to spotlight whatever it is. Wanna just hold the flashlight?"

She adjusts her head on her pillows. "I don't know, sweetie, I'm pretty tired these days."

I say, "I could carry you to the canoe. I could put you in there with pillows and blankets. Then I'd do all of the paddling. It'll be like last time when you were sick."

Grandma smiles. "Those were fun nights."

"Yeah, I'll paddle and you'll tell stories," I say. "I always loved your stories. They always made me happy."

She turns her face away from me. Says, "I don't know if I'm

strong enough to do anything like that right now. I don't feel good if I'm moving."

I lean over and kiss her forehead, and when I do, I realize that she's crying.

"It's okay, Grandma."

"I'm just so tired," she says. "I probably need my sleep now."

"Okay." I stand up.

She still has her head turned away. "Good night, sweetie."

I feel bad about pushing her. I want to say I'm sorry, but I don't. Instead, I just say, "Good night, Grandma."

After I close her door, I go out on the back porch and stare at the lake. I try not to cry myself, but I do anyway.

On the other side of the glass, Grandpa jumps up off the couch and slides the glass door open. He says, "The Giants have two men on base. Only one out."

"Good, Grandpa."

"No, it's not good. It's excellent. You have to come in and watch this."

"No thanks. I'm going down to my tent now."

"With two men on base?"

"Yeah," I say. "But let me know what happens in the morning, okay?"

Grandpa doesn't understand how I could walk out on a game situation like that. He looks at me like I'm trying to eat soup with a fork.

I say, "Goodnight, Grandpa." Turn and walk down to my tent.

I keep my tent flap open. Try to read but can't. None of the books I have seem interesting. After a while, I hear Grandpa come out on the porch. I click my headlamp off and watch him pack a bowl. He smokes it down, then packs another and smokes that one down too. I lie on my bag and watch him puff. With the porch light in his face, he can't see me down the hill.

He goes back inside.

I have to piss, so I get up and slip on my shoes, walk up the hill and down the street to Mr. Tyler's house. No one's out at this time of night. I look both ways but don't see anything moving—no cats, no people, no cars, no dogs.

As I'm pissing on Mr. Tyler's porch, I think about the time he called Creature "a dirty little coon."

WHAT HAPPENS THEN?

"HEY, CREAT. WHY DO YOU write about those Russian princesses?"

"I don't know, baby."

I say, "You have to know something. Some reason."

"I do," he says. "I do."

"And that is . . ."

Creature spins his basketball in his hands. He says, "I guess it's like this: they didn't have any power."

"Who?" I say. "The princesses?"

"None. Everything I read about them, they were powerless. Being a Russian princess is like being some no-name skinny-ass clothes model in New York City. You just put on whatever clothes they give you, walk out on that runway, and look as good as you can. Then you walk back to wherever you stay all day and do jack-shit nothing for the rest of your time. Maybe you smoke some cigarettes. Maybe you don't eat too much. That's it."

"Is that right?"

"I think so."

I say, "If that's how it was for the princesses, then why do you write about them?"

"I guess I like to put me there too. With them. What if we had love affairs? What if we had powerful love affairs? What's the difference in our lives?"

"The difference between you and a Russian princess?"

"Exactly." Creature taps his chest with his index finger. "What do I have?"

"You've got basketball."

"Right," he says. "Basketball could bring me money. It could bring me wealth. Same as being a Russian princess."

I shake my head. "It's different."

"How?" he says. "Tell me."

"I don't know. You get to play, for one thing. You *get* to. You don't *have* to."

Creature spins his ball in his hands. "Tell me, baby, what do we have here? What power? What influence? We live in a fucking trailer park in a middle-class town in the western United States. You and I are shit on by everyone at school unless they're afraid of us. We go to Taft, a trashy, rich-person school."

"Yeah, but we've got basketball, man."

"And the princesses, well, they get to be princesses. So tell me: What happens if you take that one thing away from us? What happens if we lose our *one* thing? What happens then?"

T. S. ELIOT AND BASKETBALL

I BIKE TO MEET CREATURE at the Washington-Jefferson Bridge courts, and these are the rules:

- Shirts vs. skins
- All by ones to eleven
- Winner's outs
- Call your own fouls
- Winning team stays in

I lock my bike and find Creature shooting on the far rim. He says, "We're gonna be 'a pair of ragged claws tonight, scuttling across the floors of silent seas.'"

I nod. Take a warm-up shot.

"Nothing?" he says. "T. S. Eliot, baby. 'All the women come and go, talking of Michelangelo'?"

I say, "My poet is Rajon Rondo."

"Yeah, whatever," he says. "Let's find some big men to run with."

Creature and I pick up three forwards and wait to get in on the next game. Creature says, "Pick and cut through for easy layins and dunks." Then he points at me and says, "You play the point and I'll take the two, got it?"

"Yep."

"Off the ball," he says, "I'll commit murder. Plus, we'll run the pick-and-roll up top. If I'm not open on the roll, you pop or hit one of these big guys underneath. Keep the other team honest, right?"

"Right."

Creature's only 6'1", but he dunks bigger than 6'1". And on the first pick-and-roll, that's exactly what he does. His man slides in front of me, and I hit Creature over the top for an uncontested dunk down the middle of the lane. The rim is reinforced, no breakaway, and Creature takes a moment to do a slow pull-up on the double rims. He yells as he drops down. And then the rout's on. We win that first game 11 to 2, the other team never figuring out how to stop Creature.

The next game is the same. And the next. I pass to the three big men a little more because I want them to stay interested in playing with us, but Creature's always my outlet on the break. I don't have to shoot, so I almost never do unless they drop two to the paint on the pick-and-roll.

Fourth game. Some thug-looking guys from Portland step in.

I play defense, dribble, and pass. Bring it up top to reset. Drive to draw the defender. I love this part of a game, when I get to run everything but don't have to take a shot. I start to get into a flow where it's just me. I'm myself and I'm alone, and there are motions when I have the ball and motions when I don't have the ball, and I think about my footwork, my body position, square up my shoulders, backpedal with my butt low, point at the cutter, play the left-side top of the two-three zone.

Sometimes when it's like this, I don't hear anything, or I guess I hear things and I react to what I hear, and I talk to my teammates, but even that isn't conscious. Even that part of my brain goes away somewhere, and then there's just this flow of the game and everything I love about it.

Creature snaps me out of my head. He yells, "I'm eating your entrails right now, bitch," and he's wagging his finger in a gangbanger's face, and the gangbanger looks pissed. Then I can hear. And I'm with everybody else, and one of our bigs seems worried.

Two possessions later, Creature dunks and does another pull-up on the rim. Says, "I'm just getting so damn tired from all these dunks on you."

"Fuck you," the gangbanger says, and takes it all the way to the rim at the other end, but one of the bigs blocks his shot.

"Foul," he says.

"What?" Creature jogs up next to him.

"I called a foul, motherfucker."

"Even though he blocked you clean and clear as day?"

The big looks at the gangbanger, then back at Creature. "Whatever," he says. "He can choose to call that."

"No," Creature says. "Everyone and *your* mother"—he taps the gangbanger's chest—"knows that wasn't a foul."

"Keep talking," the gangbanger says, "and I'll cut your mouth out with a razor blade."

"Oooh," Creature says, "talk dirty to me, baby. I like that," and he winks. "I guess we'll check you the ball, then."

I step over next to Creat as we set up on defense. I say, "Chill a little. Let's roll these guys and get on to the next game."

"Really?" he says, and he says it loudly enough for everyone to hear, even the people on the sidelines waiting to take next. "You think this guy is getting tired of me dragging his limp dick up and down the court?"

Someone courtside yells, "Boom, Creature! Damn!"

And Creature smiles at me. "Sorry. I had to say that."

Everyone laughs but the gangbanger. When the next ball goes out of bounds, the gangbanger says, "Keep talking, I'll wreck you. You'll see."

Creature steps up eye to eye with him, right there on the baseline, and the game stops. Everyone can tell that Creature is as athletic in a fight as he is on the court. His hands are huge for his size and he leaves them open before he fights like he might do anything. Maybe rip a man's arm off. Maybe break his teeth. Gouge out eyes with his thumbs.

Creature says, "We could just squabble right here, P-Town boy. Right now. Is that what you want?"

That gangbanger doesn't know what to say. He isn't in his hometown, on his home court. He can't just call for backup, and I see his eyes flicker back and forth as he looks at Creature and considers his options.

I step up next to both of them and say, "Hey, boys, can we just play some more ball, huh? Give this one up?" I try to allow them both a chance to step away. Then I use a phrase I saw my uncle Henry use once outside a bar. I say, "Y'all both look tough enough to me."

And that does it. It works.

"All right," Creature says, and nods. "I think we're done here."

After that fourth game ends, we play the next game and win, but not like we should. Creature keeps looking over at the gangbanger, who's on the sideline now. Creature keeps flexing his chest, winking at him, kissing the air when he hits a shot. And twice Creature gets beat on fast-break layins at the other end while he's showboating to that sideline.

"Creature," I say, "the game's right here, man. It's right here."

This side of Creature annoys me. Even in league games, in games that count, he can get like this. And when he does, I spend all my time thinking about him. I can't lose myself in the game the way I want to. There's no flow. No rhythm. No pace. And we don't dominate like we should.

Creature says, "I got this, baby. I got this locked down."

"You better," I say, "'cause this is garbage."

We win the fifth game 11 to 7—sad to me because the fifth opponent is the worst we've played yet. I have to use our three bigs over and over because Creature isn't setting quality screens anymore, and we certainly aren't killing anyone in the pick-and-roll.

In the sixth game, my bigs are tired and we get run off the court. The gangbanger walks off somewhere near the end of the game, so Creature can't talk trash to him on the sidelines anymore. Creature tries to step it up after that. He scores three baskets in a row, but it's too late. We lose the game 11 to 8.

On the sideline, Creature and I share a jug of SunnyD. I say, "You've got to focus better than that, man. You were trash out there."

"Focus for this?" he says. "This isn't even real basketball.

This isn't a D-1 game or even a high school game. No, baby, I don't have to focus for this. My mind's full of poetry and that's all that matters right now. I'm just too T. S. Eliot."

"Hey, T. S. Eliot," I say, "remember the other day when you told me that some people aren't worth the scars on the backs of our knuckles?"

"Yeah," he says. He takes the SunnyD from me and chugs three gulps. "But what I say and what I do are two totally separate things. I'm a hypocrite. I'm a complicated human being. It's like my writing. I don't even talk like that, you know?"

IVY DREAMS

MORE PEOPLE HAVE COME TO play and there's a crowd, a long wait to get back in. We're standing on the sideline, waiting for our turn at another game, and I'm pissed. I don't like to wait to play basketball when we could've stayed in the whole time. Creature's next to me, his arms crossed. He doesn't joke around or say anything to me now because he knows I'm frustrated.

We're standing there, the crowd all around us, when I see, past Creature, someone coming through, pushing through, and it's the gangbanger, and I see the flash of silver in his hand.

"Run!" I yell. "Creat, run!"

Creature breaks to my right and I follow him. We swim through people, other players warming up, stretching, people milling around, standing in circles, drinking. We bust through all of them, keeping our heads low, sprint past the first bridge pylon into the dark side, and I look back and see that the gangbanger's there, coming through the last of the people.

Years ago, under the north end of the bridge, someone shot out all of the lights, and whenever the city fixes them, someone shoots them out again. So it's dark above us, and we run along the horseshoe pits in that gray dark, more careful now, slower, trying not to hit anything in the dark, knowing it's hard to follow anyone there, past the old playground and the chained-up bathrooms. I look back again to see if there's anyone following us. I could see an outline against the backlight if he was there, but he's not.

"We're good, man. Let's keep going a little farther, but we're good now."

At the fourth pylon, we cut up and slide in behind the big cement pillar above the ivy slope. "Watch out for needles," I say. "Don't just sit down here."

Creature and I scrub our feet back and forth on the bare patch of ground beneath us, trying to kick syringes or shards of glass aside if there are any. It's impossible to see, so we both edge our shoes back and forth, clear space until we're sure there's nothing on the ground there, then we sit down.

Creature says, "So what did he go get?"

"Some kind of silver pistol. I don't know. I just saw it and booked."

Creature says, "Probably went back to his car and got it."

"Yeah, I guess he got fed up with *somebody's* trash-talking."

"All I have to say is that it was his fault. He was a weak-ass little punk. Couldn't play defense and was too scared to fight. So he had to go get himself a pistol to even things up."

"Creature, that's how it is sometimes. You know that."

"True. But still . . ."

In the dark, I can see the outline of Creature with his

arms wrapped around his legs. We're both leaning back against the cement. I'm still sweating from the basketball game and the running down here, but it's colder against the cement, in the gap under the bridge. I rub my legs with my hands to keep warm.

Creature says, "Sorry about tonight."

I'm still frustrated, annoyed that we lost games and had to run away, but I say, "It's all right."

"I should've chilled out. You were right, baby." He bumps my knee. "Huddling here isn't as fun as playing ball, is it? Sorry about this."

I say, "Don't worry about it," and this time I mean it. Creature's out of control sometimes, gets a little crazy, but it's still fun. He's not boring, at least.

There's a spark in front of us, down the slope, 30 feet. Another spark, but the lighter doesn't catch. Someone gets out a butane, and it flames blue. There are three people down there, all of them wearing layered, heavy clothes. Two men and a woman. One of the men holds a straight glass pipe. He puts the butane flame to the end, clicks it, inhales on the other, and the rock bubbles. He hands the pipe to the man next to him, and that man takes a drag before handing it to the woman. The three of them pass the pipe and the lighter until the rock's killed.

Creature says, "Do you think about her a lot?"

"Yeah," I say.

"Do you look for her?"

"Sometimes. I can't help it. But she might not even live here anymore."

I can't see the three people clearly without the lighter

going. I see the outlines of them. One of them sitting down. The other two walking away.

Sometimes when I think I see her it's like I've swallowed a piece of glass and I wonder where it's going to cut me. I picture the glass going down my throat, through my esophagus, the sharp edges of it as it enters my stomach, and I wonder where it will lodge, or where it might cut through. Sometimes I feel that piece of glass in my intestines, working its way down, and I start to think that it's really there, that I really swallowed a piece of glass.

Creature says, "I'm not trying to be a dick, but that woman down there looks a little bit like her."

"A little," I say, "but she's not shaped right. Even in those clothes, I can tell. Something wrong about her shoulders, the way she holds her head."

"Yeah?"

"Yeah, but for a second, I thought so too."

ALTERNATIVES To COLLEGE

I WALK THROUGH THE AUTOMATIC doors. Walmart's the toughest because the workers are looking for people to take stuff, and there's a man stationed by the carts. I look at him and smile. That's always my strategy. Don't try to be invisible, because ducking my head or hurrying by would seem shady. Better to seem friendly and casual. Like a regular customer.

I walk through the aisles. Look at the electronics, but I don't want to take something with a strip on it. I pass through the book aisle next, but none of the books seem very interesting, plus they're all bulky. I go through the office supplies, put a mechanical pencil in my pocket, a glue stick, and an eraser. Then I walk up front.

I wait in line for the self-checkout. When I see the worker look the other way, I slide by like I already purchased everything. And that's when I grab a 12-pack of Coke, put it on my shoulder real obvious, look right at the cart man again, smile, and walk out.

Even though I act relaxed and I probably look relaxed, it still gives me a rush. I know it's weird that it doesn't get old for me, but I don't do it that often anymore, just every once in a while, and I guess that makes it better than doing it all the time. I don't know, though. I guess it's wrong too. I guess stealing, even little things, is wrong.

THE LOVE SONG OF A SHADOWBOXER

TRIM THE HEDGES. RAKE. WEED-WHACK against the uprights. Edge the lines. Check the 2-in-1 level. Refill. Fill the mower with gas. Run it on full, not empty, so the engine isn't gulping the bottom-of-the-pan silt.

I look up and she's in the window, looking down. I shade my eyes to see her better, but she's gone. I blink and wonder if I imagined her being there in the first place. The window curtains never moved. There wasn't any sure sign.

I go back to work on the yard. Look up a few times, but I don't see her after that.

The Pervert's Guide to Russian Princesses
Princess #23 (Revised Draft)

Princess Leonilla Bariatinskaya, I knew you first from the portraits painted by Franz Xaver Winterhalter. The one at the Getty Museum is my favorite, you in ivory and pink and purple. You lay back like you're waiting for me. You finger those pearls around your neck, staring out of the canvas. There's nothing proper about you, nothing reserved, nothing to remind me that you're royal, but royal you are.

I gave you Michael Jordan's number because you're known as both physical and cerebral. You've always been famous at the Russian court for your intelligence and your eyes, eyes that could pick apart a defense. I know that you can tell if the other team is set up in a 1-2-2 zone or a box-and-1, and if I was going to face-guard any one player, it would be you. But you'd anticipate that.

You witnessed the pillaging of the Tuileries, the overthrowing of Louis Philippe in 1848. You wondered at the swallowing of jewels and the lack of violence on the part of the king. You moved with the seasons, making your way through Europe with children and tutors and expensive luggage. Ours was a strange love, always waiting for Ludwig to go away, for his business to separate the two of you. And I was always chasing you, you looking over your shoulder, hoping for a glimpse of me coming after you.

I traveled with you that one time in the horse-drawn coach to Rome, the wagon wheels jolting over the Dolomites, another rhythm for our bodies, me too tall to lay out, but you improvising. And a year later, we were alone in the bathroom of the Sayn Castle, the stonework cold against our nakedness. I put you on the countertop, you sucking in breath at the shock of the stone, and me saying, "Ooh," as my thighs hit the cold.

I liked to count the pearls on your neck, one kiss for each pearl, refusing to touch you until all of the pearls had been accounted for. You undressed yourself while I kissed you, the layers of your clothing like the complications of royalty, all title with no power, and you saying over and over, "If only, if only . . ."

THE BALLAD of BASS AND CARP

I GRAB MY FISHING POLE and flip the canoe. Paddle south, down-lake, to one of the boggy ends. It's dark down there, no street-lights or back-porch floodlights. The blackberry overgrowths on both sides are walls that no one crosses on land. The lake's water is shallow 30 feet from the shore, and I drift the canoe, looking for eyes on top of the water. I scan with my headlamp, but I see nothing.

I paddle a deeper channel, cut to the east toward the oldest house on the lake, an original farmhouse from the end of the 19th century. The old lady who lives there has never repainted the slat-board siding, and she lets her grass grow to two feet in the spring. She won't hire me to mow even though I've offered her a deal a few times. But I kind of like the way her place looks.

At night, the long grass of her backyard is deep and dark, blackish, and paddling up to it, I can see the trails and burrows animals have cut into the field from the water. When my canoe scrapes a gravel shoal, I spook a couple of deer in front of me. They pop up and run, two blacktail does bounding through the high grass and disappearing around the side of the farmhouse.

I shine my headlamp along the lake's shelf. The bank overhangs in a few spots and it's difficult to tell what I'm seeing. I scan for caiman eyes, but don't find any. Then I paddle back out into the middle of the lake and drop a silver spinner 20 feet off the stern of the canoe. I know I'm not going to get a strike without spotlighting, but I wedge the pole behind my leg anyway so I can grab it if anything sees the lure and bites.

One lamp is lit to the north of me, up-lake on the east side, on a dock, and I paddle slowly, trolling the spinner, making my way toward the light.

When I get a hundred feet out, I see that it's Natalie reading a book. She has a Coleman lantern next to her, the light shining on the side of her face. She looks serious as she reads, her head bowed, and I paddle slower. It's nice to see her without her phone, with a book instead, and I try to paddle up without getting her attention.

When I'm 20 feet out and I think she hasn't seen me yet, she says, "Don't you ever wear a shirt?"

I look down at my bare chest lit up by her lantern, wishing I'd brought a shirt with me. I say, "I guess not." There's no moon, and the full surface of the lake is black. Little ripples tap against the side of my canoe, making a *psht-psht* sound. I say, "What are you reading?"

"*Catcher in the Rye*. Required summer reading for English class."

"What high school?"

"Starting Taft in the fall."

"Starting? Then are you a freshman?"

"What?" she says. "No, I'm *not* a freshman. I'm a transfer. A junior. Do I look like a freshman to you?"

"No," I say. "It was just how you said 'starting.'" I paddle a J-stroke to bring my canoe closer to her dock. "Where are you transferring from?"

"A better place," she says.

"Where's that?"

"Lake Oswego."

I laugh. We beat the Lake Oswego basketball team by 30 points in a preseason game last year.

Natalie says, "What are you laughing at?"

"Nothing." I put my paddle in the water and pull the starboard side of my canoe a little closer. Then I reverse the stroke and slide the canoe back out.

"You really love that boat, huh?"

"This canoe?" I slap the hull with the flat of my hand. "Yeah, I do."

"Did you name it?"

"Huh?"

"You know," she says. "Boys are always naming their cars. Giving them stripper names like *Candy Baby*. Shit like that."

"No," I say. "I didn't even think about that. Maybe I should, though. My grandma gave it to me, and she has cancer, so maybe I'd name it for her."

"Your grandma has cancer?"

"Yeah."

"Wow. That's terrible. I'm sorry."

"Yeah," I say. "It's pretty sad."

Natalie looks down at her feet. She has her thumb in her

book, holding her place, and I wait for her to set it down. I tell myself that if she sets her book down, I'm going to paddle the canoe to the dock and hop up next to her. But she doesn't set her book down. She keeps her thumb marking her place. So I wait.

I say, "You like to read outside?"

Natalie looks over her shoulder and nods her chin in the direction of her house. "I don't like to read inside *that* house. That's for sure."

"Why not?"

She looks right at me, right at my eyes, and she doesn't blink.

I look away. Turn and stare out across the lake. The lights on the back porches of the mobile homes on the west side are like cheap imitations of stars.

My fishing line zips and my rod bends. Then the pole rips overboard. "Oh, damn." I stash my paddle and dive in after my fishing pole. Catch it as it drags across the top of the water. When I get ahold of the pole, I lean back against the weight of the fish, tread water, and sidestroke back to the dock. I have to kick my legs hard, grip the pole in my off hand and paddle with my right. When I get to the dock, I hold the pole up. "Take this."

"What?" Natalie's laughing so hard that she's bent over.

"Just take it."

Natalie is still laughing, but she grabs it, and I turn around and swim to my canoe, take hold of the side, and push it back in. Then I pull myself up onto the dock, grab the bowline, and hitch the boat to the cleat. Natalie's holding the fishing pole but not controlling it, letting it whip one way, then the other. She hasn't reeled the fish in at all.

I say, "You've gotta hold that steady and reel it, or that fish will snag the line or break it off. Or break your pole."

"Oh, okay." Natalie tries to turn the reel the wrong way and it won't go. Then she cranks it the other way and starts to bring the fish in. As soon as she starts reeling, I can tell that the fish is a carp. The fish makes heavy S movements in the water, but doesn't jump or make a run.

Natalie reels until the fish breaks the surface 10 feet away. "Oh my God. It's huge."

"Yeah," I say, "big, big carp out here. They're no good to eat, but they're fun to catch."

"Why can't you eat them?"

"Well, you can," I say. "I've eaten them before. But they taste like mud. And in this lake they kind of taste like goose-poop mud. Plus, there's lots of bones in them."

"That's a great combination."

"Yep." I reach down and wet my hands. Natalie has the fish next to the dock, and I take the line and pull it in. Then I reach the fish, put my left thumb in the roof of the mouth to hold it, and with my right hand, I pull the treble from its lower jaw, the barb making a wet click sound as it tears through the edge of the lip.

Natalie says, "Oh, that's nasty."

"Yeah, not the best sound, huh?" I hold the fish at the waterline. Because it's a carp, it doesn't struggle to swim away. I say, "Do you want to release it?"

"Not really."

"You don't?"

Natalie exhales. "Okay." She kneels down next to me. "What do I do?"

She smells good, her hair, like some kind of shampoo or

conditioner when it's wet. I breathe in the smell of her. Say, "Wet your hands, then put your hands over the top of mine. I'll slide my hands away and you'll be holding the fish."

She follows my directions. Doesn't say anything. I slide my fingers back and out of her way, and she holds the fish in her hands. That carp has to be at least 10 pounds, one of the biggest I've ever seen in the lake.

I say, "Now with one of your hands, stroke down the side of its body, real mellow."

She pets the fish with the tips of her fingers. "Like this?"

"Yeah. Now run your fingers down the side a little harder and the fish will flip its tail and swim away."

She pets twice more, and all of a sudden that carp whips its tail and rips forward into the water. Natalie screams and pulls her hands back. "Oh my gosh," she says, and sits back laughing. "That scared the shit out of me."

"But that's how you know you're doing it right. Cause if you pet the fish right, it'll snap to life just like that."

She shakes her head.

"Cool, huh?"

"Pretty cool, but it still scared me." She smells her hands. "And oh wow." She smells her hands again. Makes a face.

"Not so good?"

"No," she says. "Smell yours. They smell phenomenal."

"We can get some of that smell off in the water, but mud or sand or something helps even more." I reach down and pull some algae, scrub my hands with it, and rinse them in the water. I smell my palms and fingers and they smell a lot better. I grab some more algae and do it again.

Natalie raises her eyebrows. "Does that work?"

"Sort of. Mostly."

She scrubs with algae too. As we're leaning over and scrubbing our hands next to each other, I can smell her again, a little bit of whatever she cleans her hair with, and the fainter smell of her skin. I dated a girl the year before, during basketball season, but that girl sprayed a lot of flowery perfume in her hair and on her neck. Every time I kissed her it sort of overwhelmed me, like we were kissing in the Glade aisle at Target. But Natalie, whatever she uses and however she smells, I like it.

Natalie scrubs her hands three times and rinses them. Sniffs and wrinkles her nose each time. "It's still not all the way gone."

"No," I say. "You might need a little soap to get the rest off."

"But it's better, I guess. It doesn't make me gag now."

I sit down and let my feet dangle in the water. Natalie sits down next to me.

I say, "I meant to ask you—why do you hate bass so much? You said that you hate them, remember?"

Natalie kicks her feet in the water. "They eat frogs."

"And you like frogs?"

"Yeah," she says, "I love frogs."

"Why's that?"

"I know it sounds weird." She shrugs. "But I guess I always did. At my old house on the edge of Lake Oswego, there was a slough nearby, and I used to catch frogs there pretty much every night in the summer. I'd go down and catch one, hold it, sing to it. . . ." She scratches her nose with her forearm. "I guess I was a strange little girl."

"Sounds normal enough to me."

"Well, anyway, I loved them. And I heard that bass eat

frogs, that they rip their legs off sometimes and leave the rest of them to die. So I hate bass. Fuck bass."

"All right," I say. "Fuck bass. Kill 'em all."

Natalie smiles. She says, "Do you go to Taft too?"

"Yeah."

"And do you play any sports?"

"Basketball."

"Wait," she says. "You play basketball?"

"Yeah, that's pretty much all I ever did growing up. All I ever do now."

Natalie says, "I don't know why, but I didn't think of you as a basketball player." She tilts her head and looks at me.

I look out at the water in front of us, the black ripples bigger with the wind, yellow lantern lines on black. I hate it when people don't think of me as a basketball player. I know that's stupid since they wouldn't know unless they were watching me play, but somehow I wish it were more obvious. If I looked like Creature, they wouldn't even ask me if I played.

"Sorry," Natalie says. "I didn't mean anything by that. There just aren't a lot of basketball players under six feet, you know?"

"It's fine," I say. "Don't worry about it."

"You probably get that a lot, huh?"

"Yep."

"Sorry." Natalie splashes the water with her feet again. "Sometimes I just say things."

I point to the scar on her knee, half lit from the lamp. She leans back and lets the light fall directly on her leg. Now I can see that the scar is one long line with four dots to the side.

I say, "What's that from?"

She shakes her head. "Long story. Maybe I'll tell you some other time." She stands up. "But I'm gonna go wash my hands now." She smells her palms again and makes another face. "It was nice hanging out, though." She picks up her lantern by its handle. Grabs her *Catcher in the Rye*.

I stand up. "I'll see you around?"

"All right," she says, and walks up the dock.

WALLFLOWER

IN MY TENT, I CAN'T stop thinking about Natalie, can't fall asleep. I keep thinking about how it would feel to kiss her, the smell of her hair when she leaned down next to me, her strong legs, those brightly colored bra straps, how she loves frogs and swims after them in the dark, how she reads alone at night on her dock, and the light of the lantern casting shadows across the angles of her body.

I imagine her in my small tent with me, how the tent would fill with the smell of her, her breath, her lips, her body on top of me, the good weight of her. Then I'd turn and roll on top, feel her underneath me.

I think about all of that, and pretty soon I'm wide, wide awake.

TOMBSTONE BLUES

WE SLEPT IN A DUMPSTER the first two times we got kicked out of motels, but that makes it sound a lot worse than it was. The Dumpster was mostly filled with cardboard, and the first time we slept in there, we slept between a new refrigerator box and a big brown box that said FRAGILE. Both smelled like paper.

We put our two suitcases in the Dumpster with us, our army blanket, and our sleeping bag. We swam down four layers in the cardboard before we laid out the blanket and pulled it flat, then settled in next to each other with the sleeping bag over the top of us.

I was fine until my mom said we had to shut the lid. I didn't want to do that.

She said, "You want someone to see us in here?"

"No."

"Or to toss bottles in on top of us?"

"No," I said. "We can shut it."

So she shut the lid.

Then the Dumpster didn't smell as good. It still smelled like cardboard next to us, cardboard on both sides, but there were other smells that came through. Smells from the corners, smells from below us on the Dumpster's floor. And it didn't feel like there was quite enough air in there either. But we slept all night. We were fine.

We slept in the same Dumpster the next time, but it didn't smell as clean as before. When my mom closed the lid that second time, the bad smells were almost too much to fall asleep. But we were between layers of cardboard again, so I knew it could have been worse, and I finally did fall asleep. I had to pee in the middle of the night. I woke up having to go, and the dark of the Dumpster was too dark, and the smell of something near my head was overwhelming. I don't know what it was. But my mom was asleep, and I didn't wake her up. I kept counting to 100, waiting for morning, and at some point I fell back asleep with my hands between my legs, and I had a bad dream before I woke up and it was daylight. I'd peed my pants during the dream. I knew I was too old to do that, so I didn't tell my mom in the morning. I kept turning sideways so she wouldn't see the wet on the front of me, and I let it dry like that. Then it itched all day.

Walking down the street, we both smelled terrible. My mom said, "We can't do that again. Something's not right in that Dumpster."

I nodded.

So after that, we slept down by the river anytime we got kicked out of a motel.

YOUR FEET

THESE I DON'T KNOW WELL. But I worry about them because of what I've heard.

It rains 200 days a year in this valley. If you live outside, your feet will be wet. If you have bad shoes, your feet will be badly wet, always wet, soaked through and staying wet, never less than damp. Most of the fall, all of the winter, and most of the spring. Your socks will mildew, then mold, then rot. Your rotting socks against your skin will begin to rot your skin.

Your skin, once pink, is now white, thickened and spongy. I've been told that they call it "trench foot" because soldiers stood in water-flooded trenches for months during the wars. Trench foot is what the homeless have.

You need to change your socks. You need to air out your feet at least twice a day. You need to let your shoes dry, or find a second pair of shoes and trade off, back and forth.

But you don't have extra shoes. Extra shoes isn't what you're trying to score.

LiKE COYoTES iN PDX

I CAN HEAR THE SCREAMS from four houses away and since I'm the youngest resident on the loop, I get there first.

Maribel Calhoun is screaming, "Oh help me, God! Help me!"

I run around the side of her house and up her back stairs. When I jump onto her porch, I almost step on the caiman. It's right there on the porch, its head up. The caiman hisses as I plant my foot next to it and I jump, hurdle over a chair, and jump again. I slide behind the screen door. Pull that door back like a shield and stand behind it. "Oh my goodness. . . ."

Mrs. Calhoun is right behind me, inside her house, the back door cracked open, and her nose sticking out. She's still saying, "Oh God, oh God . . . ," but she's also crying and gasping for air, staring at the caiman, and now that I'm safely behind the screen door, I stare too.

And what we see isn't pretty.

The caiman has a cat, or what's left of a cat. The body

doesn't have a head anymore, and the right front leg is gone too. The caiman's halfway through its meal, and it's standing over its food, defending what it's caught.

"Ma'am," I say, "is that your cat or someone else's?"

Mrs. Calhoun's crying too hard to answer me.

I say, "It's okay, ma'am. It's all right." But it isn't exactly all right, at least not for the cat. Or for Mrs. Calhoun. There's a small crocodile on her back porch and a headless pet in front of us. I know it's wrong, but I have an urge to laugh. I bite my lip. Say, "Let's scare it off, okay?" I step out from behind the screen door and move forward. I yell, "Go on! Get!"

The caiman hisses. Opens its mouth. The bright peach of its gums is lined with an incredible set of teeth, top and bottom. The thing has grown in the last couple of weeks, and the mouth seems to have grown the most. I yell again, "Get out of here! Go!"

It still has its mouth open and it takes a couple of steps toward me, hisses again, and opens that mouth wider. I slide back behind the screen door. Look at Mrs. Calhoun, her nose and her glasses showing in the crack of the door. I say, "Well, that didn't work. Do you have a shovel or a rake or something?"

She keeps staring at the caiman. She isn't screaming anymore, she's just sort of whimpering and hyperventilating. She hasn't said a word to me yet, and she doesn't answer me now.

I say again, "Ma'am, do you have a shovel or a rake I can use?"

Just then, Bob Thomas, the neighbor from the other side, shows up. He's tucking in his shirt as he comes around the corner. When he sees the caiman there on the porch, he says, "Holy jiminy!" He sneaks in from the right side and slides in next to me behind the screen door.

I say, "It's impressive, huh?"

He says, "It's like a crocodile. Where the heck did that come from?"

"I have no idea," I say. "Weird, huh?"

Mr. Thomas pulls a small black pistol out of his pocket.

"Whoa," I say. "Are you gonna shoot it?"

He waves the gun back and forth in the air. "This isn't real. It's a starter's pistol. I'm a volunteer for the middle school track program. Better plug your ears, though." He takes a step toward the caiman, which doesn't back up at all. Mr. Thomas says, "Hope this works."

He shoots the gun and the caiman lurches like it's been shot with a real bullet and sidewinds off the porch and down the steps. It takes off across the grass, and Mr. Thomas and I get to the porch's railing just in time to see the caiman disappear into the undergrowth of the brambles near the water's edge.

"Holy smokes alive." Mr. Thomas whistles. "That animal is something."

We both stare at the blackberry bushes like that caiman might come back out, but it's gone. Mr. Thomas says, "We better help Maribel with her cat."

I point at the torn-up carcass.

Mr. Thomas kneels down and examines the carnage. "Or what's left of her cat."

"Right."

I find a shovel in the shed, and Mr. Thomas goes over to his house to get bleach, paper towels, and a white plastic Walmart bag. He holds the bag open and I slide the shovel underneath the body of the cat, lift it, and drop it in the bag. Then I take the bag from him.

"That was sad," Mr. Thomas says. "She really loved Mr. Fluffers."

"Mr. Fluffers?"

"The cat," he says.

"That was the cat's name?"

Mr. Thomas smiles. "Kind of a gruesome end for a cat named Mr. Fluffers, huh?"

I put my hand over my mouth and Mr. Thomas stifles a laugh too. We both hold our breath and look at our feet. Mr. Thomas puffs his cheeks out and swallows. He says, "Should we do something with that bag?"

"Probably."

The neighbors are all showing up. There's about a dozen of them now in the side yard or on the bank by the lake. They've got flashlights and they're shining them into the undergrowth. I hear someone say, "I think I see its big, white eyes."

Everyone huddles next to him.

"No," someone says, "those aren't eyes. Look. Those are PVC caps."

Another neighbor says, "I don't think any of us are safe anymore."

Mr. Thomas flips on the porch light. "We better bury Mr. Fluffers. Maribel doesn't need to see that body again."

One of the neighbors goes back to his house to get more shovels. Another neighbor says, "Maribel would like it if we were to bury it in that open space over there, and if she wants me to, I could make a little cross for it."

Three of us dig a hole. The neighbors who aren't digging keep giving us directions on how to dig, tips on how to pry out rocks, suggestions for depth and width. I dig most of the grave, try to get it done quickly, and let them sort out the details while I finish. When the hole's about three feet deep, Mr. Thomas says, "That's probably good enough," so I stop.

There are maybe 20 people in Mrs. Calhoun's house now, and they all come out for the burial. I put the Walmart bag in the bottom of the hole and Mrs. Calhoun sprinkles a little dirt on top of the plastic. Then I shovel in the rest of the dirt.

Mr. Thomas says a few words about cats in general, things like: "We know they love to eat mice," and "I'm sure he played so much with yarn when he was a kitten." Most of the women cry and the men look serious. Then I pat the dirt with the flat of the shovel to smooth it out.

One of the neighbor men says, "Mind if I pray over this?"

Mrs. Calhoun nods and the man prays for a long time, talking about souls and heaven and angels and demons and animals and purgatory and the coming of the new kingdom in Revelations. Then he says, "Amen," and we all say, "Amen," and that's the end of the service.

When I get home, I go straight back to my grandma's room. She's sleeping, as usual, so I start to close the door. But as I do, she opens her eyes and says, "Wait, sweetie."

I say, "Oh, sorry to wake you, Grandma."

"No, no, I was awake. I slept all day, so I'm fine. Come back in here and talk to me. Tell me what's new with you?"

"Well," I say, "guess what happened at Mrs. Calhoun's tonight?" I sit down on the side of her bed.

She scooches herself up onto her pillows. "What happened?"

And this is what I've wanted, what I was hoping for. This is why I put the caimans in the lake in the first place. I wanted stories for Grandma, stories to tell her, stories to talk about.

I get in bed next to her and tell her all about the caiman and Mr. Fluffers, about scaring it off and digging a grave.

When I'm done, Grandma makes a clicking sound in her teeth. "Well, that is just plain wild. That is"—she shakes her head—"that is ridiculous."

50-FOOT MONSTERS

THE NEXT DAY, THE KILLING of Mr. Fluffers is on the morning news. A news van is parked in front of Mrs. Calhoun's house when Creature and I dribble down the road toward Gilham Park. We stop and watch the station interview a few neighbors, who are happy to be on television.

It shouldn't be much of a story since the remains of the cat are already in the ground and the caiman's nowhere to be seen, but Mr. Gilligan tells the news crew that he "saw the monster," and it looked to him "like a 10- or 12-foot alligator."

"10 or 12 feet long." The newsgirl repeats that in a serious tone.

"Yes," Mr. Gilligan says. "Someone musta released it when it was little and it's been growing fat for years on the geese and bass and ducks and whatever else it can eat in this lake."

The newsgirl nods like she's listening to a church sermon. "And what do you think will happen next, sir?"

Mr. Gilligan blinks a couple of times. "Well," he says, "it'll probably be 15 to 20 feet long by summer's end, so it's only a matter of time before a person gets eaten."

The newsgirl likes that quote a lot, and she shakes her head before turning to the camera and frowning. She pauses for effect, then says, "There's a monster in this lake, and we haven't heard the last of it yet. People may be next."

After the cameras are turned off and we start dribbling down the road, Creature says, "Wait, why didn't you interview with that news lady? I thought you and Mr. Thomas were the only ones who were actually there on the porch with it and saw what it was."

"Yeah, I don't know. I don't want to be on the news."

"No 15 minutes of fame for you, baby?"

"No thanks," I say.

"I guess last year you got your 15 minutes of glory, didn't you."

"Of glory?" I say.

"Okay, 15 minutes of infamy. Sound good?"

The Animal Control vans are out at the lake when we come home from our workout. Creature and I stand and dribble and watch them. They search and talk to each other. Search some more.

I mow and weed out the borders of two east-side homes in the afternoon, and every once in a while I stop and look back across the lake at the Animal Control officers searching for the caiman on the trailer-park side.

It's Friday, so when I finish my yard work, I knock on the front doors of all my houses to collect my money for the week. Seven pay me in cash and two pay me with checks. Three people aren't home. At Natalie's house, I put on a clean T-shirt and smooth the wrinkles. But no one answers the door.

I bike back to my grandparents' house and stuff the bills in my jar, hide it again in the zip-up throw pillow at the bottom of the bed. I have hundreds of dollars in there from the last two summers, and the only time I spent anything was when I needed new basketball shoes last winter. Other than that, I've saved it all for my mom, in case I need to help her out someday. I daydream about that. Getting her an apartment. Getting her on food stamps. Maybe the Oregon Health Plan too. Or sometimes I picture myself just giving her the cash and telling her that it's all for her, that I earned it for her, that I want her to have it, that I want her to get her life together and live better. Sometimes I picture all of the men who treated her like garbage, and I want to hand her that fat jar of money and say, "It's gonna be okay, see? Look at all of this. You could just set yourself up with all this money. Get an apartment for a couple of months. Get a job and start over again."

When I walk out to my tent, I look around. Everyone's out on their back porches tonight, and I can hear the neighbors next door to me on the other side, the Quincys, talking about the Animal Control officers. Both of the Quincys are half-deaf, so they yell everything. It isn't hard to hear an entire conversation when they talk to each other.

Mr. Quincy says, "Did you hear what that one officer said earlier?"

"No, I did not," Mrs. Quincy says.

"Well, he said that a dog probably killed that cat last night."

"A dog?"

105

"Yes, and he also said that the old people nearby were probably too senile to know what it was."

"Oh my goodness," Mrs. Quincy says. "Did the officer really say that?"

"Honest to goodness," Mr. Quincy says. "I heard it myself from Mr. Anderson."

I smile to myself, duck down, and crawl in my tent. Lie on my sleeping bag and think about how everyone's got a story now, something to talk about, something more than what they're going to eat, their aches and pains, and their medications.

PLANKS

I GO DOWN TO THE park and run a free-throw drill. Two full-court sprints dribbling the basketball, then two free throws. 50 sets is a game. 100 free throws total. It takes more than half an hour and I'm sweating hard.

The park's drinking fountain is on the wall of the bathroom building, and on the other side of the bathrooms, there's Natalie. She's set up orange cones in the grass, and she's dribbling a soccer ball right and left through the set, turning, dribbling back, and cracking shots off the wall of the bathrooms. I watch her hammer one shot and go retrieve the ball, dribble to the top of the cones, and turn to do it over again. She's wearing a bright orange sports bra and soccer shorts. She looks super strong. Tan and scary pretty.

She stops when she sees me.

I say, "What's up?"

"Hey." She rolls the ball back onto the top of her foot and stalls it there, flips it to the other foot and stalls it on top of that foot too. Then she juggles it a few times, back and forth, before stomping it to the grass.

I look at that thick brace on her right knee. "What did you do to that knee?"

"Tore the ACL last year."

"Oh, man. How?"

She rolls her ball up and juggles it a few more times. "At practice."

"Practice? Not even a game?"

"Nope."

I shake my head. "That's rough."

She shrugs. Stalls the ball on top of her foot again, lets it roll slowly off the front of her foot, and settles it underneath the toe of her cleat.

I say, "You're going to play for Taft, then?"

"I hope so. If my knee's healed up," she says. "It's been 10 months, but it's not that strong yet. We'll see."

While I talk to her, I spread my fingers and try to palm my basketball. But it keeps slipping. I spin it and try again.

Natalie says, "So how often do you practice basketball?"

"Pretty much every day."

"Really?"

"Yeah," I say. "I'm a point guard, so I have to."

"You're pretty good," she says. "I watched you sprint and shoot some of those free throws. You made almost every one."

"I missed seven."

"Right," she says. "Never mind. That's total crap. You better keep practicing."

I smile.

"Speaking of," Natalie says, "want a challenge?"

"What's that?"

"I'm just asking. Want a challenge or not?" She smiles, has a look on her face like she might've slipped something into my food.

"I don't trust you, but okay."

"Don't trust me?"

"No."

"Okay, fine. You're scared? We won't do the challenge, then." She puts her hands on her hips.

"No," I say. "Let's do it. I like challenges."

"Okay," Natalie says. "Here's how it'll be. We do four exercises, one right after the other, no resting. And it's a competition between you and me. Last one still exercising wins the comp. First person to stop loses. Got it?"

"All right. What are the four exercises?"

"Push-ups, then pull-ups on that bar"—she points to the playground bar a few feet away—"then squats to 90 degrees, then a plank on your forearms. Got it?"

"Got it." I smile. I'm feeling confident. Anything with push-ups and pull-ups is an automatic win for me. I've been doing them all spring and summer. I can do a lot of both, and there's no way Natalie can come anywhere close to beating me on those. The other two exercises I don't do too often, but how hard can they be?

We walk over to the edge of the playground. Natalie says, "Push-ups, then jog to the pull-ups, then jog back and go right into squats, right?"

"Right."

"No rest. You ready?"

"Ready."

"Then go."

We both drop down and start pumping out push-ups. We're

on the same rhythm at first, but on number 13, Natalie slows down. She does maybe 10 more, but a lot slower on those last few, and I keep cranking, feeling good. By the time I'm in the mid-30s, she's finished and I see her jog over to the pull-up bar and start doing pull-ups. I keep doing push-ups, pass 40, pass 50, then start slowing down. I go hard, do as many as I can, the last few really slow, and get to 63 before my shoulders give out.

When I stand up to jog over to the pull-up bar, Natalie's already back from her set of pull-ups. She's behind me in the grass, doing standing squats, dropping to 90 degrees and back up. I go over to the pull-up bar and do 17 pull-ups, which isn't my record but is still pretty good for me for a single set.

When I jog back to start my squats, Natalie's still doing hers. Her face is a little sweaty, but she's smiling and still doing squats at a good pace. If I had to guess where she was numbers-wise at that point, I'd say well over 100.

She and I do squats next to each other. I pass 100 and she passes 200. I pass 150 and she passes 250. She starts to slow down then. The muscles in my quads and butt are hurting bad, but I can't show her that they are because she's still going on squats. I try to squat to the same depth, but I'm starting to fall apart. Finally, Natalie drops down onto the grass, props herself up on her forearms, and goes into a plank position. I do a few more squats, just out of pride, then drop down next to her.

I don't do well. I start shaking right away. My stomach starts to sag, and Natalie says, "Straight. Bring that up."

I straighten my body for maybe 10 seconds, but then it starts to sag again.

Natalie says, "Get that shit up or it doesn't count."

I straighten one more time, but I have to will myself straight, and when I look at Natalie she's still in a perfect plank position and I have no hope of winning. I fight as long as I can, but my body breaks down and I slowly sag to the grass.

I lie there panting, then say, "You win. Good game."

Natalie smiles, rolls over onto her back, and lies there breathing. "Good game."

I stay down a long time, lie there, watching Natalie. I watch her abs rise and fall, watch the lines of her ribs, then her chest expanding and dropping.

I say, "You knew you were going to win, didn't you?"

She's looking at the sky. "I always win."

"But what if I won?"

"You didn't." She smiles. "But small consolation: you made it further than any other guy I've competed against. I've always done so many squats that the guy has to start his plank first. And by the time I drop down, he's already defeated. But you're competitive. I like that."

"So did I worry you, then?"

Natalie shakes her head. "Oh, hell no. I knew you'd suck at planks."

"What?"

Natalie smiles again. "You were horrible at planking, super weak, and I knew you would be because all guys are." She pops up to her feet, walks over and grabs her cones and soccer ball. "I'll see you around," she says.

"Yeah," I say. "I'll see you around."

LOCUSTS

GRANDMA AND GRANDPA ARE GONE when I get back from the basketball court. I wish there was a basketball game on TV, but even the NBA finals are over. I'm stiff from the workout competition with Natalie, and I can tell that tomorrow I'll be sore.

I make a three-inch-thick sandwich with turkey and salami slices, cheese, and lettuce, and I mix a big cup of cold Tang. Then I go down to my tent and get the latest book Creature left for me, *Drown*, and I bring it back up to the house and sit on the couch in the living room, reading and eating. The first story is nothing like anything I've read before. The books that Grandma always gives me are slow at the beginning, and almost all of them are set in Europe, in Russia or France or England, a long time ago. But this book is on the island of the Dominican Republic and it starts right off with violence and cussing and a little bit of sex stuff. The older brother's always getting into trouble, always trying to do things he shouldn't, and the little brother's always following along. I like the book a lot, and I sit on the couch and read the next two stories. I'm still reading when my grandma and grandpa get home.

I hear them in the driveway, and Grandpa yells, "Hey, Travis? Are you home?"

I open the front door. Go out on the porch.

Grandpa's trying to get Grandma out of the car, and he's struggling to lift her. I jump down the steps. "I've got this, Grandpa. I've got her."

"She's a mess," he says.

And she is. She has a big smear of vomit down the front of her shirt, chunks of pink in her lap. "Oh, Grandma, I'm sorry."

She says, "No, sweetie, I'm sorry. I smell terrible." Her voice sounds like she swallowed a few pieces of sandpaper.

I say, "I don't care about that." I get my hands underneath her armpits and pull her out of the car and to her feet. Then I slide one arm behind her back and one arm underneath her knees. "Let me lift you."

"Thank you, sweetie." She doesn't weigh much anymore, maybe 105 pounds, 110 at the most, and it's not hard to carry her up the stairs and into the house. I take her to the bathroom and set her down on the toilet. "Here, put your hand on the counter. Hold on."

Grandpa's behind me. "Thank you, Travis. I can take it from here. I'll get her into the shower."

"Okay."

Grandma says, "This looks bad, but I had fun today."

"That's good, Grandma."

"I really did," she says. "We had so much fun today."

* * *

Out in the kitchen, I take off my shirt and put it in the sink. Soak it in warm water and dish soap. Then I take a rag and wipe my chest and shoulder where a little bit of vomit soaked through my shirt. I smell there and wipe again.

I used to clean my mom up like this, but she didn't ever say thank you. Usually she was asleep, her vomit down the front of her. I'd come in from playing basketball or just shooting alone on the back court, and she'd be asleep against the wall, the room smelling terrible.

I'd feel my head filling with blood and then my head would be tight, too tight like that blood was trying to push out from behind my eyes, and I'd have to lean against the wall for a second so I wouldn't pass out, but then I'd stand back up and I'd get her clothes off and fight her weight as I worked her into the tub. Then I'd run the water and fill the bath, wake her over and over as the water rose. I'd say, "Mom, you've got to wake up and clean yourself off. You have to." I'd put a washcloth in her hand. But she wouldn't wake up, and I'd stop the water before it was too high, then I'd sit in there, in the bathroom with her, and wait for her to open her eyes.

Sometimes I wouldn't eat dinner afterward because I wasn't hungry anymore. My hands would feel sort of numb and I'd lie on the bed and open and close my fingers, and hope for that feeling to go away.

THE CAMPS

I SEARCH AGAIN IN THE morning. I have my backpack filled with cookies, the money jar, cold pizza wrapped in foil, dinner rolls, an old Gatorade bottle filled with ice cubes and mixed Tang. I bike down to the DeFazio Bridge, Alton Baker Park, check the Mill Race, the spillway bridge, the picnic area. Find two people sleeping in the middle of the island, both of them men in their 20s, one without a shirt on, a rash covering his back, yellow pus in the cracks.

I hike the river paths on the north bank, the fish camps, the sloughs. Trash heaps. Find a young woman passed out like she'd been hit in the head with a rock and fell that way. But she is breathing, and her right hand still holds an HRD vodka bottle, a few ounces in the bottom like water.

An old man at the west end of the trails is reading a mystery novel with a blue cover. I nod to him and he nods back.

I keep looking. Where the cottonwoods lean over the river, a middle-aged man smokes a cigarette and stares at the water.

He's wearing a wool shirt and a down coat as if it's 20 degrees out, not 85. The July sunlight beats on his army-green jacket and he sits and soaks it up.

I say, "How's it going?" but he doesn't nod or say anything back to me.

I keep walking. Cut through on the trails east, up past the mini-boulders. There's a group of men and women with pit bulls at the picnic shelters, under the tin roof, two of the dogs growling at each other, one lunging, then the other lunging back, nearly meeting at the ends of their ties, a foot from each other, off the ground on their hind legs, snarling and thrashing and choking themselves against their collars.

I go back to the river trails, work east past the boat ramp toward the Autzen Footbridge. I look in the hollows, in the berry overgrowths, in places where she might be sleeping, check under a particleboard lean-to and a tarp shelter. But there's no one under either of those, and I don't find her, don't see her dirty hair and green eyes, don't see the lines across her forehead or her high cheekbones that are always so pink they look like the first layer of skin has been taken off with sandpaper.

I sit down and stare at the water. Feel hopeless. It's easy for me not to think about the homeless camps when I'm on the surface streets in this city, when I'm biking on the sidewalk or riding in someone's car through traffic. But down along the river, on the mud paths, at the tents or shelters, or under the bridge, I can't ignore how these people are living, how she's living right now, how the elements are always on her, how it's too hot or too cold, or the rain's soaking through everything, or the sun's cracking it open. And on days like this I can't even find her, and I worry where she could be because there are worse places than these homeless camps. There are the condemned houses out in West Eugene, the motels near Highway 99, rooms with a dozen people passed out, some on top of others, the floor littered with needles, broken bottles in the bathroom. And I can't save her from that. I can't even find her.

Biking home, I stop at a traffic light, put my foot down next to a woman at the corner of the 76 gas station. Her cardboard sign reads:

GOD GIVES FOOD AND SHELTER

I give her all the food in my backpack.

The Pervert's Guide to Russian Princesses
Princess #29 (First Draft)

Princess Catherine Yurievskaya, you sit tall in your photograph, your thick hair pinned up, your head tilted with the weight of it. You are in a formal dress, but I will cut that off of you with a pair of scissors. I don't want you to be formal forever.

You became a professional singer in France after you left Russia, and you will stand next to me in your slip, dressless, and sing while you look out the window of our house in the country. I will rub lotion into your hands as you sing in French, and when I turn your palms up, I will see the lines of your life extending like a cottonwood tree over a river.

The fighting of the Whites and the Reds passed your city and you wandered between the armies. You walked for miles, hungry, alone, your face like a young girl's even though you were 39 years old at the time of the Revolution. No one knows your age now, and to me, you are ageless. I cannot see the lines around your eyes or the creases across your forehead. Your lines vanish like disappearing ink.

You were wronged at birth, born to a mistress of the tsar, illegitimate and unrecognized until Alexander II married your mother when you were two. For a year you were the favored child. A toddler. Then the emperor was assassinated and that favor went away. Was that your one blessed year? I want to give you another year like that. Then another year after that.

You will ask me to take off your slip and pour lotion on your back. You will ask me to rub your body as I rubbed your hands, next to the window. I will cover your skin in lotion, the glistening of the lotion like jewels under the moonlight.

You will ask me to lay on top of you and be still, the weight of my body holding you solidly to the earth.

NERDS

CREATURE FOLDS THE PAGES AND puts them in his pocket. "What do you think?"

"Honestly? I think that one was kind of sad, man."

"Yeah, I know," Creature says. "When I read the true details about her life, she seemed super sad. Only two family members attended her funeral."

"Only two people?"

"That's what I read. But what do you think about the pages?"

"I don't know. I'm not a writer."

"Well, did you like it?"

"Yeah," I say. "I was interested the whole time, so that's a good sign, right?"

Creature pulls the pages back out of his pocket, unfolds them, and looks at them again. He says, "'Cause I'm not sure if this entry fits with the rest. The tone's a lot different on this one."

"I don't know, man. Maybe that's okay, right? I mean, I'm not a writer, but everything doesn't have to be the same, you know?"

Creature leans his head back and thinks about that. Then he nods and puts the pages back in his pocket.

I say, "You really like reading about Russian history, huh?"

"Yeah," he says, "it's super interesting. I never knew anything about Russia until I read a few things online last year, and now I'm hooked. The Revolution was crazy. How they executed the Romanov family and all that? It was like a purge, like an extermination."

"And you put some of those facts in the book. Some of your facts are real, right?"

"All of them are real but the love stuff. The sex stuff. And I try to make those parts ridiculous. I want my guidebook to be disguised history, like a complex basketball play. Entertainment on top, but reality underneath, something about these lives, these women. Complex."

"That's cool," I say. "I like complex in certain situations. Like basketball."

"All right," Creature says, "like basketball. So give me an example."

This is a game we play sometimes. He gives me a challenge, and I have to answer it quickly.

"All right," I say. "How about . . . Let's see. . . . Set up the high pick like it's a pick-and-roll for the four and the point. Point baits with a jab step. Roll the four off to the top of the key as the other three run double backdoor cuts. The five screens for the two. The two screens for the three after. So the pick-and-roll is the first bait, and the first backdoor is set up too. Defenders come high and run through. Then the second backdoor is the layin or dunk. Two ball fakes, and the assist comes on a bounce pass or an alley-oop."

"Oh, baby." Creature laughs at me. "You're as nerdy as I am with writing and Russian history."

"Like you always say, Creat, I know what I like."

MAYBE THIS IS NOTHING?

THE GAMES UNDER THE BRIDGE tonight aren't good, no quality players, and Creature dominates without trying very hard. In one
game, the high pick-and-roll fools the other team four times in a
row and I hit him for layups and dunks, until it doesn't fool the
other team on the fifth run and I pop a long jumper off the screen.

Creature shrugs and says, "That kind of night, I guess."

There isn't a single good game.

Afterward, while we're unlocking our bikes to go, I see
something in the ivy on the lit-up side of the nearby bridge
pylon. "Hey, Creat, what is that?"

He looks. "I don't know."

Something pink. I walk up there. It's the hood of a jacket.
A woman's jacket. The woman is mostly hidden by the ivy.
She's sloped downhill, her feet high, her head low, and she's
passed out. One sleeve is rolled up and the needle is still in her
arm, attached to the syringe.

Creature says, "Is it her?"

"No."

"Are you sure?"

"Yeah." I kneel down. "What should we do?"

Creature says, "With a passed-out junkie? Nothing. I'm sorry, but there's nothing we can do about that."

"Is she still breathing?"

"I don't know," Creature says. "Come on, baby."

I lean in and listen for her breath. Watch her chest to see if it rises and falls, and it does. "She's still breathing."

"Okay, then let's go. Come on."

"No, hold up." I stand and look at her. Think.

Creature says, "Look, Travis, I get why you care so much, but really, there's nothing for us to do here. We can't fix this or even really help her."

I hold up one finger. "Just a minute. I'm gonna turn her right-side up and onto her side."

"Why?"

"So she doesn't choke if she pukes."

"Okay," Creature says. "Just don't get poked with that needle or some shit like that, all right? And junkies sometimes have needles in their pockets too."

"I know."

I take hold of the woman's ankles and I pull her downhill and rotate her around until her feet are below her head. Then I find an old sweatshirt in the ivy, tilt her on her side, and prop her head up on the sweatshirt. "There," I say.

Creature says, "Okay. Now you're ready to go?"

"All right."

We walk down and get our bikes. Pedal across the river at Maurie Jacobs Park, then over Delta Highway on the Neon Bridge, back to the trailer-park loops.

MiSSiᵒNARiES

I PARK MY BIKE BEHIND the shed and go inside to make some food. Grandpa's in the living room watching the game of the night on ESPN. I make a sandwich and go in next to him. Eat and drink a glass of water while the Indians bat during the 7th inning.

Grandpa stands halfway up, teeters, and falls back onto the couch.

"Grandpa?"

He tries to stand again and makes it to his feet this time, but has to lean over and steady himself by holding the coffee table. He mumbles, "I just . . ." He sounds like a voice recording played on the wrong speed.

"Grandpa, what the hell?"

"I just . . ." He giggles and stands back up. Balances. Leans over and holds the table again. "I took some . . . I smoked a little . . ."

"A little?"

"I just . . ."

"Grandpa, what did you do?"

He sits down on the coffee table. Puts his hands out in the air, feeling for something invisible. "Her pills were . . ."

"Wait, you took Grandma's pain pills?"

"A few."

"Grandpa, if you do all this stuff at the same time, you might die. You understand me?"

"Die," he says, and laughs. He puts both hands on his knees to steady himself. Laughs so hard that he's shaking.

I stand up. "I'm going back out."

I leave the house and slam the door. Hop off the porch, get my bike, and start pedaling. I don't have anywhere to go, so I don't go far, just down to the Chevron to grab a Coke. I park my bike and lock it next to the bathrooms. Walk around the corner to the front door. There's a man handing out some kind of pamphlet, and he hands one to me. I start to read it and the man says, "It's about the battle that changed the world."

I hold the pamphlet. Look up.

"Son," he says, and points at me, "there will be things beyond your control in this life. Things you can't handle."

"Excuse me?"

"You'll need help," he says. He's still pointing at me. "This world is dark and difficult. The road is not easy. And there will be things beyond your control."

I laugh in his face. "Things beyond my control?" I look at the pamphlet in my hand. It has a picture of a man on his knees holding a big black book. In the upper right-hand corner it says SEVENTH-DAY ADVENTISTS.

The man says, "Things far beyond your control. You're young, though, so you don't know it yet, but this world is difficult. When you grow up and move out of Mom and Dad's house, when they're no longer cooking for you and doing your laundry, and making your life easy, you're going to find out a whole lot about yourself and the real world."

"The real world . . ." I shake my head. I can feel the anger in my body like ripples on a pond, the circles spreading out, expanding, going to the edges of my skin.

"See," the man says, "you don't believe me now because your life is so easy, but in the real world, the world you don't understand yet, there will be . . ."

I punch him.

I don't even think about it. I just punch him. And it's a good punch, one of those shots where it lands right where I aim and everything about it feels perfect, from how I throw it to where it lands. I catch the man on his chin and his head rips sideways and he goes down quick against the wall, and I know he's knocked out the second he falls.

Then I take a step back. The man is crumpled in front of me and his Seventh-day Adventists pamphlets are spilling onto the cement. There's a gust of wind, and a few of the pamphlets flap and skitter away like small birds.

Someone across the lot yells, "Hey!"

I turn.

It's one of the gas-pump attendants. He's walking toward me from the far pump. He says, "Hold it right there."

But I sprint around the side of the building to my bike, pull the key out of my pocket, unlock it quick, and hop on. Start pedaling. I look back and see the guy coming around the corner. He yells, "You better stop right there."

I don't. I bike behind the Carpet Store to the alley that leads to the Home Depot. It's dark in that alley, between the industrial Dumpsters, and I slow down to think about where I should go next. But there's nowhere to go. So I bike the cross-road to the trailer park, the hedge, and the back entrance to the loops. I pedal to my house, park my bike behind the shed, and walk down to my tent.

This is one of those times when I know that things are going to be messed up no matter what. Like when they couldn't find my mom and the Department of Human Services lady told me they were going to put me in what she called "a temporary placement." And then those two years. I thought things would be better now since I called my grandparents and I'm living here.

But nothing erases the bad. Nothing puts it away forever. The bad is like one of those overgrown Himalayan blackberry patches that we have everywhere in western Oregon. You can cut it back or even burn it to the ground, you can burn it and dump salt over the top, but it doesn't matter. It's coming back. That things has roots, it has incredible unseen roots that live and wait in the dark underground, and it's only a matter of time before it's up again, before that thing is growing three inches a day, snaking along the surface, then hoisting itself into the air on unseen wires, animated, and the bright green thorns along the stems are thin and sharp as razor blades. The only way through the thicket is to take the cutting.

SiGN oN THE CRoSS

NIGHTTIME. LYING ON MY SLEEPING bag. I hear someone's footsteps in the grass. Flip-flops clicking against the bottoms of someone's feet. My tent flap is open—I never zipped it closed—so I wait until I can see who it is.

"Creature?" I say.

"Who's Creature?" It's a girl's voice.

"Natalie?"

"Yeah?"

I scramble to my knees and crawl out of my tent. "Why are you . . . ?"

"I don't know," she says. "Maybe because I had a really shitty day." Her face is lit from the side by the porch light. Her eyes are pure black.

"Yeah?" I say. "I had a shitty day too."

Natalie says, "Wanna trade stories, then? See whose day was more messed up?"

"All right, let's do it."

We sit down on the bank above the lake. There's a warm breeze blowing from behind us, little ripples in front of us.

"You go first," I say. "Why was your day so terrible?"

"Stepdad," she says. "He's a dick. But worse than that, he's weird."

I wait for her to say more. Stare at the lake. The lights from the houses opposite are rippling on the water. The reflections are orange and yellow.

I say, "So your stepdad?"

"Yeah, my stepdad. His name's Will, and he's a real piece of shit."

"Because . . ."

"I don't know. It's hard to explain. He acts nice, seems nice. He has a good job, and he dresses well. We have a nice house and all that. People seem to like him, or at least his friends do, but I don't like his friends."

"But your mom does?"

"She seems to. She seems to have bought in to that whole nice-house, nice-car crap. But I feel like she doesn't see who Will really is."

"Is he good to her?"

"Mostly."

"Mostly?"

Natalie takes a deep breath. "He gets pissed about stupid little things sometimes. But then he's nice most of the time."

"Okay," I say. "And . . ."

"Well," Natalie says, "he makes me uncomfortable."

I wait for her to explain.

She says, "See, most of the time I just get a bad feeling, but today it was obvious."

"What did he do?"

Natalie sighs. "It's embarrassing."

"It's fine," I say. "You don't have to tell me." I shrug like I don't care. But the truth is, I really want to know.

"See," she says, "I went to the park to do a soccer workout, and it was super hot today—you know how hot it was—and I was totally sweaty and gross. So when I got home, I wanted to take a shower. I didn't even think about it. I just went into the bathroom and took a shower. But when I finished, when I turned the water off and pulled back the curtain to grab my towel, he was right there. Will was right there."

"What do you mean 'Will was right there'?"

"He was right there in the bathroom. He was pissing in the toilet right next to me, while I was finishing showering."

"He what?"

"Pissing. Peeing. He was peeing in the toilet next to the shower. I saw his . . ."

"No."

"Yeah, I saw it," she says. "How creepy is that?"

"Real creepy. Weird too. You weren't joking."

"No," she says. "That's fucked up, huh? He was standing there over the toilet . . . just holding his, um . . . He was just shaking it off."

I want to ask if Will's thing was soft or hard. I'm curious, and it matters. I want to ask about that, but I also don't want to ask a girl I still don't know that well that question. Then I think of something else. "Wait," I say. "Do you only have one bathroom in the house?"

"No. We have four."

"Four bathrooms?"

"Yeah."

"So why did he use the one where you were showering?"

"Exactly," she says. "What the hell?"

"Were other people home? Was your mom home?"

"No. She was still at work."

"So it was just the two of you home. You have four bathrooms, and he took a piss in the one where you were showering."

"Right."

"Wow. I don't know what to say about that."

Natalie picks up a handful of gravel and throws it in the water in front of us. She says, "I can't believe he saw me naked."

"Shit."

"Yeah," Natalie says. "I screamed and cussed at him, and he acted like it was some kind of big misunderstanding. A mistake. He kept saying how sorry he was and that he just went to pee without thinking, that he just walked in there by accident."

"No, no, no," I say. "No way."

"I know, right? Fuck that. It wasn't a mistake." Natalie takes another handful of gravel and sorts the rocks in her hand. Moves the little ones toward her thumb, the big ones out to her fingertips. Then she tilts her hand and lets them fall off.

I say, "I'm sorry. That sucks."

"Yeah, it does."

"That's messed up."

Neither of us says anything for a minute. There are black lines on the water in between the ripples of orange and yellow light. The lines shift, and above them, on the east side, the windows of the houses are wide and bright.

Natalie stands up.

"What is it?"

"Shhh." She sneaks forward.

I stand and try to see what she's seeing.

She crouches down by the edge of the water, on the left side of my little gravel beach. She reaches into the long reeds, reaches with both hands, then stops.

I say again, "What is it?"

She lunges and clasps something in her hands. Stands up. "Got it."

In the dark, I can't see what she's holding. "What is it?"

"A frog." She sits down again. "So why was your day wonderful?"

"Well," I say, "the highlight was when I punched a Seventh-day Adventist."

"You what?"

"I punched a missionary guy."

Natalie cups her other hand over the frog's head and looks straight at me. "Really?"

I nod.

"Was he hurt?"

"I don't know if he was hurt for real, but I know I knocked him out."

"What the . . . How hard did you hit him?"

"Pretty hard. I knocked him out and then I took off. Ran to my bike and pedaled away."

Natalie shakes her head. "But why'd you punch him in the first place?"

"It's sort of hard to explain," I say. "My grandpa . . ."

Natalie waits for me to explain. She pets the frog some more. "Your grandpa was there?"

"No, no. It's a long story."

"Well," she says, "I'm kind of in a hurry to get back to my stepdad's den of perversion, so I don't really have much time right now. . . ." Natalie pushes me.

"All right," I say. "I'll explain then. My grandpa gets high."

"Your grandpa?"

"Yeah."

"High? Like, smokes weed?"

"Yeah."

Natalie giggles. Then she stops herself. "I'm sorry. That's not funny."

"He gets high every day, smokes my grandma's medical weed. She has a card since she's been sick."

"And he smokes hers?"

"Yep."

"Every day?"

"Yep. He smokes a ton. Gets super high."

"This is your grandpa we're talking about? An old man?"

"Right, I know. It sounds like something a person would make up, but I'm not. He smokes all the time, and my grandma's not doing well. But Grandpa doesn't seem to be worried about that. He just watches baseball and smokes weed. Eats Doritos or brownie batter. And tonight he took a bunch of Grandma's pain pills and got all messed up. He couldn't even stand right."

"Like, he was wobbly?"

"And mumbling."

"Oh damn," Natalie holds the frog in one hand and points back at my house with her other hand. "Do you live with them all year? With your grandma and grandpa?"

"Yep."

"Full-time? Even during the school year?"

I nod.

Natalie sets the frog down. Nudges its back to make it jump toward the water. Then she wipes her hands on the grass. "And this missionary guy, he said . . ."

"He said that my life was too easy now but that soon enough I'd realize what the real world was like—how difficult life can be."

"Wow," she says. "Super condescending."

"I let him talk for a minute, but then I just punched him."

Natalie laughs. "Sorry, but that's pretty funny. And maybe he learned a good lesson, right? Maybe he'll learn how to talk to people."

"Maybe," I say, "but I've got to stop punching people. I can't afford to do that anymore."

"Wait, is this something you do regularly? Is my shirtless neighbor boy secretly a UFC fighter?"

We both laugh, and I shake my head. Natalie's next to me, her smooth, strong legs six inches away. I want to run my hand up and down those legs, but instead I look away. Creature told me once that if you want a girl, do the opposite of everything you think of, the opposite of everything you want to do. He also said that ignoring a girl for a minute or two will do wonders. I force myself to look away from Natalie, and try not to say anything.

While I'm still looking the other direction, Natalie leans against me, bumps my shoulder with hers. "You and punching, huh? You might have a little bit of a problem?"

"I guess I might even punch myself. You never know." I smile at her.

Her shoulder is still touching my shoulder. I like the way she feels leaning against me. A breeze comes from behind us and I consider putting my arm around her. But then I think of Creature's advice and I lean away again. I don't want to, but I lean just far enough away that Natalie and I are not touching anymore.

Natalie's phone buzzes and she taps the screen to check the text. "It's my stepdad."

For some reason—just a reaction—I grab her phone out of her hands and throw it over my shoulder.

"Hey," Natalie says, "why'd you . . ."

"I hate those things. Plus, your stepdad sounds like a dick."

"True," she says, and kisses me. Just like that.

I've kissed girls before, but it's been a while since I have, and I'm not expecting it. Natalie kisses me and I kiss her back, and she's holding my face, and she tastes like mint ChapStick, her lips and the tip of her tongue. I smell the mint on her lips and the lake water on her hands, and the smell of torn grass.

We slide onto the ground and roll over. I roll up on top of her, and her body feels long and lean underneath me, strong, and I love the feeling of our bodies against each other, and she's still holding my face in her hands and she's kissing me hard. I'm kissing her too and I can feel the dark of the sky changing above us and the ground moving underneath our bodies like everything is tilting and spinning fast.

Natalie rolls us over, and then she's on top of me. She kisses me slower then, sucks at my bottom lip, kisses the side of my neck.

I open my eyes. See the night above the outline of her head, the first stars pricking through the deep blue.

She kisses me on the mouth again, then stops and pushes up. Says, "I've been wanting to do that for a while now."

I want to be kissing her again. I want to take her shirt off, want to feel her skin against mine.

She puts her hand flat on my chest. She says, "I like my no-shirt neighbor boy."

"If you want me to, I could put my shirt on more often."

"No, no, it's okay," she says. "Don't wear too much clothing. It'll probably restrict your movements or something, make you claustrophobic, might even mess up your basketball game."

"Right," I say. "I'll just keep my shirt off for basketball purposes, then."

"Good," Natalie says, "and that way I'll be able to continue objectifying you." She smiles and leans down, kisses me once more, then stands up. "Where'd you throw my phone?"

We search around in the grass for the phone. It takes a while to find it, and I'm glad I didn't throw it farther. It's wedged in a wide crack in the dirt between two big clumps of grass. I hand it to Natalie. "Here it is."

"Thanks." She checks her texts, then locks the screen and slides the phone into her bra. It's those little things that girls do sometimes that devastate me: sliding a phone into a bra, adjusting panties under a skirt, redoing a ponytail.

Natalie turns and walks down the footpath toward the blackberry growth.

I say, "Want me to walk you home?"

"No," she says. "I'm okay. I've got mace on my keychain and it's only old people who live here. I think I can mace an old man all by myself."

"But what if your mom's not home yet?"

She turns around and looks at me, walks backward as she talks. "Then I'll mace my stepdad."

I laugh, but it's not funny.

She puts one hand up and waves, then disappears into the shadows of the blackberry growth.

CANOE RIDE

THE MORNING IS LIKE A new box of nails, dew silver on the grass. I walk up to the house to see if Grandma is awake. In her room, she's sitting in bed, eating saltine crackers, sipping at a cup of Sprite.

I say, "Good morning, Grandma."

"Oh, good morning, sweetie."

"Feeling all right?"

She smiles. "I'm doing just fine."

I sit down on the edge of her bed and she stops eating.

"No, no. Keep eating, Grandma."

She takes another bite of cracker.

I pat her leg. "Is today good?"

"Yes. I think we should take a short canoe ride together."

"Perfect." I stand up. "I'll be ready in five minutes."

I grab pillows and a blanket from the closet, jog down the hill, flip the canoe, and set up a spot for Grandma in the front of the boat. Then I push the canoe to the edge of the water, slide the bow in, weight the stern with a rock, and jog back uphill.

Grandma's still sipping Sprite in bed.

"Are you ready?"

She raises her eyebrows. "Ready as I'll ever be."

I help her to her feet. Support her as she shuffles out of the room, down the hall to the back door.

Grandpa's in his study, modeling. He calls out, "Where are you all going?"

"Short canoe ride, Grandpa."

"Is that a good idea?"

I ignore that question. Slide the back door open and lift Grandma off her feet. "I can carry you from here."

"Are you sure, sweetie? Even down the hill?"

"Definitely."

I carry her down the hill through the long grass, past my tent, careful not to trip on any of the gopher mounds, the ruts, the bigger river rocks. I wade out into the water and set Grandma in the front of the canoe, on top of the pillows. Pull the blanket over her. "Are you comfortable, Grandma?"

"I'm perfect, sweetie."

"Good." I push off and jump in. The canoe rocks back and forth as it glides out. I hold the paddle. Wait for the glide to slow.

I stroke to the middle. The canoe cuts across green glass, no wind and no fish jumping. South of us, a family of ducks steps off a mud peninsula, swims out past the shallows into the algae patch.

"This is wonderful," Grandma says.

"Yeah, it's pretty nice out here." I say this as I scan the top of the water for caiman eyes, for the swish of a monster's tail.

"Oh no, sweetie," Grandma says, "it's more than nice."

I can't see her face, but I know she's smiling. I can hear the smile in her voice, see the way she tilts her head a little bit as if the smile weighs something, as if it pulls her head just a little bit off center.

KERMIT WASHINGTON

WE'VE HAD THIS MEETING SET up since the end of school. I wrote it on the calendar that I keep in the kitchen and circled it in bright red pen. It should be a good meeting. Coach always liked me. But I haven't talked to him since school got out, so I'm nervous. I make myself eat a bowl of cereal and drink a glass of water to try to settle my stomach before I leave, but I still feel like I could puke.

I bike down to the high school and lock my bike outside the gym. Go in the west-side door and onto the hardwood. I don't see anybody in there yet, and I'm 15 minutes early, so I start dribbling. Right-handed, left-handed, crossovers, behind my back, and cutting. I dribble out to the three-point line, then cross up an imaginary defender, drive, and lay the ball in off the glass. Then I do the same sequence but finish with a reverse layin to use the rim as protection against shot blockers.

Coach comes in. He says, "Can you do that with your left hand? If you come right to left?"

"No. Not as well, but I've been working on it." I dribble back to the three-point line. Run the crossover, drive, and hit the layin left-handed. Then back to the three-point line, crossover, drive, and reverse layin with my left, but I miss the shot. The ball rolls off the front of the rim. I rebound and put it back with a power layin. Say, "Let me do that again."

Coach smiles and nods. "Go, Russell Westbrook."

I run the play four more times. On the first, I hit the reverse layin. Then I miss again. Then I hit two in a row.

"Good," Coach says. "Now let's go to my office."

I was just getting a sweat going and his office is hot. He reaches into a mini-fridge under his desk and pulls out an orange Gatorade. Hands it to me.

"Thanks, Coach."

He waves me off. "Let's cut to the chase here, T. Let's talk about last year."

"Okay, Coach."

"Do you know why you made varsity as a freshman?"

I take a drink of Gatorade. "Is it because I was a year older than most freshmen?"

He smiles. "That probably didn't hurt you. But no. Most sophomores don't make varsity either. There were two reasons that you made it, and I'll give you a hint: neither of them had to do with your shot or your ball handling."

"Well, I was going to guess my ball handling," I say. "I wasn't going to guess my shooting, that's for sure. But it's getting better."

Coach smiles again. He has a way of smiling that doesn't show any of his teeth. It's like his face turns into a map of cracks. He says, "Your handles are better than your shot, that's true, but it didn't have to do with that."

I wait for him to tell me.

"See, T, after tryouts, we came up with two words for each player in the tryout pool. Things like 'shooter' or 'rebounder,' 'mistake-prone,' 'defender,' 'lazy,' or 'foolish.' And do you know what our two words were for you?"

I shake my head.

He holds up two fingers. Touches the first finger and says, "Quickness." He touches the second finger and says, "Passion." He smiles again. His face cracks into a dozen lines.

"Thanks, Coach."

"No, don't thank me. You earned those two words. Those were the words that all of the coaches agreed on. We needed a guard quick enough to stay with any guard in the league, and we also needed a kid passionate enough about the game of basketball to go out and bleed on that floor, to dive for loose balls, run through screens, play help defense. And that's why you made varsity."

"Thanks, Coach."

"The problem is"—he pauses—"we didn't know that you'd make someone else bleed on the court too."

I hang my head when he says that. I hate to think about that night. I hate to think about the lost season, how much I let everyone down, how I let that player get to me. I say, "It was a big mistake, Coach. I'm real, real sorry about that."

"Now I understand," Coach says. "I know what he said about your mom, and I get how fired up you can be during a ballgame. Believe me, I understand all that. Your passion is infectious out there. But still, you can't do what you did. You can't act like that."

"I know, Coach. I really do."

"See, because he was running the other direction, there was

so much force in the punch. He ran into your fist, and it looked like his head was going to come off."

"I know, Coach. I jammed my wrist when I hit him. My wrist didn't loosen up for a week."

Coach nods. "Did you see the video on YouTube?"

"No, Coach. I didn't want to see that. Creature told me."

"It went viral. The video has a little bit of game footage to start, then the punch, then the paramedics on the court and a long shot of a girl holding her hands to her mouth and crying."

"It sounds horrible." I hang my head even more. It's like someone's placed a 45-pound weight bar on the back of my neck and it's pushing my head down.

"Yeah, that video is horrible," he says. "And it might even be why you got such a harsh penalty from the league."

I nod.

He says, "There was a punch like that a long, long time ago in the NBA. A forward named Kermit Washington punched another forward, a guy named Rudy Tomjanovich, and it ended up being Washington's defining moment in the league."

I flinch when he says that. That weight bar is still pushing down on my neck and I can't look up at Coach.

"But," Coach says, "we won't let that happen to you. I won't let that happen. You were just a kid last year, a freshman in high school, and it was a mistake. So that's not what I think of when I see you. It really isn't." Coach takes a deep breath and lets it out. "When I look at you, I see a young player who's passionate about the game, someone who works three times as hard as the average player. You're on the short side and you don't have Rajon Rondo–size hands, but you have a lot of talent and you also love the game. And that matters. Big-time. You hear me?"

"Yes, Coach."

"So that incident? That punch? That suspension for the rest of the season? It doesn't mean much to me now. It's over. You hear me?"

When he says that, it's as if that weight bar slides down a little, settles on my shoulders, not just the back of my neck, and I can lift my head. I say, "Thanks, Coach."

"This is a new year," he says, "and if you keep working the way you do, then you've got a shot at All-League as a sophomore. Then, who knows from there?"

I don't say anything but I smile pretty big when he says that. I want All-League bad, but I never tell anyone about that.

Coach says, "That's the truth. You could earn that. And I'm excited about the coming season." He leans over and takes another Gatorade out of his mini-fridge, opens it, and gulps a big drink. He sits back and sighs. "Now, honestly," he says, "how's your anger?"

"Coach?"

"I mean, when was the last time you got in a fight?"

I hesitate a little because I know I can't tell Coach the whole truth. I lower my head and say, "I don't really fight, Coach."

"You don't?" he says. "Let me put it this way: When was the last time you punched someone?"

The Seventh-day Adventist pops into my head. I can see his head spin when I hit him, the way his mouth was open halfway as he lay slumped against the wall. But I can't tell Coach about that. I have to lie. I say, "I haven't hit anyone since that basketball game."

"You haven't? Are you sure?"

"That's the truth, Coach." When I say that, I can feel my eyes wanting to twitch, like I want to blink a lot or something,

145

and I remember how my science teacher last year told us about the physical signs of lying. So I make myself look Coach right in the eyes, and I don't blink, and I don't look away.

He says, "So you've been avoiding trouble altogether?"

"Yes, sir," I say. Another lie. He doesn't know about shoplifting either. *But*—I ask myself—*is it trouble if I never get caught?* In my head I go back and forth on that one, and in the end, I decide that it's not trouble since I don't get *in trouble* for it.

Coach takes another big drink of his Gatorade. "That's good, T. That's real good, because I want you to have a full season this year."

"Okay, Coach." I stand up and throw my Gatorade bottle in the garbage can next to his desk.

Coach leans down, picks the bottle back up, and tosses it in the recycling bin instead.

HOUSEHOLD PETS

NEAR THE CHEVRON LATE THAT evening, I see another missing dog poster. It reads:

LOST BOXER-CHIHUAHUA MIX
BLACK-AND-WHITE, NAMED LUCY
LOST NEAR AYRES LAKE ON SATURDAY
REWARD OF $100
CALL (541) 554-6095

I shake my head. Feel sort of bad. There was a dog that hung around one of our motels a few years ago. He was a small gray terrier, skittish and mangy, but I loved him and I named him Chris Paul III. Sometimes I'd bring him into our room when my mom was gone. I would save a little food for him, Taco Bell meat, anything I could find in the Dumpster, or unfinished food I'd scrounged at Subway.

I'd sit on the bed in our motel room and pet behind his

ears, watch him fall asleep on my lap. We'd watch television, and sometimes a loud noise on the screen would make him pop his head up and look around like someone was trying to get him. Sometimes he'd even growl at the screen, and his ears would turn into two sharp triangles, and that always made me laugh.

But one day I couldn't find him and I searched all over. I searched behind the adult video store, the shoe outlet, and the fast-food Dumpsters. I went over to the Red Apple and the Mexican food cart. But he was nowhere, and it wasn't until I was walking home after dark that I found him.

He'd been hit by a car on 6th Street. I found him lying on the gutter grate, the storm drain, his head turned the wrong way around. He was so small lying there, and I picked him up and saw that his front leg was broken too, snapped and pushed back, and I threw a rock at the nearest parked car even though I knew it wasn't the car that had hit him.

I remember the week after he died, how I didn't want to shoot baskets or watch TV, how the motel room felt so empty when my mom was gone, how I kept looking for him each morning before realizing, once again, that he wasn't coming back.

I was thinking about this and feeling sort of bad for the people who'd lost their pets. In a way, I'd known these things might happen when I released the caimans, but in another way I hadn't. I guess I didn't really think it all through. I wanted something exciting for the people along the lake, and that is what's starting to happen.

I shake my head and jog over to Mr. Tyler's house so I can do something I don't feel bad about. In front of his single-wide, the warm stench of our collective summer's worth of urine hits me before I even leave the sidewalk. I turn in a circle and check for anyone who might see me, then hop up on the porch.

For some reason, Mr. Tyler's left his shoes there by the front door. I look over my shoulder once more, but there's still no one out in the neighborhood. I unzip my fly, whip it out, and pee long and hard into his shoes, fill one to the brim, then switch to the other, and get that shoe most of the way full as well.

SMASHING

WHEN I GET HOME, I stash my bike behind the shed. Walk up on the back porch and stop. Grandpa's pipe, the old briarroot he loves, is on the glass table. I pick it up. Smell it. Smell the burnt marijuana, the ash. I walk down to the edge of the lake.

I hold the pipe in my hand, dark-wood bowl, black stem, little white cloverleaf imprint in the middle. I snap the stem off, try to break each piece again but both the bowl and the stem are solid. My hands slip. I reach down and pick up a large pebble. Jam the pebble into the bottom of the bowl. Then I lay the stem on a wide rock and smash it into tiny pieces using another rock. Dump those off and grind the pieces into the dirt. Then I pick up the bowl, the pebble stuck in its mouth, and throw it in the lake.

I look over at my tent and see two pages pinned underneath a rock, the white paper reflecting the early moonlight.

The Pervert's Guide to Russian Princesses
Princess #31 (Rough Draft)

Mathilde Kschessinskaya, I've watched you from the front row at the Imperial Ballet, looking up your tutu as you rise on pointe, your calves flexing and your feet arching downward like commas on the sentence of the stage.

You became *prima ballerina assoluta* even though the maestro Petipa didn't like you and called you "that nasty little swine." He was afraid of you, afraid of how you could use your body. And you used your body like a goddess from an unknown religion. But I am not afraid of you.

I will build a stage of marble, smooth and straight, underneath the naked sky, and we will dance without clothes when it rains. I will watch your muscles ripple over your bones, your thin ballerina's body a perfect match for the long muscles of an NBA two-guard. I will guard you.

I know that you created scandals and rumors by passing back and forth between two dukes of the Romanov family, that you held Nicholas II in the palm of your hand, but you will stay with me from now on and never be traded again.

Your rivals mean nothing to me. Anna Pavlova, long limbed and ethereal-looking, a crowd favorite, will drink a concoction of lime juice and Ex-Lax before her next show, and she will lose control of her bowels onstage. And Preobrajenskaya won't be given another premier role either. Her pointe shoes will always be missing, her costumes torn before she walks onstage, the hair on one side of her head shaved off in her sleep. You will hear your rivals weeping after every show, asking, "Will I ever star again?"

The answer is no. Not again. Because of me.

When you decide to quit dancing, you will ask me to move to France with you, and I will agree. We will rent an artist's studio on the east side and live off bread and cheese and vegetables grown in our window boxes.

In the afternoon, you ask me to suckle your neck on a riverboat heading up the Seine. You lay back on the prow, your skeletal body arched as I put my lips to your throat.

In the evening, you will sit at a café barefoot, begging me to tickle the thick calluses on your gnarled feet, feet that will never recover from your years of dancing. I will pour water over the thickened twists of your toes, watch the drops fall from the yellow of your fungus-covered toenails.

THE FRIDGE

THE NEXT AFTERNOON, I ARRIVE at Natalie's dock in the canoe, gliding to catch the edge.

She says, "Hey there."

I'd seen her from across the lake, paddled hard. I say, "Hey back."

As I tie the bowline, I try to think of something funny to say. I want Natalie to kiss me again, but I don't know how to start a new conversation after what happened. In the end I don't say anything.

Natalie frowns. "Are you all right?"

"Yeah, sorry. I was thinking about something."

"Your face looked so serious. What were you thinking?"

"Nothing." I shake my head. "Do you have a bike?"

"A bike? Yeah."

"All right. Then do you want to go jump off Knickerbocker Bridge with me?"

"Knickerbocker? I can't remember, is that a tall bridge?"

"Not too tall," I say. "Maybe 35 feet?"

Natalie folds the corner of the page in her book. Sets it down next to her. "What are we jumping into?"

"Water," I say.

"No shit." She laughs. "I mean, is it a river, a pond, a lake, a creek . . . ?"

"Oh, right. A river. The Willamette River. The water's deep, and not too cold."

Natalie nods. "Okay," she says. "Let's do it."

"Yeah?"

She stands up and dusts off the back of her shorts. "Yeah, that sounds like fun."

"Okay. I'll paddle back to my tent and get my bike. You get your bike. If you ride south on Gilham while I ride east, we'll meet at the skate park. Sound good?"

When I get to the skate park, Natalie isn't there yet, so I wait and watch the kids skate. Most of them aren't any good, but one kid is, and I watch him do nollie kick-flip tricks on the tabletop and think about how much he must've worked to get those tricks down. I've always liked watching anyone who had to work to learn a skill. That's why YouTube sucks me in sometimes. I couldn't care less about kitten videos or the newest celebrity video of whatever it is that celebrities do, but I'll watch a snowboarder or a BMX biker who's dialed a new gap trick even though I've never ridden a snowboard or done a BMX trick in my life. I'll sometimes watch the same video over and over, just thinking about how many times he messed up before he got it down. That's what I think about when I watch skaters too. They have hundreds of attempts behind every successful stick. It's a lot like watching Michael Jordan

154

hit a double-clutch reverse layin so smooth and perfect, and people say stupid things like "It's because he was such a natural athlete." But I know better. It's because he worked harder than other people were willing to work.

I'm thinking about all of that, and I don't notice when Natalie rides up. She puts her arms around me from behind and hugs me. "You okay today?" she says.

I like her hugging me, so I don't say anything other than "Yeah." I keep watching the kid skating in front of us.

I don't know if Natalie understands how hard nollie kickflips are because she doesn't say anything while the kid's skating, but she keeps hugging me and that's good enough. When I turn around, she kisses me, one long kiss, and her lips taste like mint ChapStick again, and I feel the tip of her tongue and I want to kiss her like that all day long in the sun.

She pulls back and raises her aviator sunglasses, her green eyes wide. "Ready?"

I nod. "Yep."

I'm riding in front, leading, and I look back at Natalie and she's wearing a white tank top over a black bikini and the straps are thin and there's so much tan skin to admire, and I wish that I could ride behind her so I could look at her as much as I want to.

I smile back at her and pedal a little faster. She has her knee brace on her one leg, but it doesn't seem to slow her down. She rides fast on her 27-speed white Surly, and I like seeing her big fat smile every time I look back.

We ride along the river on the north bank, through Alton Baker Park, then down past the cottonwood grove at the footbridge. From there, the bike path winds along the field, the old landfill with the methane pipes sticking up every hundred feet, and I think about all of the homeless camps across the river, the big one behind the low-head dam, the dam's angled cement graffitied in yellows, purples, and silvers, and how my mom lived there one summer. That was when I was 10, the first time I stayed with my grandma, and I thought the house on the lake was magical, the food in the refrigerator more than I could imagine. I remember going into the kitchen even when I was full, right after breakfast or lunch or dinner, and just opening up the fridge door and staring at all of the food lit up on the shelves. I would tell myself, *I'm gonna eat that, then I'm gonna eat that, then after I finish, I'm gonna eat that and that and that until I'm so full that I feel sick.* Then I'd open the freezer and look at the ice cream.

Knickerbocker Bridge straddles the river just down from the I-5 bridge near the edge of town. On the southeast side of the bridge, the water underneath is a smooth green channel, deep and fast. The wooden railing is gouged and carved, marked with names, dates, and arrows showing where people jumped from. There's a TR, with a wide arrow next to it, and that's my jumping spot. I've never hit the bottom from there.

I say, "The police put up a NO JUMPING sign three times one year, but the sign was stolen every time."

Natalie says, "Can you get arrested for jumping, or is it just a fine?"

"I don't know."

She takes off her sunglasses. Wriggles out of her jean shorts. "Then we better jump quick."

There are some guys drinking at that end of the bridge, a little down from us. Each one's holding a 40 of Olde E or Steel

Reserve, swigging and laughing. One of them walks up, sets his bottle down on the cement, climbs over the rail, and holds on, facing me and Natalie. He has his back to the river below. He lets go and leans back, rolls through a slow backflip, and hits the water feetfirst. His friends cheer and hold up their 40s.

Natalie says, "Damn, that was smooth." She pulls her tank top over her head. Unties and reties her bikini top. Adjusts the straps on her knee brace.

She climbs up on the rail. "Are you coming or what?" She stands there for a second, balancing, putting her arms out wide to steady herself.

"You're gonna jump from the top of the rail? It's 35 feet from there."

She says, "Then I better not think about it," and jumps. Her body arcs out into the space above the water. She falls. Pulls her feet up a little before she hits and I hear the slaps of the bottoms of her feet before she splashes into the water.

The boys with the 40s cheer for her. Lean over the rail and yell, "Yeah, girl!" and "You killed it!"

I wait for her to come back to the surface. When she does, I yell, "Are you good?"

"Yeah," she laughs. Slides under the water again and comes back up. "Nothing going on here. Just a little bit of a loose bikini."

The 40s boys cheer again when she says that.

She treads water below us and reties the strap behind her neck.

When Natalie gets back on top of the bridge, I say, "That was awesome. You didn't hesitate at all."

"Well, if you hesitate, you'll panic, and you might never go." She tilts her head to the side and pounds water out of her ear. She grabs my face with her cold hands and kisses me. Her nose drips onto my nose. "Your turn," she says.

I want to impress her, and there's only one way to do it. I kick off my shoes and climb up on the rail. Stand there for a second, then turn around.

Natalie says, "What are you doing?"

"Backflip from the top of the rail."

"From up there? I don't know about that." Natalie scrunches her nose. Squints one eye closed.

I say, "I've got this."

I've done flips off people's diving boards, off small rocks into the river, off a log that hangs about 15 feet over the McKenzie, but I've never done a backflip off anything high, nothing like a bridge, and I have no idea how to land a flip from this height. Inside I'm terrified, but I make my face into a calm smile. Relax my shoulders.

The 40s boys walk up while I'm standing on the rail, my back to the water. The one who did the flip earlier says, "Get it, man. Go get it."

I can't hesitate because I know I'll chicken out if I do.

Natalie says, "Please be careful."

And that makes me smile for real. I know I've impressed her if she's scared for me. I put out my arms and lean back. No stopping myself now. I go into the flip and try to rotate slowly, but right away I know I'm going too fast. I tuck my chin and wave my arms, roll through all the way and see the water, too early, keep rolling, and I try to stop my flip but I only manage to twist my body sideways when I do that.

I hit the water flat on my left side, like hitting cement at that angle, and it knocks the wind out of me. I stay under. Let the river current take me, and I keep my eyes closed. Wait for the strike of pain to ease up, for the tightness in my body to loosen like it usually does when I hurt myself, but it doesn't, or not much anyway. My body stays tight, even when I come to the surface.

I'm downstream. Natalie's yelling something off the bridge. I go under again and come back up. My left arm is stung. Won't work. I use my right arm to paddle.

Natalie yells, "Are you okay?"

I look up and see all of the 40s boys and Natalie hanging over the west-side bridge rail, watching me float downstream. I try to yell back, to say that I'm fine, but I'm still gasping for breath. I make a thumbs-up sign with my good arm. Hold it for a second, then try to swim. But I can't swim correctly. I cripple-swim to the side using my right arm only, kicking my feet and gasping for air. My chest feels like it's supporting a large rock, like I'm lying flat and the rock's crushing me.

I make it to some rocks at the side of the river. Moss covered. I drag myself up. Breathe. Try to calm my breathing. Open and close my numb left hand. My arm feels the way it did last winter when I ran through a screen in a basketball game and hit the other team's center at a full sprint. He was 260 pounds, and I jammed my shoulder so hard I got a stinger.

I hold my left side and stumble up the bank of the river, over the mossy rocks and through the blackberries that hang above the water, scratching my legs and arms. I roll my neck and shoulder to loosen them up, to get the nerves going again. When I get to the dirt underside of the bridge, I put my hands on my knees and breathe, try to relax and get strong again before I have to face Natalie and the 40s boys.

But Natalie runs down the dirt path and meets me under the bridge. "Oh shit, Travis, are you okay?"

I straighten up when I see her. Say, "Yeah, I'm good. I'm fine."

"That looked horrible. Are you hurt?"

"No," I say, "it wasn't that bad. I just over-rotated a little."

Natalie starts to hug me, then pulls back and looks me over.

"Really," I say, "I'm fine. Let's just walk back up."

She leads me and I hold her hand with my good arm. We weave through the blackberry bushes, up the trail. Past broken glass and an old sweatshirt. One syringe and needle, and a glass cap. Human shit on a newspaper. When we get on top of the bridge, the 40s boys gather around me. "You all right, man? That was crazy."

I nod. "I'm fine."

"You need a drink?" One of them holds out his 40. "If you chug the rest of that, it'll take the sting away."

"No, I think I'm good."

The one who did the perfect backflip earlier says, "That was crazy, bro. Crazy to do a flip if you don't have the height dialed."

I nod.

He says, "I dialed 35 feet at a quarry years ago. So it's not hard for me to get it right."

I smile, but then I cough and a little bit of blood splurts out onto my chin.

"Oh damn."

Everyone steps back.

"What the . . . ? You're coughing blood, man."

"Oh my God," Natalie says. "This is really bad."

"I'm okay," I say. I wipe the blood off my chin with the back of my hand.

One of the 40s boys says, "There's a clinic not too far from here. University health center on 13th. There are doctors there."

"Travis"—Natalie grabs her shorts and tank top—"we're going there now." She picks up my shoes and lays them out, right and left at my feet. I step into them, bend over slowly, and pull the tongues to get them on. Bending over feels like pushing a steak knife between my ribs.

Natalie says, "It's gonna hurt to bike, but you have to bike fast anyway. We need to get you checked out. Okay?"

"Okay."

One of the 40s boys turns my bike around for me. "Good luck, man."

"Thanks." I get on. Hold the handlebars with my good arm.

"Come on," Natalie says. She starts to pedal.

My left side hurts so bad I feel like laughing.

Natalie yells back, "Come on, Travis."

I follow her. We pedal down off the bridge, west along the river, under the train tracks, up onto Franklin Boulevard, and down 13th. We stop in front of the clinic. Natalie clips my lock around both of our bikes. "Come on," she says. She takes my good hand. Pulls me into the clinic. At the nurse's desk in front, Natalie says, "He's got to be seen at once."

THE CLINIC

THE NURSE LEADS US INTO a room and a female doctor follows us in. The doctor points to the exam table. "Have a seat."

I sit. The nurse puts a wrap around my bicep and starts pumping. Takes my blood pressure. The doctor listens to my chest. The front, then the back. "Subcutaneous hematoma," she says. The nurse writes notes on her clipboard.

"No catching sounds." The doctor listens some more. "The lungs sound good." She holds my face. Looks in one eye, then the other. Presses my cheeks with her thumbs. "No sign of shock." The nurse continues to take notes. The doctor says, "Follow my finger with your eyes. Keep your head still."

"Okay." I follow her finger back and forth.

"Good. Now tell me what happened."

I explain the flip, and how I landed.

Natalie says, "He coughed up blood."

"How much blood?" the doctor asks.

"Not much. He sort of spit a little blood up onto his chin as he was talking to us afterward."

"Okay. We'll do X-rays now, then bring you back in here again."

The nurse walks me down to the X-ray room and they take pictures with me standing in four different directions. Then I go back to the exam room.

Natalie's waiting in there. She says, "Was that okay?"

"Yeah, they didn't mess with me or anything."

"Good."

We wait, then the doctor comes back in. "Okay," the doctor says. "Now I have a better sense of what's going on. I want you to lie back." She feels along my ribs, then pushes on my abdomen in different places. "Any pain there?"

"No."

"How about here?"

"No."

"Good," she says. She turns to the nurse. "The liver and spleen are intact. Organs are fine." She pats my leg. "Now sit back up, please."

I have to roll to my side to sit up. I groan. It feels like someone's stabbed me with scissors from behind, trying to wedge my ribs apart.

The doctor runs her fingers up my back. I wince. She says, "There?"

"Yeah."

"And there too?"

I pull away from her.

"And there?"

I wince again. "Yeah."

163

"And probably the most right . . . here." She pushes on a rib with her fingers and I feel something like a heated spike going in.

I open my mouth and drool with pain.

Natalie says, "Is that necessary?" She has her arms crossed.

"Yes." The doctor turns around. "I had to know if I had the right location. Sometimes the bruising isn't a perfect indicator."

I breathe and try to relax.

The doctor turns back to me. "Do you have pain anywhere else?"

I say, "My arm went dead, but it's a little better now."

She rotates my arm. Nods and says, "When a person hits a surface violently, he's going to burst a few small blood vessels at the very least. Thus, the blood you spit up. But your lungs sound fine and your left arm is fine as well." She looks down at the clipboard the nurse is holding. "In layman's terms, you deadened the nerves when you hit so hard on your left side. You have significant bruising on your back. Cracked ribs. At least three. Maybe four. There are fracture lines on three on the X-ray, and a spot on the fourth, the one that hurts the least. See the color coming in there?" She has me look in the mirror to see the bruising.

There's a dark color all down the left side. Four of the ribs are marked by dark lines going across.

The doctor says, "You need a lot of rest. But in four to six weeks, you'll be good to go."

"Four to six weeks?"

"Yes," she says. "Don't do anything significant for three or four weeks at least. Do you understand me?"

Natalie says, "He's a basketball player. A good one."

The doctor smiles. "Well, don't play any basketball this month, okay?"

I don't say anything.

"This is important," the doctor says. "It's summer right now, and basketball's a winter sport, right?"

I say, "If you want to be good in the winter, you have to work hard in the summer."

"I like that attitude," the doctor says, "and I'm sure that's true, but three or four weeks off won't kill you."

Natalie looks at me. "It might."

Before we leave, the nurse comes back with two Vicodin and a prescription for 40 more.

We walk out of the clinic to the bike rack. Natalie says, "What's your grandpa's phone number?"

I shake my head. "We're biking home."

"But the nurse said . . ."

"Trust me. I'm fine. We're biking."

ALL THE WAY HOME

THE BIKE HOME IS BRUTAL. Normally I can do it in under 20 minutes, but it takes me a full 45. Natalie keeps slowing down and riding next to me even when that means she's riding in the street instead of the bike lane. Cars honk as they drive around her. She flips them off.

When we get to the skate park, I say, "I'll see you tomorrow?"

"No," she says, "I'm biking you all the way home."

The Vicodin is kicking in and I'm starting to feel hazy. "I'm okay. Really."

"All the way home," she says. "And that's final."

We bike up Crescent Avenue to Green Acres. I slow one more time at the entrance to the trailer park. "I'm good now. Really."

"Just tell me," Natalie says. "Which way from here?"

I call the park a trailer park, but there aren't that many trailers. Most of the houses are single-wides or double-wides,

166

manufactured homes, a little better than trailers, but still not well built, not nice houses. As we ride past the first few, I'm hoping Natalie doesn't notice the plastic porch railings and Astroturf lawns, the pressboard siding and carpeted porches, the prefab slide-and-lock picket fences, yard gnomes, windmills, and pink flamingos stuck into the fake grass. I think of Natalie's white-carpeted stairs, her hardwood floors, her clean front porch.

She says, "Which one is your house?"

"A little farther."

When we get to my grandparents', I see how ugly the mini Tuff Shed is, with its peeled red paint and a big dent on the driveway side. On the porch, there are fake flowers in metal stands on the railing. I say, "My grandparents have a thing for fake flowers."

Natalie laughs. "They're cute."

We park our bikes on the side of the house and go to the front door. Walk inside. Grandpa's watching baseball. He looks up and clears his throat. Stands quickly. "Well, uh, hello, young lady."

"Hi." Natalie smiles at him.

"My name's Roy." He holds out his hand.

"Natalie."

"Please sit down." He points to the recliner.

"Okay. Thanks."

I look around the room and notice how cluttered it is. Junk mail sliding off the desktop in the corner. Magazines, dirty plates, and milk-crusted drinking glasses on the coffee table. Laundry in a pile at one end of the couch. I walk over and start to pick it up, forgetting about my ribs. I groan and stop.

"Hey," Natalie says, "let me do that."

Grandpa looks confused. "No, no, he can . . ."

"Seriously, I've got it." Natalie takes the laundry from me. Turns to my grandpa. "Where do I put this?"

Grandpa goes to get a basket. Brings one back and she dumps the laundry in. Grandpa takes it to my room and comes right back. He points at me. "What's wrong with you? She's a guest."

Natalie says, "He cracked four ribs. Fractured them."

Grandpa adjusts his glasses. "How?"

"He hit the water wrong when we jumped in the river."

"Must have been a big jump." Grandpa shakes his head. He points to the chair and the couch, and Natalie sits down again. I have to sit slowly, leaning on my good arm first and lowering my body into a sitting position. I can feel each place where my body parts connect, and none of them feel well put-together.

"That doesn't look good," Grandpa says. "You better rest. Watch this game."

"I'm okay."

"No," Natalie says, "you listen to your grandpa. You need to do nothing for a while. Your grandpa can go get that prescription and I'll make you some food. Does that sound good?" She turns to my grandpa.

He stands up again. "Yes, ma'am. That sounds like a plan."

I pull the prescription out of my pocket and hand it to him.

Grandpa says, "I'll go get this and come right back." He looks at Natalie. "You sure you're okay here?"

"Just fine." She smiles.

"Grandma's asleep. If she needs anything . . ." Grandpa looks at both of us now.

Natalie says, "I'll get her anything she needs."

"Thank you," Grandpa says. He puts on his YELLOWSTONE NATIONAL PARK hat and grabs his car keys. "I'll pick up some Tang too, and we're almost out of bread and sandwich fixings. Maybe I'll get some more eggs and milk."

"Thanks, Grandpa."

He wears his hat high on his head, like a trucker. He adjusts the bill, smiles at Natalie, then leaves.

"He seems nice," Natalie says.

"He is nice. He just . . ."

"Smokes a lot of weed?" she says.

"Right. At night. In the day, he's fine." I lean forward to grab the TV controller.

Natalie says, "If you need anything, just ask me, all right?"

I watch a TNT reality special on the NBA Summer League while Natalie makes me a ham sandwich and the last of the Tang. When she comes in with the food, she says, "How's your pain?"

"Those pills work." I feel like clouds are floating through, more and more clouds, my mind puffy and my eyes heavy. "Yeah, I'm not hurting too much."

"Good," she says.

I'm watching the show and I'm eating, and Natalie's sitting next to me, and I fall asleep. I don't even know when. I don't know if I finish my food or if we say anything else. When I wake up, there's a baseball game on and it's dark outside. Grandpa's on the couch next to me.

I blink. Try to wake up all the way. "Where's Natalie?"

Grandpa says, "She left after a couple of hours. You were sleeping the whole time."

"Oh."

"Real pretty girl," he says.

My pills are on the coffee table. I say, "I should probably head to bed."

"Okay," Grandpa says. "Sleep in tomorrow and heal up, all right? No basketball."

"Right." I pick up the prescription. "Thanks for getting these."

Grandpa waves me off but doesn't look up from the TV. There's a Giants game on, and the Giants are up to bat.

It hurts to open the sliding glass door. My back feels like it's been tightened with sharp metal screws. My left shoulder won't rotate all the way. I use my good arm to close the door. Then I walk down to my tent.

I have to piss but I'm too sore to go over to Mr. Tyler's, so I piss in the blackberries near the water's edge. Go back to my tent. Take a big drink from my water bottle and crawl in. Then I think of something. I put on my headlamp and prop myself up, open the prescription bottle, dump the 40 pills onto my pillow, and sort them into groups of five. The last group only has two pills, not five. I make sure I didn't lose count. Count out by fives again. But there are only 37 pills in there. 37 out of 40. Three missing.

I look through my tent flap at the house. I can see the back of my grandpa's head as he watches the Giants game.

ZEUS

BEHIND THE MOTEL. I WAS maybe 60 pounds, just a little kid, holding a garbage bag, walking toward the Dumpster. Zeus was slumped against the front. He was wearing a yellow Oregon Ducks shirt. Purple tutu. Bare feet. A sombrero on his head tilted low.

There was an empty Mickey's bottle between us like a single bowling pin on a lane of black asphalt. The bottle was shining bright green in the sunlight. I dropped the garbage bag and picked up the bottle. I didn't know if Zeus had already seen me. Sometimes he was awake and sometimes he wasn't.

I stepped forward and swung, but he wasn't sleeping and he caught my arm. Worse, he was laughing, and he tilted his head back and I saw his missing top row of teeth. I hated how his bottom teeth jutted into the space when he opened his mouth, how those teeth reminded me of the dead nutria I found down on the riverbank the night my mom forgot me after a score.

GOING D-1

CREATURE COMES TO THE TENT at 8:00. He says, "Bright shiny morning, baby. Sun like an egg yolk, and you didn't even get me for practice? It's already eight o'clock."

I groan as I roll over. Reach to unzip the tent with my good arm, and even that hurts. "I'm hurt, man."

"You're what?"

I get the zipper open. Look at Creature. "I'm hurt." I roll to my knees and crawl out of the tent. I have to stay on all fours for a second before I sit to my right, lean on my good arm. I don't have a shirt on, just my basketball shorts.

Creature sees my back and the huge bruise there. "What the hell did you do to yourself? That thing's huge."

"I know." I struggle to stand up. It feels like someone's wedging apart my ribs with a set of screwdrivers. "I tried to do a backflip off Knickerbocker yesterday. Landed wrong and cracked four ribs."

"Oh damn." Creature puts his hand over his mouth. "I'm sorry, T."

I shake my head. "I'm an idiot."

"That looks painful, baby."

"It's not the best feeling I've ever had."

"Let me look at it." Creature inspects the bruise. Measures it with his hands. "That's maybe 15, 16 inches long. Six inches wide. That thing's gnarly. Wait," he says, "did they say anything about basketball?"

"Doctor said I had to rest for three or four weeks. Not to play at all this month. But I won't wait that long."

"Good," he says. "Your skills would be dull as dull."

I don't say anything.

Creature nods, palming his basketball in his left hand. "So I guess I'll check in with you later?"

"All right." I crawl back in my tent. Take a Vicodin and sip some water. Read until the pill kicks in. Then fall back asleep.

NOTIFICATION

WHEN I WAKE UP, IT'S stifling hot and I can tell that I've been sweating for hours in my sleep. It might be 11 or 12 o'clock and I'm even more sore than I was this morning. I moan as I crawl out of the tent and stand. Stagger to the house and strain to open the back door. No one's in the living room and I go into the kitchen. There's a note saying that Grandpa took Grandma to an appointment at the hospital.

I make two large cups of Tang. Gulp them both down. Stand and lean against the counter, feeling a little bit better. Less thirsty. I get the peanut butter jar out of the cupboard and eat a few spoonfuls. Then I drink some water to unstick my mouth.

I go to the phone and look at the calendar for the number. I don't want to call, but I know I have to. If I don't, he'll hear about it from someone else. So I dial.

It rings twice, then he answers. "Taft High Athletic Department, athletic director here, how can I help you?"

"Uh, Coach? It's Travis."

"Hey, Travis, how's it going?"

"Not so good, Coach."

There's a long pause. Coach says, "What happened?"

"Well . . . see, I jumped off a bridge into the river, and I got hurt."

"How hurt?"

"Not too bad. I mean, bad, but not too bad. I cracked four ribs and I'm pretty sore. I can't play basketball for three or four weeks. Or at least that's what they say. I'll play sooner, don't worry."

"Okay," he says, and exhales. "I'm sorry that you're hurt. But it's July right now, not the worst time in the world to be dinged up. You'll be healthy by October."

"And that's not all," I say.

There's another pause. "Go on," he says.

"I have to admit something."

"All right, then."

"I just want to be honest with you . . . so I needed to tell you that I punched someone."

"Punched?" he says. "Who?"

"This missionary sort of guy. But not the good kind of missionary or anything like that."

"A missionary?"

"Yeah. He was handing out Seventh-day Adventist pamphlets at the Chevron."

"And you punched him?"

"Well, he . . . it's hard to explain. He said something terrible to me."

"So that justifies you punching him?"

"I guess he said something pretty bad, and I just . . . I'm sorry, Coach."

Coach exhales long and slow on the phone. "This is bad, Travis. I'll just be honest with you too then. That's a two-game suspension to start the season."

"Really?"

"Yes, really," he says. "Those are the team rules and everyone knows them. There are consequences for getting in a fight. Doesn't matter who you fight with. Our players and our team, we have standards. So you ended last year with a suspension and you'll start this season with a suspension too."

"But it wasn't really a fight. And it wasn't at school."

"I know. But it's good to have solid consequences for our actions."

"Okay," I say. "I guess."

Coach pauses for a long, long time, then he says, "Travis, I want to be in your corner. I like you. I believe in you. But you've got to stop making these mistakes. These are big mistakes. And you now have two huge marks on your record. Do you understand that?"

"Yes, sir."

"And these things matter. Do you want to go back to juvie? Do you want to lose another season of basketball and any shot you have of playing college ball?"

"No, Coach."

"Then you can't make any more mistakes," he says. "None from here on out."

"I know, Coach. I really do."

"Because I can't stand by you forever. You're a good kid and you could be a great player, but at some point I'll have to draw a line in the sand, and you're starting to take me there."

* * *

After we hang up, I take two oranges out of the fridge and go sit in the living room in the big recliner chair. Peel the first orange and eat it slice by slice, worrying about Coach and what he must be thinking about me.

On the table in front of me, there's a big orange pill bottle: Grandma's pain pills, the ones she never wants to take. I pick it up. Three-quarters full. Read the label: PERCOCET. I don't know if that's stronger or weaker than the Vicodin I'm on for my ribs. I open the bottle and look at the pills—round, smaller than my Vicodin. Since Grandma won't take that many and Grandpa shouldn't, I steal my three pills back. Put two of them in my mouth and swallow.

PAST MISTAKES

I PICK UP THE NEWSPAPER, sit back, and read the sports page. After a while, I realize that I'm sort of floating in the room, that my body's lifted a little, and I'm smiling at nothing. I don't want to move. My ribs don't hurt much at all. The recliner is the most comfortable seat in the world. I peel the second orange and start to eat that one.

I realize that someone's knocking on the front door. I don't know how long that's been going on. I look at the door and it seems to shift in its frame. Another knock. I push myself up to my feet with my good arm. Walk over. I'm made of pieces of wood bolted together. The skin on my arms has hardened into grains, a sheen of electric varnish over the top.

I open the door.

Natalie's standing there with yellow flowers in her hand. She says, "I know it's cheesy, but I bought these flowers for you since you're hurt."

"Oh," I say. "Thanks."

She looks great. Wearing a blue tank top. Thin yellow bra straps. Short jean shorts. She steps in and kisses me, says, "How's the pain today?"

I pull her close, pull at the belt loops on the sides of her jean shorts. "I feel good right now. I feel all right."

She's wearing a little perfume, and it smells good in the small space by the door. She says, "Were you super sore this morning?"

I nod.

She says, "Your smile's kind of crazy. Are you on those pills?"

"Yeah." My smile's so big that I have to wink one eye to keep it from cracking my face open.

She says, "You crashed last night. I sat with you and your grandpa for a long time but since you never woke up, I finally went home."

"Sorry."

We stand there and kiss in the space next to the door, and Natalie's body is against me and her chest feels good against mine, and her hips are so strong and the pills are heavy in my brain.

Natalie stops us. She says, "I don't want to hurt you."

"I'm all right."

"But you should be careful today." She squeezes my arms but doesn't hug me. "I don't want to hurt your ribs."

"I'm not hurting."

She kisses me again. "Only because of the pills." She takes my hand and leads me into the living room. "You smell like oranges."

I point to the orange peels.

Natalie says, "Come on. Let's sit you down. You need to rest today."

I'm a wooden puppet, folding my jointed arms and knees. Natalie holds my elbow as I bend to sit.

Once I'm settled, Natalie turns and lies back, her head on the couch's armrest. She lifts her legs and places them across my lap. "Is that okay?"

I run my fingertips along her calves and shins, then back down to her ankles and feet. Natalie closes her eyes. I trace up her leg to the scar on her right knee. "Does it hurt?"

"Not too much. Just a little when I do my stretches."

"And you'll be ready for tryouts?"

"I hope so. I've been working so hard, and there's still a month."

Her scar has one long line and four little circles around it. I trace the line with my finger. The pills make her legs feel like warm plastic. I blink and look at the scar again. Touch each little circle. "Was the surgery bad?"

"No," she says. "Not bad at all. The lying around after the surgery was terrible, though." Natalie tilts her head off the edge of the couch. Looks back at the room behind her.

I watch the rise and fall of her chest. See the edges of her bra under her arms. Yellow underneath the thin blue of her tank top.

I say, "How long did you have to lie around?"

"Three months of nothing but flexibility rehab, three months of light strengthening, and three months of fitness and strengthening. It hasn't been my favorite year."

"I'm sorry."

"I lost the entire season." She lifts her head and looks at me. "Hey, are you looking at my chest again?"

"Maybe." I look away.

But when I look back at her, she's smiling. "I don't mind if you look."

My eyes feel heavy. Start to close. I force them wide again.

She says, "Those pills are super strong, huh?"

"Yeah."

"My mom takes those, and she does that eyes-shut, eyes-wide thing that you just did."

"Your mom's hurt?"

"Not at all," Natalie says. "She used to have a little back injury. Nothing major, no blown disks or anything. But it hurt some. I think the pills got her through other stuff, though. And she still takes them every once in a while."

I don't say anything. The pills make it hard for me to come up with new questions.

Natalie says, "But enough about my awesome family. How much time were you out last season?"

"I lost the whole season too. All but the first few games."

"Were you injured?"

"No, I got a league suspension."

"Really?" Natalie props herself up. "This should be a good story."

I shake my head. "Just me being stupid."

"No. I want the whole story."

"Okay," I say. Take a deep breath. "I was the backup point guard, but I was getting more playing time each of the first five games of the season. And in the fifth game, still before league play started, we were going against the Catholic school."

"Is that the school with all the rich bitches?"

"Yep."

"Okay, I've heard about their soccer girls already."

"Right. So they had a junior point guard, a good player, a slick guard, but a dickhead. And he talked a lot of trash. Said all kinds of stuff. I was matched up on him for the entire second quarter and he kept talking trash and it started to get to me, some of the stuff he was saying."

"Well, what did he say?"

"It doesn't matter." I look away.

Natalie leans forward and looks at me. "What did he say?"

"It really doesn't matter."

"It doesn't? 'Cause it seems like it does."

"Not really. People talk trash. I shouldn't have reacted to him."

Natalie raises her eyebrows. "Okay then. So forget what he said. What did you do?"

"Well, during halftime, I thought a lot about his trash-talking. I should've been focused on the game, focused on my team and our game plan, on winning, but I let that one guy bother me way too much."

"Then?"

"Then when I subbed in halfway through the third quarter, I waited for my chance and I punched him."

"Wait, you lost an entire season over a punch? One punch? Isn't that a little bit excessive?"

"Well . . ."

"Well what?"

"It wasn't exactly a fight. And it was way more than a punch."

"What do you mean?"

"I mean, I hit him when he didn't have the ball, hit him when he was running downcourt going the opposite direction, so there was a lot of force behind it. And he wasn't looking. He didn't expect it. On film, it looked really bad, like my punch came out of nowhere. And on the play before, he switched on a screen so he wasn't even guarding me. It looked like I targeted a player for absolutely no reason."

"Did he get hurt or did it just look bad?"

"He got hurt. He went to the hospital. He was knocked out and didn't come to for more than an hour. Then he couldn't play for another month because of concussion syndrome."

"Damn."

"Yeah, it was sort of crazy. There was a local news crew at the scene and they caught the whole thing on tape. I got arrested the next day. Charged with assault three. I went to juvie for a while."

My hand is resting on Natalie's leg. She reaches down and squeezes it. "You really do punch people, huh?"

"Not normally. Or, I mean, sometimes."

Natalie squeezes my hand again. "Hey, Travis," she says, "look at me. It's okay. We all mess up sometimes. We all make mistakes."

"It was a big mistake, though. It was a whole season."

"Yeah, well, I lost a whole season because of my mistake too."

"How was yours a mistake?"

She purses her lips and that scar wrinkles under her eye. "You wanna know how I really got this scar on my knee?"

"Didn't you tell me already?"

"Sort of. I didn't lie about it. But I don't tell people the whole story either." She lets go of my hand. "I stole my teammate's boyfriend."

"What?"

"At a party."

"The teammate who tore your knee in practice?"

"Yeah." Natalie wipes her eyes with the back of her wrist. "She was my good friend too, and I don't even know why I did it."

"So she was dating this guy, and you . . ."

"Saw him at a party. I'd been drinking a lot. And I didn't even like him."

"But still you did something?"

"Yeah, we did. And when she found out, she was pissed. But she waited until practice to get me back."

"What'd she do?"

"We were scrimmaging and I was playing in the midfield, defensive mid. I went to slide-tackle her and I missed. Normally a striker like her would step over a missed tackle and continue her run, but she stepped on my knee, or, more like, she stomped on my knee."

"On purpose?"

"Seemed like it. And it popped. MCL and ACL. The MCL was torn partially, but the ACL was gone." Natalie puts her two index fingers together, end to end, to form a straight line. Then she makes a clicking noise with her mouth and moves one finger sideways.

"That's messed up. Did she ever apologize?"

"Later. We both did. But we were never close again. She kept dating that guy and she finished the season as second-team All-League. I had surgery and did rehab."

"That sucks."

"Yeah, well . . ." Natalie rubs her eyes with the heels of her hands. "Fuck it, I guess. Right?"

"It'll be better this year. Success during the season is all about practicing in the off-season. Creature and I always talk about that. And you're doing it. You're working hard now."

"Who's Creature?"

"My friend Malik. But his nickname for AAU was 'The Creature.' Now everyone but his mom calls him that."

"So he's a basketball player too?"

"He wrecks."

Natalie laughs. Wipes her face on her tank top. "'The Creature'?"

"You should see him play."

Natalie pulls her phone out of her pocket and touches the screen. "Whoa," she says, and sits up. "I should walk home now. I didn't realize what time it was. I said I was only going to be gone for 20 minutes."

Natalie gets up and opens the sliding glass door. I struggle to my feet and follow her out. On the picnic table, there's a dented 7UP can blackened in the middle where someone has used a tack to poke holes. Natalie picks it up and smells it. "Is this a weed can?"

"Yeah," I say, "I think that's what it is."

Natalie laughs. "Your grandpa's a blazer!"

"But how'd he know he could use a soda can?"

"Well," she says, "he probably checked on the great wide interwebs. Googled 'How can I smoke marijuana without a pipe?'"

"BOB DYLAN'S 115TH DREAM"

I'M READING AN OLD ISSUE of *ESPN The Magazine* when Creature comes to my tent. He says, "I'm sorry you're hurt."

I put the magazine down. "It's fine." I try to stretch my back a little but it's too stiff. "If I could only play basketball . . ."

"I know."

Creature has a backpack on. I point at it. "What's with the pack?"

"I decided to camp with you." He drops his pack to the ground.

"Yeah?"

"My first camping ever."

He pulls a Coleman flannel bag out of his pack, unrolls it, then reaches back in the pack for a mini *Star Wars* pillow. It's one of the old ones with Darth Vader on it. A red lightsaber. Blue background.

"Was that your mom's pillow when she was little?"

"She loves Darth Vader, baby. Any black man." Creature winks at me. "And this pillow just proves I'm a camping pro."

I scoot my bag over and try to organize my things. Make a stack of magazines and books, put my headlamp on top. Shove T-shirts to the corner. Keep both tent doors open, east and west, so the tent will air out and we won't feel like we're sleeping in the same bed. I say, "Here. Lay your stuff on this side. The breeze'll come through."

Creature puts his bag down, his *Star Wars* pillow at the head. Gets his water bottle out of his pack and sets that next to his pillow. Then he pulls out a flashlight and turns it on. It's not quite dark yet, but he shines it in all the shadowed spaces in the tent. "Does anything ever crawl into your sleeping bag out here? Snakes or spiders or anything like that?"

"No."

"You sure?" he says. "I mean, I've seen some huge bull snakes out here by the lake. Five feet long."

"Yeah, but they don't come in the tent."

"Okay."

Creature keeps shining the flashlight. Spotlights a tiny spider down by our feet. "Can we kill that thing?"

"The spider that's smaller than a baby mosquito?"

"First," Creature says, "baby mosquitoes bite the shit out of you. Second, spiders are spiders. They're all evil and sketchy."

"Okay." I grab the spider and throw it out of the tent.

"What the fuck was that?" Creature puts his fist to his mouth. "You just threw it out right next to our heads. You know that thing's just gonna crawl directly back in, right?"

"No it won't."

"Yes it will." Creature shines his flashlight on the long grass next to the tent, searching for the spider.

I say, "You want to hear a messed-up story?"

Creature does another sweep with his flashlight. Rechecks the corners of the tent. "No," he says, "I don't want to hear a messed-up story."

"It's good, though."

"Good enough to scare the crap out of me for the rest of the night?"

"Maybe."

"That's what I thought. And here's what'll happen. You'll tell your little story. Then, in a while, you'll be sleeping like a baby and I'll be wide awake staring into the darkness, waiting for something to crawl onto my face and bite me in the eyeball."

"Man, Creat, you sure are fun to camp with."

Creature rolls up onto his elbow and takes a drink of water. "Okay, fine. Tell me your stupid story."

"Okay," I say. "So you know how I did that wilderness experience for teens out of juvie?"

"Right. And that's why you like to camp so much now."

"Exactly. So, one day, they showed us how to build primitive shelters and had us each make our own shelter and sleep in it for a night. No sleeping bag or anything, just survival-style, right?"

Creature shakes his head. "I can tell this is gonna be a bad story. I don't like it already."

"It's fine, man. Just listen. Anyway, I built a good shelter. Spent all afternoon and evening making the structure and filling it with insulating grasses. And I felt pretty sure I was going to be warm enough."

"But you weren't, right?"

"No, that wasn't the problem. I crawled in there just before dark, got all of the grass around me, made a pillow out of the grass for my head. It was comfortable enough and I fell asleep. But in the middle of the night, it rained."

"How much? Did you get soaked?"

"No, I didn't. That wasn't the problem either. It rained a fair amount, but the counselors had taught me how to make a good shelter, and the rain slid off the outer layers of ponderosa bark to the side, and it was fine."

"You know what?" Creature says. "I'm good. You don't have to tell the rest of this story. You were warm enough. You didn't get wet. Great story. THE END." He turns his flashlight on once again and checks the seams of the tent above him.

I say, "I guess the rain filled all of the holes in the ground. There wasn't any water that came in the shelter or anything like that, or at least barely any water, but the rain went in all of the holes in the ground all around. Filled those holes. And the desert toads came up. They were calling to each other, croaking wild and crazy, and I could hear them as soon as it stopped raining."

"Frogs? Okay. Frogs are fine. I thought this was a horror story, but frogs? I can handle frogs." Creature clicks his flashlight off and lies back on his pillow. Sighs.

"But other things got flooded out of their holes too."

"Oh no, no, no, no. Fuck that. What other things?" Creature turns his flashlight back on. "No, man, no. I don't want to hear this story anymore. I told you that already. And that's final. Good story. Great story. And it's the end now."

I say, "Other things got washed out, but I didn't see them right away. I was listening to the toads croak, and I started to fall back asleep. Then I felt something crawling on me inside the shelter."

"No! What the . . . ?" Creature sits up. "Fuck this! Stop talking."

"I had a light in my survival kit—the counselors made us carry our kits everywhere—but my kit was outside the shelter, and I didn't want to have to wriggle out of all of the insulation to grab it. So I tried to ignore whatever it was and let it crawl on past. But soon enough something was crawling in my hair too."

"Seriously, T. What the hell, man?"

"So I had to get out and find my headlamp. I shook those two crawling things off, pushed all of the grass aside, and wriggled out of my shelter. There wasn't much of a moon, and I couldn't see until I got my light on. But when I did, oh my gosh . . ." I stop talking. Shake my head.

"What? What was it? No, don't tell me," Creature says. "It's cool. Don't tell me. I'm good." Creature holds his flashlight against his teeth. "No, wait, tell me. I have to know."

"Big red spiders."

"Oh no, no, no." Creature taps his flashlight against his forehead. "No, you're making this up. Tell me you're making this up."

"Big red spiders by the thousands."

"Wait. Why? Why would there be thousands of spiders anywhere?"

"They were all crawling in the same direction, and my shelter was in their path, so a lot of them were trying to climb over it. I shined my light around and I couldn't believe it. Even if I wanted to squish them, to kill them all, I couldn't. It would've been impossible. I would've been crushing spiders for hours." I start to laugh.

"What the . . . ?"

"There were too many."

Creature says, "I'm done with this story."

"And I just stood and watched them. It was sort of cool in a crazy way."

"No, man. No." Creature shines his flashlight directly in my eyes. I block the light with my hands, laughing hard now. He says, "That's not cool. There's nothing cool about that. Cool is meeting a girl who plays point guard. Cool is reading a book you can't put down. Cool is dunking for the first time. It sure as hell isn't thousands of spiders crawling on you when you sleep."

"No, but it was cool in a weird sort of way. They were all going the same direction. I asked the counselors about it, and they said that those big red spiders were just common ground spiders in central Oregon, that when it rains enough, they all get flooded out of their holes. So they come up and move. All together. They pick one direction to go to safety, and everyone goes that way. One counselor called it 'a migration.'"

Creatures shivers. "I'm not into that. I'm not into that at all."

I say, "I didn't like them crawling on me. And I waited until they were all gone before I got back in my shelter."

"What?" Creature sits all the way up. "You did what? What the hell is wrong with you?"

"I had to sleep, man."

"No, you did not have to sleep. You could've kept your flashlight ready. You could've kept watch all night. Or you could've gone back to the cabin."

"But I didn't want to chicken out."

"Just tell me this: Who would've judged you? No one.

When you see thousands of big red spiders, you bail. That's it." Creature's sitting on his butt, his arms wrapped around his knees. "Now I'm not going to sleep for a week. That was a messed-up story. Thanks a lot."

"Those kinds of spiders don't even live here."

"But there are other kinds. Are there any poisonous spiders that live here?"

"I don't know."

"T, you have to tell me, baby. I can't go to sleep if you don't tell me."

"I really don't know. Probably not." But there are poisonous spiders here, and I do know. I know of at least three kinds of poisonous spiders that live in western Oregon, but I don't say that.

"Are you sure, baby?"

"Yep. We're good. I've slept more than 50 nights straight out here. Trust me. We're good."

Creature breathes and looks around. "Maybe we should close the tent doors."

"Okay."

We zip them closed. Then the tent feels small, a little small for both of us lying in there.

Creature checks the tent one final time and turns his flashlight off. "I'm trusting you, all right?"

"Good. Now let's go to sleep."

Creature lies back and I close my eyes.

MiLKY WAY

A LITTLE WHILE LATER, AFTER I've fallen asleep and gone through part of a dream, Creature nudges me. "Wake up, T." He's propped up on his elbow.

"What is it?" In my dream I was playing basketball against a team of blue herons, hundreds of them, a few dozen guarding me, others flying in front of the hoop. I couldn't get a shot off.

"After your scary-ass spider story," Creature says, "you're not sleeping if I'm not sleeping."

"What?" I'm still thinking about all of those blue herons.

"Because," he says, "you're the one who told that horrible story about spiders."

I'm lying on the west side of the tent, fully awake now, watching the sky. Creature's by the east door, a light wind coming through the mesh. I say, "I had a counselor at that camp that was obsessed with the stars. Always trying to teach me the constellations."

"Yeah, you've told me about that. But where'd you live before that? With your mom."

"The motels mostly. West Eugene in the weekly places."

"Oh, I know some of those. We lived in a few the year before we came to this trailer park."

I say, "Is that when your mom got disability?"

"Right." Creature lies back down and folds his hands behind his head. "For the mental stuff. But it was good news since we got enough money each month to leave the motels. They were shit."

"Yeah," I say, "dirty and old. Cops always there."

"And the manager of one of them was racist too," Creature says. "I heard him call my mom a 'nigger lover.' Heard him say, 'Look what you did to your kid, mixing him up like that.'"

"Yeah, fuck that."

Creature laughs. "It's like the Deep South out there on the west end of town."

"That's sorta true."

I unzip the tent partway to lean my head out and look up at the sky. The stars multiply above me and the light of the Milky Way begins to glow. "Milky Way," I say, and Creature leans out on his side.

I say, "How's your book coming, Creat?"

"Good. I have a new entry. Want to hear it?"

"You've got it with you?"

"Yeah." Creature turns on his flashlight and sits up. Reaches into his backpack and pulls out two folded pages. Lies back again. Adjusts his head on his Darth Vader pillow and clears his throat.

The Pervert's Guide to Russian Princesses
Princess #37 (First Draft)

Natalia Pavlovna Paley, you will be my first blond princess—dyed blond, but I won't tell people. I won't tell them about your Hungarian blood either. I'll let you be the American that you always wanted to be, as all women in New York are American, born or immigrated.

Many historians see you as the most beautiful Russian princess, a fashion girl, a model, but I won't reduce you to your looks. I won't talk about your catlike eyes, your *Mona Lisa* smile, the way you lean forward and put your face in your hands. I'll barely notice your long, thin body and the perfect swell of your breasts. When you are with me, I'll trail my fingers between your legs without noticing your thighs. I'll wait for you to dab perfume on the insides of your ankles and wrists, then smell your limbs with my eyes closed.

You were married to Lucien Lelong, the fashion magnate, a man who had no interest in women, and you tell me that he did not touch you. A "white marriage," they call it. He touched only men. He was interested only in what men could offer, but not you.

You come to my room in the motel at night. I am asleep on the bunk above the water heaters in the boiler closet. It is more than 80 degrees in that room, and I sleep naked. You have a key and you slip in without waking me. I do not know that you are there until I hear the sound of your jeweled dress hitting the floor, followed by the softer sound of your slip falling away, the layers of your clothing slipping, and then the quiet nothing of your nakedness in the dark room, in the space next to my bunk.

I am awake and I wait with my eyes open. When you come to me, I will look. I will see the outlines of your shoulders, the outline of your hips. The only light in the room is the switchboard's red light marking you ready. You stand next to me, my eyes open, and you tremble, goose bumps on your skin, and you say, "I have never felt the weight of him."

My weight waits.

You swim into my bunk with me, our bodies sinking the springs, the thin mattress sagging to a U, both of us in the low curve together, and we have to fight the blanket that's caught between us like the differences of our lives.

You say again, "I never felt the weight of him," and I don't tell you that I've read of your affairs with Serge Lifar and Jean Cocteau, two men who are also only interested in men. Was it an affair, then? I want to ask you about that, about what brings you to men who do not want you. I want to ask you, Why? Or, Why now with me?

I know that there is nothing real in your stories, and that what is real is now, no words, no stories, but this bunk above the water heaters, the sweat of us in the heat, the warm damp, the tangle of our bodies.

LiSTEN

I THINK ABOUT MY MOTHER, my mother who sleeps somewhere along the river in a tarp camp, braved against wet, my mother who rolls herself in a blanket, tucks her hair into her sweatshirt collar and slides the hood on, folds the sleeves of her sweatshirt over her balled-up fists to keep out the cold.

Sometimes I get mad or jealous when I think about other people's parents, but mostly I get confused. Why are some people the way they are, while other people are like my mom? It's easy to say it's the drugs, but what was before that? Maybe we need to ask more questions.

I'M ONLY BLEEDING

I LEAN FORWARD, POST MY good arm on the couch's armrest, and push myself to a standing position. The pills cut the pain but not the stiffness, and I walk like an old man to the kitchen. I make sandwiches, double the meat, and cut thick slices of cheese. Add lettuce and tomato, mustard, but no mayonnaise. She hates mayonnaise.

I wrap the two sandwiches in wax paper and slide them into a brown lunch sack. Then I put some Doritos in a Ziploc, and throw in an apple. I open the refrigerator and look around, but the only thing I see to drink is one of my Gatorades. So I grab that. Pick up a backpack from the floor in my room. Put my jar of cash in the bottom, everything else on top. Zip it closed. It doesn't weigh much, but still I slide it onto my back so slow. Loosen the straps until the bag's not touching the long bruise on my back, but dangling from my shoulders and hitting my butt instead.

I step back to the coffee table and take one more Percocet out of the bottle. Swallow it dry and look for my Tang glass. But it's empty.

I go outside, grab my bike, and get on. Sitting there hurts, even without anything touching my back. I wince a little as I start to pedal, but the stabbing pains in my ribs are muted by the pills. The pain is there but far away, like it's happening to someone else, and I pedal slowly through the park toward the entrance.

The bike ride is three miles to 1st Street, near Washington, near the courts, and I struggle the whole way. The third pill kicks in and makes me feel like everything around me is covered in tinfoil, bright shiny in the sunlight, but my back and ribs are too tight. Pulses of tightness radiate up into my neck. My left shoulder is sore and stiff as I keep it extended to grip my handlebars.

I get off my bike at the bridge and lock it. Walk under the shadows. Start looking for her. On the pylon wall there are blue letters that say BOB MARLEY 420. A mural of his face above them, a blunt hanging from his lips. Around the back of that wall, someone wrote PHILOSPOHY IS LOW-HANGING FRUIT, and another person drew a line through the word "fruit" and wrote TESTACLES in its place.

I walk the ivy paths, check the overgrowth near the Maple Garden. Look across to Delta. There are three homeless men there, drinking Steel Reserve in 24-ounce cans, all of them at least 10 years older than my mom. I don't find anyone else in that area, so I look along the construction site, where the skate park is being built, always out of funding. On the underside of the ramp, I find a young couple, a boy and a girl close to my age, both of them with split hands, yellow cracks oozing at the ends of their fingernails.

The girl's drooling.

The boy says, "Got a smoke, bro?"

I shake my head.

"Money?"

I shake my head again.

I try both bathroom doors near the second bridge pylon, but they're locked. The graffiti on the door reads YOUR MOTHER SUCKS IT AND SWALLOWS. An orange spray-painted dinosaur is stenciled above the door handle. Below that a blue penis going into two slits that I'm guessing are supposed to be a vagina. Black trees and red paint underneath that reads MURDER ROBOTS KILL.

I check along the fences and blackberries that run the railroad tracks through the center of the park. There's a woman about my mom's age, but she has thick dark hair that's dreadlocked down to her waist and she's reading Proverbs from the Bible out loud.

I say, "Do you know a woman who goes by Sally down here?"

"No," she says, "but I know a few women. Is she your age?"

"Older," I say. "Twice as old. I'm trying to find her."

"Don't know, but the Lord will provide." The woman taps the Bible with her finger. Flips the pages back to an earlier chapter. "The 23rd, you know it? 'The Lord is my shepherd'?"

"I think I've heard that."

"My name's Medusa," the woman says. "Medusa reading a Bible, huh?" She laughs like a lit cigarette. Coughs with her tongue out. Takes a deep breath. "So if it says here that the Lord will provide?"

I reach into my bag and pull out one of the sandwiches. "Do you need some food?"

Medusa smiles, two front teeth missing. "Are you the Lord, then?" She laughs again.

I hold out the sandwich and she takes it. Then I keep walking.

Check the benches along the west side, up to the courts. There's no one playing in the middle of the day, and I look at the double rims and the graffiti against the girders. There's a painting of a knife slicing open a face, the eyeball popping out. Underneath, it says THE EUG—187.

The bridge traffic above me is constant, the *clunk, clunk* of the cars and trucks, and I look around again, but I don't bother calling her name because she'd never hear me anyway. I walk west through the Whitaker neighborhood for a couple of blocks, check alleys and along fences where the hedges are thick, but I don't find anyone other than an old man sleeping faceup in the middle of an alley, his arms outstretched to each side, his hands open like he's nailed in that position.

I walk back to the bridge. At my bike, I open the Gatorade and drink half of it. Unwrap the other sandwich and eat it, lean against the wall, and finish the rest of the food. A homeless man walks by me as I eat and says to me, "Keep your head up, brother. I've been there too."

Then I get back on my bike and ride home.

Before I head down to my tent, I walk over to Mr. Tyler's house and take a piss. Since I'm too sore to run away, I don't go up on his porch. Instead, I hide in the shadow between his car and the side of his house, whip it out, and piss all over the hood of his Buick. With the pills making me drift a little, I rock back and forth and feel the piss surging, watch it splash over the shiny silver, smell the urine and metal as my piss runs off the hood and leaks through the seam, down into the engine compartment. I smile to myself as I finish, standing there staring at the car's hood. Then I zip up and walk back to my tent.

CRIME AND PUNISHMENT

IN THE MIDDLE OF THE night, I wake up to a noise. I don't know what it is, just that the noise wakes me. Something's there. I sit up quickly and a shock of pain jolts through my rib cage. I groan, suck in a breath, pant, and try to relax my back and ribs while looking out into the dark. I get onto my knees and lean on my good arm. Feel like someone is trying to take apart my rib cage.

Something hisses.

I look but can't see anything. It hisses again, not far away. It's so dark that I don't know exactly where it is even though I can hear it. I get low and look for its outline. Then I see it. More than four feet long, the caiman looks like it's grown, and it's just outside my left-side tent door, only a few feet away.

I want to zip my tent door closed, but I don't want to startle the caiman. I look around for a stick, but there's nothing between me and the small crocodile. I have a knife somewhere in my things at the other end of the tent, and I think about that knife but I don't move to get it.

I stay still. Wait.

The caiman stays still too. He closes his mouth and opens it again. I scooch down a little toward my pile of stuff, closer to my knife, and the caiman waddles forward and hisses again. I stop moving then. He's only two or three feet from me, right outside my tent, close enough that he could step inside. He stays there, mouth open.

I have no idea what to do. I stare at the outline of that open mouth, a mouth half as long as the body behind it. The caiman's not the biggest animal I've ever seen, but it's crazy-looking. It could take my hand off, or my whole arm if it got ahold of me and thrashed a little.

I notice something hard under my right hand, glance down, and see it's Grandma's copy of *Crime and Punishment*. It's a hardback, has some weight to it. I slide my fingers underneath the book, raise it slowly, so slowly, until it's next to my head.

The caiman waits there, not hissing, just there, mouth open, at the edge of my tent door. I count in my head—*one, two, three*—then I swing. Hard. Bring the book down on the caiman's nose, at the end of its top jaw, and the caiman's mouth closes. It backs up a little. I throw the book at it, but I miss. I scurry back, crawl inside and fumble for the zipper, zip the door closed, then turn around and zip the other door closed as well. The caiman is scrabbling around out there, hissing and thumping its tail, and I feel around for my headlamp until I find it by my pillow.

Then I notice the pain in my ribs again, and realize that I'm wheezing and wincing from a feeling like box cutters separating cartilage in my back, like three or four people are back there cutting me open at the same time. I try to move into a more comfortable position. Get back on my knees, then lean forward. Rest on my hands. My head is low, next to the tent's air vent. I look out, try to see the caiman, but can't. I shine the light through, and then I see it. The caiman's only five feet away, on the grass, the hardback book in its mouth. It's attacking *Crime and Punishment*, and the book is hanging lopsided from its jaws while it turns in a circle. The caiman releases it, then snatches it up again, ripping off the front cover. It's grunting as it takes the book apart. Then it thrashes its tail and waddles a few steps, dropping off the bank, down onto the gravel by the lake, and I can't see it anymore.

I take two Vicodin pills and lie down on my side. Listen for the caiman, but he's gone.

In the morning, I'm sore and stiff, and I groan as I sit up. My ribs feel worse than ever. I peek through the open two inches of door on my left side. Turn around and look out the right-side door, opening it a crack, making sure the caiman isn't waiting for me.

After I piss into the lake, I look around for the book. Or what's left of it. The first third is just a wad of papers that I find in the blackberries. I pick them up, most of them single sheets, all of them torn in half. Then I look around and find the rest of the book up the shore 30 or so feet, lying next to a small rock. The back cover is still connected to the second half of the book, but it has gouges at an angle from the caiman's teeth. It looks like it's been chewed on and dragged around by a big dog.

I take what's left of the book up to the house. It's still early and my grandparents aren't awake yet. I put the remains of the book in a plastic grocery bag and set it next to the phone. Then I write a note:

> *Grandma, the book you loaned me is in this bag. Sorry that it looks like this. But I thought that if anyone would think it's funny, that CRIME AND PUNISHMENT looks like this, it's you.*
>
> *Travis*

ON THE ROAD AGAIN

I TAKE TWO MORE VICODIN and walk to Natalie's. Knock on her front door.

She opens it and smiles. Takes my hand and walks me upstairs to her room. She's wearing a loose white shirt with the collar cut out, the open collar slid all the way to the edges of her tan shoulders. I can see both turquoise bra straps as I follow her up the stairs.

Her room is white. Bright white paint. A brass bed painted white. White bedspread. Four white pillows. Her white pine bookshelf is lined with an even row of hardbacks. No room in my grandparents' house looks anything like this. There are no clothes on the floor. No plates or wrappers. No crumpled newspapers. No magazines.

On a table on the far side of her bed is an aquarium with water in the bottom. Lily pads on the surface of the water. A flower and two vines. A frog at the waterline on the side of a hanging platform.

"My mom's gone." Natalie kisses me. "Are you hurting?"

"Not too bad."

"Are you on painkillers?"

"I just took some not too long ago."

She peels off my shirt. "Lie on my bed. Facedown. Let me see your back."

I lie on the white bedspread. It's thick and soft. Natalie sits next to me, runs her fingertips along the bruising on my back. "It still looks pretty bad."

"I need it to heal quick."

She walks around the bottom of the bed and comes to the opposite side. Lies down facing me. She runs her fingers along my arm. Says, "I think it can take a long time to heal ribs."

I prop myself up on my good elbow. Wince a little.

She says, "I'm sorry you're hurt."

"It's okay."

She kisses me. We're kissing, and our bodies are next to each other. We kiss and I run my hand up her shirt, feel her abs, run my fingers over her skin and muscles. Then I slide my hand up, onto her bra. She presses into me, and I slide up on top of her. I run the tips of my fingers underneath the lace of her bra, against the soft skin. We're kissing and my fingers are against her bare breast. She's shifting against me and I'm breathing hard, she's breathing hard, and she feels so good underneath me, her legs spread, and everywhere our skin touches it's like I've added nerve endings.

She shifts once more, breathes into my mouth, and I'm heavy on top of her, pressing, her underneath me. I kiss her neck and reach down to pull her shirt up over her head, but she drops her elbows, leans away, and breathes. Stops. Looks away.

I stop.

She pushes my shoulder and slides out from under me.

"I'm sorry," I say. "I just—"

"I know," she says. "It's fine."

"Wait."

"Everything's fine." She stands up. "Sorry. You should go."

"Now?"

"Yeah." She's looking at the wall, but the scar under her eye is twitching.

"I'm sorry I—"

"No, you're fine. It's fine. You should just go, though, okay?"

"Natalie, I'm—"

"Will you just fucking leave?"

I stand up. Hold my hands above my head like she's got a gun pointed at me. "So I guess I'll just go then?"

"Thank you," she says, and walks out of her room. I follow her. She leads me back down the stairs to the front door.

At the bottom of the stairs, I say, "Want to talk later?"

"Sure. Or whatever. I don't know." She opens the front door.

"Look. I'm—"

"Stop." She puts her hand on my chest. "It's fine. Really. Don't worry about it." I walk out the door and she shuts it behind me.

IN MY HEAD

MY WALK BACK AROUND THE lake is like doing the difficult part of one of those 1,000-piece nature puzzles. The bottom part of the puzzle is fine, where the mountains and trees and rocks are, that's easy enough to complete, but the whole sky is one color of blue, and all the pieces look the same at first. As I duck under a blackberry vine, I say to myself, *What the hell just happened?*

The girl I dated last year was named Maggie. She was a freshman, nine months younger than me. But she seemed older. She was into all kinds of stuff and she made me nervous. She liked to steal her stepdad's Marlboro Reds and smoke them in her room and say, "If he catches us smoking in here, he'll kill us both." He was a big, scary guy who'd played defensive line for the University of Oregon, and he never looked anyone in the eyes, and I wanted to say, "But I'm not the one who's smoking, you know?"

Maggie and I didn't go out for very long, but we still went

pretty far whenever we were making out. That would've been cool if she'd let me lock the bedroom door, but she never did, for whatever reason, and I'd sort of look over my shoulder the whole time we were in her room. I'd have her shirt off and she'd put my hand down her pants, and she'd be moaning and asking me to do things to her, and I'd be so nervous that someone was about to walk in that I couldn't do anything at all. The room would be full of smoke from her stolen cigarettes, and I didn't even want to take my shoes off in case I had to run.

Maggie dumped me as soon as I got back from juvie. We'd only been going out for four weeks before that, but still, I was pissed. She said her stepdad saw the news coverage of the punch and told her that she couldn't have me over to her house anymore. She was chewing bubblegum when she dumped me and she shrugged and said, "It's not like we're a good match anyway. You're kind of a pussy, you know?" She blew a bubble and I wanted to grab that bubble and pull the gum out of her mouth.

I watched her after that. I watched her at school, and I watched her flirt with guys. I watched her walk down the hall with her new boyfriend after they started dating. She saw me watching her one time when they were kissing against the lockers in the back hallway. She looked over his shoulder and saw me there, and I could tell that she liked me watching her, and she reached between his legs and looked right at me.

So I tried not to watch her after that. But all spring long I thought about her, wondered what we'd be doing if we were still together. The weird thing was that I didn't even like her that much, but still, I thought about her a lot. I don't like to admit it, but a girl can get in my head like that.

If I had to pick between Natalie and Maggie, though, I'd

211

pick Natalie every time. Even though she practically shoved me out the door and slammed it in my face today, I'd still choose her. 'Cause it sort of makes sense. Maybe she doesn't want to do too much when we make out. Maybe she gets nervous. Maybe she starts thinking too much. I do that sometimes, I think too much, so I understand. And anyway, there's lots of reasons for a girl to act like Natalie did today, so I guess that's all right. There's a little bit of mystery in it, and mystery keeps things interesting.

NEIGHBORHOOD WATCH

I GO UP TO THE house. Slide the back door open and enter right as Grandpa's coming in the front door opposite of me.

"Grandpa?"

"Yeah?"

"Where were you?"

"Community meeting. Everyone in the neighborhood got together to discuss the lake monster."

"You still believe in that?"

"Everyone does. The Bufords lost a cat this week. Shanahans think they might have lost their schnauzer, Billy. And Animal Control isn't helping at all. Animal Control doesn't think there's a monster."

"Well," I say, "it's a pretty crazy story."

"Oh no," he says, "there's a monster, and that's a fact. Some kind of crocodile monster. There's been more than half a dozen sightings now."

I say, "I'm not so sure."

"But weren't you there at Maribel Calhoun's? Didn't you see it?"

"I saw something, but I'm not sure what it was."

"Well, we're going to set up a lake guard. Take turns patrolling the bank. And we'll see who's right."

"Okay," I say. "Do whatever you want."

"Oh we will," he says. "And you might not want to sleep out there anymore."

"I'll be fine," I say, and walk into the kitchen, open the refrigerator, and grab the end of a block of cheese. Then I pull some Ritz crackers out of the cupboard. I keep my back to him since I'm smiling so big. I say, "Don't worry about me."

SLIP PAST THE CHEESE GIRL

I TAKE TWO VICODIN AND try to read. But I stare off after the pills kick in. It's evening, cooler than most, when I step out of my tent, and I put a hoodie on. Zip it up.

Then I walk out the lake loop to the entrance road. Walking feels better than biking since I don't have to hunch over. I cross Green Acres, go up the dentist's drive, through the hedge, and past Little Caesars. I walk around the corner to the Market of Choice.

Up and down the aisles, I don't know what I'm looking for. Then I see the chocolate display. All of the bars are the imported kind, from Europe, the Caribbean, or Africa. There's a store worker at the cheese display next to me, but no one is posted at the chocolate.

I pretend to read labels, but I'm really watching the cheese girl. She keeps talking to customers as they come by, offering different cheeses, always looking around. But when she finally turns her back to grab another box of toothpicks behind her, I slip a chocolate bar under my sweatshirt, take a few steps, then slide it into the front of my basketball shorts.

CODEPENDENCE

MY RIBS ACHE ALL THE time. I swallow pills. Ice three times a day for two weeks. I lie on the couch or take a chair out onto the back grass and sit in the sun. I take naps. I try to do as little as possible and heal my ribs.

I don't hear from Natalie. I think about going over to her house so many times, but I don't know what I would say.

The only noise in the house is Grandpa's snoring. He's asleep in his chair in the study. The door to Grandma's room is closed. I go into the kitchen, make a big glass of Tang, and drink it. Grandma's Percocet pills are sitting out on the counter again. I open the bottle and take four pills. Put three in my pocket. Pop one in my mouth and swallow it dry. Then I go into the living room and turn on the computer. Watch Michael Jordan highlight videos on YouTube. Then Damian Lillard videos. Then Jason Kidd's. Chris Paul's. Steve Nash's. Magic Johnson's.

Take another Percocet.

I quit the Internet and turn the computer off. Hear Grandma coughing and I walk down the hall and into her room. She's sitting upright, reading a book with a magnifying glass. Holding a handkerchief to her mouth with her other hand.

"What are you reading, Grandma?"

"*Persuasion,* sweetie. Jane Austen. It's always been one of my favorites."

"You and Creature. I've never reread a book."

"Sometimes the story is good enough, or the writing. I could read *Persuasion* 50 times and still enjoy it."

I sit down on the edge of her bed. Ask her the question I've been wondering about. "Was my mom always into drugs? Even when she was younger?"

Grandma places her bookmark and closes the book. Sets it next to her. Puts the magnifying glass on top. She shakes her head. "No, sweetie. She went to parties a little bit during high school, but it was your father who got her into drugs."

"Are you sure?"

"They started seeing each other again when you were six or seven, and that's when everything turned ugly, sinister. That was when you moved out to that motel in West Eugene. Do you remember that?"

"Yeah," I say, "I remember that place. But why'd she take him back?"

"She told me that he had just returned to town, that he had a job for the first time in a long time. She said he had only been drinking in small amounts, very little in fact, and that he was looking at a promotion at the mill. I told her that it still didn't sound good, the drinking part, because I knew him, but she would never listen to me."

"Did he really have that job?"

"Probably not."

"I don't remember him. I remember the motels, but I don't remember which guy he was."

"You wouldn't remember him. He never acted like much of a father."

Sometimes I wonder about him. Wonder what he looks like, how tall he is, if he likes to play basketball the way I do. But I don't want to tell Grandma about that, so I change the subject. "How are you feeling?"

She makes a little clicking noise with her mouth. "Not good, sweetie. But I know that now. I know that for sure. So I've made peace with it."

"What does that mean?"

"I'm not going to make it much longer. The doctor told me that at my last visit, and I know it's true. I've known it for a while." She reaches for my hand and I let her take it. "It could be a year. It could be six months. But it's coming."

I squeeze her hand. "You can fight this some more."

"No," she says, "but you two will be okay without me. You'll still have my retirement pension to live on until Grandpa dies. And he is as healthy as a horse."

"Sort of."

She looks up. "Sort of?"

"Well, I don't know if you've noticed, but he's high every night."

"Oh, sweetie, I'm sure it's not every night," she says, "and it's not like he's drinking anymore."

"Was that worse?"

"Oh yes. God yes. That was a lot worse. He lost his job, he lost his engineering license, and he was a terrible person to be around. Until he went to the rehab center and got sober, the kids didn't even like him."

"Then he went back to work after that?"

"Some," she says, "but mostly he stayed home. Among our generation, he was the first househusband. I laughed when 'househusbands' became a popular term because I thought that must mean 'men who've lost their jobs.' He learned to cook well enough, though."

"He doesn't cook anymore."

"Well, sweetie, we don't need him to."

"Then what's changed from when he was drinking all the time?"

Grandma sighs. She looks tired and I feel bad for pushing her like this.

I say, "I'm sorry, Grandma."

She smiles, but she doesn't look happy. "What he chooses to do, he chooses to do. And I'm not going to stop him. Not now. Not this late."

I squeeze her hand again. "You're not going to die, Grandma."

"Oh, sweetie," she says, "we're all going to die."

"I mean . . ."

"And some of us," she says, "are going to die sooner rather than later."

JOKER MAN

After Grandma falls asleep, I go to Grandpa's study. He's in there building a model World War II ship. He's gluing a railing on the front when I walk in.

I say, "You know that my mom's a junkie, right?"

He sets the glue down and looks up. "Yes," he says.

"Is that worse than what you do? Smoking all of Grandma's medical weed? Taking her pills?" Even as I say that, I get a twinge of guilt. I don't like being a hypocrite, and maybe my pill stealing lately is the reason that I'm bringing this up now.

I look away from him. Look at all of the different planes and ships he's built over the years. Models are on every shelf, all the way around the room. When he finishes a really nice plane, he hangs it by fishing line from an eye hook in the ceiling like it's flying. There are a dozen of those planes in the room, all hanging at different heights.

I look back at Grandpa, and he looks back at his model. Doesn't look up at me. He fits the railing in place on the model's deck and slides it into its grooves. Clamps it with his fingers. He says, "You know what, Travis, your grandma doesn't even want what the doctors prescribe. She never uses it. And anyway, marijuana is nothing compared to heroin."

"Nothing?"

"No," he says. "There isn't even a comparison. Do you understand that? Those two things aren't in the same league."

"But what's the difference if you have to smoke it every day?"

He shakes his head. "I don't have to smoke it every day."

"You don't?"

"No," he says.

"Then why do you?"

"Well, maybe I *choose* to smoke it regularly."

There's an F-14 Tomcat in front of me. I touch the nose and the plane wobbles on its line. "So you're not addicted?"

"No."

I look at him. "But if you smoke it every day, what's the difference?"

He turns his ship in his hand. Sights it from the stern, then the bow. "A lot," he says. "A whole lot. I just do it because it helps with my hip pain."

"Your hip pain?"

He looks at me. "You know I had a hip replacement surgery."

"That was a long time ago. And didn't they give you painkillers for that?"

"Yes, but not enough. And when they ran out, instead of getting my own medical marijuana card, I just used Grandma's. So it's the exact same thing. I could've gotten my own card, legally, so what's the difference?"

"I don't know," I say, and shake my head. I touch the F-14 again and it spins. "I guess you must understand things a lot better than I do." I stare at Grandpa for a second, but he keeps his head down. Stares at the model in his hands.

I walk out.

He calls after me as I walk down the hall. "It's the same thing, Travis. It's the same exact thing."

SHRAPNEL

I GRAB MY BASKETBALL AND go out front to the driveway. My ribs don't feel good, but I have to shoot. I feel like I'm one of those pressure-cooker bombs that terrorists make, and if I don't play ball soon, I'm going to explode nails and metal pieces all over everybody and everything.

I shoot with my right hand. I try going up on the left side one time, but my left arm is too stiff to work right and I get sharp pains when I raise it above my head.

I shoot short, one-handed power layins on the right side of the backboard. Two-foot shots. Then three-foot. Move out to five. But anything farther than that hurts too much, so I stay there, shooting short shots, one-handed, off the backboard. Then I move in and shoot two-foot swishes, trying not to let the ball hit the rim. I give myself one point for each perfect swish and count games to 10 in my head. By the third game, I start to relax. Nothing has ever made me feel as good as doing something right on the basketball court.

"Are you supposed to be doing that?"

I turn around. Natalie's there with her arms crossed.

I say, "It feels okay on the right side."

"Does it?"

I shrug.

"You should wait," she says. "You should heal up all the way, then start working out again."

I say, "I just had to shoot a little." I spin the ball in my hand. Try to palm it and it almost sticks. The ball slips off the pad of my middle finger.

"Are you all right?"

I spin the ball again. "Maybe."

"I'm sorry about what happened at my house a couple of weeks ago."

I take a shot and miss. "It's okay."

"I mean, I'm not sorry about what happened. I'm sorry I just pushed you out the door like that. It's sort of hard to explain."

I step in closer to the hoop. Make a short shot. Catch the ball as it comes out of the bottom of the net. "Really, it's all right."

Natalie still has her arms crossed. She says, "I made a lot of mistakes when I was younger. Too many mistakes, and I don't want to be like that anymore."

I nod and look at her. "All right."

"And I like you, Travis, and I don't want to . . . I don't know." She tilts her head back. Sniffs.

I take a step toward her. I say, "It's okay. It really is."

"I just did so many shitty things, you know?"

I don't know what she means, or not exactly, but I nod my head.

"So can we just relax a little bit?"

"Relax?"

"Yeah, I know this sounds like a cliché movie or something, but can we just take it a little slower?"

I nod and spin the ball in my hands. "Yeah, we can do that."

"I mean, would that be okay for real? Because sometimes people say it is, but . . ." She wipes a tear with the back of her wrist. Her scar looks a brighter shade of pink.

"It's fine," I say. Step closer to her. "It really is."

She puts her hands on my face and kisses me. "Thanks for understanding."

I grab the front of her shirt with one hand. Hold my basketball against my hip with the other. "So do you want to hang out today?" I pull her closer to me. Kiss her.

"No, I've got to do this charity thing." She sniffs again. Smiles.

"What charity thing?"

"A feed-the-homeless thing under the bridge."

My mouth goes dry when she says that. I say, "Why are you doing that?"

"It's part of the local food-bank program. My mom sets these things up for her philanthropy work."

"Philanthropy?"

"She feels obligated or something. That's what she says. But they're cool. The events, they're good. I don't mind them."

"So you give out food?"

"Pretty much. A lot of the people are drug addicts or alcoholics, but most of them are nice enough. They thank us a lot. And the few who are really crazy or high . . . they don't bother me much."

I overgrip the basketball with my one hand like I'm trying

225

to crush it against my hip. I realize that my other hand is flexing too hard, twisting her T-shirt. I relax my grip.

Natalie says, "I came over to ask you if you want to come along. Do you?"

I shake my head. "No thanks."

"Why, are you doing something else today?"

"Uh . . ."

She says, "Homeless people are people too, just like us. You'll see."

"Yeah, I know about homeless people."

Natalie kisses me again. "So come with me, then. In the summer, we do these things once a week. And by now we know all of the regulars, so we see a lot of the same people. You'll get to know them too. It's pretty cool."

"No, I don't think I can. Sorry about that."

"But you're not doing anything. Is this about what happened at my house?" Natalie pulls away from me. Takes a step back.

"No," I say. "It's not about that."

"It isn't? Are you sure?"

"No," I say, turn, and take a shot so she can't see my eyes. "I've got to help my grandma today. She's got a doctor's appointment."

"She has a doctor's appointment on a Saturday afternoon?"

I forgot it was Saturday. My story doesn't seem likely but I stick with it. I say, "She does. She has one today. An important one."

"Really?"

Before I think about it, I say, "The thing is, cancer doesn't know what day of the week it is."

Natalie's eyes narrow when I say that. She crosses her arms

again. Nods her head slowly. "Okay," she says. "I see. Never mind. Just thought I'd ask." She turns around and walks to her car. Clicks the UNLOCK button.

Creature dribbles up then. I hadn't seen him coming down the street, but he must've been right there. He stops in front of Natalie's car. Looks back and forth between me and Natalie. "Are you two all right?"

"Oh we're fine," Natalie says. "We're great."

"Creature," I say, "this is Natalie. Natalie, this is Creature."

He smiles.

Natalie shakes her head. Says, "I gotta go." She opens the driver's side door and gets in. Starts the car, whips a U-turn, and drives off.

"Whew," Creature says. "That momma was pissed."

"Yeah."

"But she looked good, baby."

"Fuck you, Creat."

"I'm just saying." He puts his hands up and makes an innocent face like after he commits an intentional foul in a league game.

I say, "And don't make that face either. That just means you fouled me on purpose."

Creature dribbles through his legs. "What was she so mad about?"

"It's a long story." I turn and shoot one-handed from 10 feet out and swish it, but swishing the shot doesn't make me feel any better.

"You don't have to tell me." Creature dribbles up the driveway and takes a shot from 15 feet. Misses. Rebounds and dunks. "It's cool, baby. I've been around girls. I get it."

227

We shoot for a few minutes. My ribs hurt on every shot, but I shoot anyway. I don't care that they hurt.

Creature's phone goes off; Jay Z's "Death of Auto-Tune" is his ringtone. Creature picks it up off the ground and reads the screen. "I gotta go, baby."

"Can't shoot a little?"

"No," he says. "But I'll catch you later, all right?"

HOLLiS BROWN LIVED ON
THE OuTSIDE OF TOWN

MY MOM PLAYED BOB DYLAN CDs—only Bob Dylan CDs—the whole time we lived in the motels. She knew all of the words. She had every album, plus 13 live albums, the *Biograph* collection, and two of his greatest-hits tapes.

One time she said to me, " 'Like a Rolling Stone' is called the greatest song of all time, but what about 'Ballad of Hollis Brown'? What about 'Shelter from the Storm'? What about 'To Ramona' or 'One Too Many Mornings'?"

I liked all of those songs. All of them were good to me. But sad. I said, "Isn't 'Hollis Brown' that one song where he kills his whole family?"

"Yeah," she said, "but you understand where he's coming from, you know?"

She leaned down and started *Biograph*'s third disc on the portable CD player that she kept on the nightstand by the bed. Each time we moved, the CD player and her disks were the first items she put in her oversize Walmart bag. Sometimes—when we were in a hurry—those were the only items we moved.

WiLL

WHEN I WAKE UP, IT'S evening, and my back's stiffer than it was before I fell asleep. Shooting hoops probably wasn't the best idea.

I roll to my knees, get to a sitting position slowly, drink some water. With my good arm, I reach and feel my ribs with my fingertips. I can just touch the spot where they're cracked, and pushing on them sends little pulses of pain into my shoulder and neck.

I feel bad about how I talked to Natalie. I tear a blank page out of the back of one of the novels Creature left for me and write a note:

> *Natalie –*
> *I'm sorry about earlier. It's nice of you to do some-thing for the homeless and I shouldn't have acted like that. I don't know why I did.*
>
> > *Sorry,*
> > *Travis*

I walk the lake trail through the blackberries, then around the north end to her house. Go up to her front door and knock.

A man opens the door. He's about 40 years old, curly haired, clean-shaven, wearing slacks and a white button-down shirt. He's holding an iPad. He says, "Can I help you?"

"Yeah," I say. "I'm Travis. I know Natalie. Is she here?"

"No. She went out with some kids from school." The man looks down at his iPad and types something.

That doesn't make any sense. Natalie hasn't been to school yet. I say, "Some kids from school?"

"Soccer teammates." He doesn't look up from his iPad. He says, "They left maybe an hour ago."

He's staring at that screen, and I look at the top of his head. His hair is starting to gray and thin out. This has to be her stepdad, the one who waited to see her coming out of the shower naked. I get an impulse to punch him. With his head down, he wouldn't see it coming and I could probably knock him out with one shot.

He looks up. Says, "Do you need me to tell her something?"

I hold the note out. "Can I leave this for her?"

"Sure." He takes it.

"Thanks," I say. Turn and leave.

ENTER THE DISTILLERY

I'M ASLEEP WHEN NATALIE COMES to my tent and shakes it. "Hey, you."

"Yeah?"

She unzips the door. Crawls in. Pulls my sleeping bag open and slides in against me. Kisses me, her mouth like a distillery. I was sleepy before that, but now I'm awake.

We kiss for a while—she kisses like she's drinking me. It feels so good but she smells like wood alcohol. I say, "How much did you drink tonight?"

"A little bit." She giggles. She gets up on her knees and takes off her shirt. Puts my hands on her breasts, over the top of her bra. She straddles me. The insides of her thighs are hot.

She kisses my neck. Says, "Too bad I'm such a fucked-up girl."

"You're not fucked up."

Her hair brushes across my face. She kisses the other side

of my neck. "I am. I'm fucked up in the head." She breathes into my ear.

We're kissing again, and her whole body is on top of me, rubbing against me. She feels incredible in my sleeping bag like this. But I don't like to think of her as fucked up in the head.

I pull back. "What about the other day? What about when you stopped us at your house?"

She puts a finger to my lips. "Shhhh." She giggles again. Sits up. Dances a little to music that isn't playing. Then she bends down, puts her mouth next to my ear, and says, "Don't you wanna fuck me?"

I do. I want to. But that's also what Maggie used to say when I was with her in her bedroom and she wouldn't lock the door, and I don't like that memory, how it makes me feel sort of off balance, like after you get off a spinning ride at the county fair.

I say, "Maybe we should just chill a little bit."

Natalie sits up again, and this time she doesn't dance. The face she makes is like watching people go away. She starts to cry. No sound, just tears.

"Hey," I say, "it's okay. It really is."

"No, I'm just so . . ." She wipes her eyes with her hands. "I'm just . . ."

"Really, Natalie, it's okay. Come here."

She wipes her eyes again, leans her head down, and rests it against my shoulder. She says, "This just . . . I don't even know."

I hold her there, and she stays, her head on my shoulder, my arms around her. She breathes deep, in and out. Settles her body against me.

I'm wide awake, her long legs on either side of me, her breasts against my chest, all of her skin against my skin in that sleeping bag. I'm awake, staring at the ceiling of the tent.

She falls asleep like that, breathing against my neck, pressed into me. Asleep and breathing deep. I hold her amid the smells of liquor and shampoo and sweat.

I AND I

IN THE MORNING, MY RIBS hurt. I shift to get more comfortable. Feel Natalie on top of me, my left arm asleep underneath her. I scooch some more, trying to find a position where my ribs don't hurt, but Natalie's heavy on top of me.

She moves her head and groans. Mumbles, "Shit."

"Are you okay?"

"Yeah," she says. "I'm okay. I might've gotten hit by a train, though."

"You might've had a little bit to drink last night."

She rolls off of me, lying on her back, breathing deep, her chest rising and falling in her bright orange bra. She says, "I don't feel so good."

I watch her breathing. The sun's risen, and the tent is already warm.

Natalie says, "Did we . . ."

"Did we what?"

"You know." She turns toward me. Pinches the bridge of her nose. "Did we?"

"No," I say. "We didn't. You were kind of sad last night."

"Oh, I'm sorry, Travis. I was a mess."

"It's okay."

"No, it really isn't. I'm sorry I was like that, that I came here like that." Natalie rubs her eyes with her fingertips. "I was really upset, and I went out with those girls, and I acted like an idiot. I'm sorry."

"It's okay. Really."

"No. It's not," she says. "I don't want to be like that anymore. That's what I meant a couple of weeks ago. I don't want to be like that. I don't want to be the party girl. I don't want to drink and all that. And, you know . . . other stuff." She shakes her head and pinches the bridge of her nose.

"It's wasn't all bad," I say. "I like having you here now. I like that you slept in my tent, and you look really good in that bra."

"You're sweet." Natalie smiles, her eyes closed. She's still pinching the bridge of her nose. "I'd kiss you right now if my mouth didn't taste like a sewer system. I need some toothpaste and a 7UP. And in a minute, I'm gonna go home to die."

THE ART OF SEDUCTION

CREATURE SAYS, "THE GUIDEBOOK'S ALMOST done. It's good, man. Just the way I want it. I wrote this essay today called 'How to Save a Sad Princess from a Russian Marriage: Seduction 101.' It might end up being the opening to the book."

"Do you practice your seduction techniques on Jill?"

"Shut up," Creature says. "You know how that went. And I'm trying to quit that. I am. But she seduces me." He pretends to be Catholic and makes the sign of the cross. Kisses his fingertips after.

"So," I say, "in this metaphor, in this intro to your guidebook, are you the Russian princess, then?"

Creature tilts his head back and laughs. "Maybe," he says. "Maybe I am."

I think of the last Russian princess pages he left for me.

The Pervert's Guide to Russian Princesses
Princess #43 (Revised Draft)

Princess Irina Alexandrovna, I hear you were a shy and tongue-tied girl with deep blue eyes and dark hair. Nicknamed Baby Rina. Treated like a baby. But I don't want you to be a baby, or shy, anymore. Others will hold you like a baby, 120 pounds in their arms, but I'll take the bottle from their hands and shatter it against the wall.

You married a man who dressed in women's clothing, who—people say—scandalized society. So I know that you are daring. What would you not be willing to do? I've studied you. Asked that question. Studied you some more. And I know now that you wouldn't kill Rasputin, that you said no, that you are not a murderer. But what will you do with me? That is the real question.

On Saturday afternoons, I won't let you be Baby Rina. You'll be a woman. We'll fumble with each other's clothing while we dial the tsarina on the phone, laughing as we go back and forth, the phone on speaker, both of us trying to talk normally, but giggling to ourselves, and the tsarina saying over and over, "What's going on over there? What's so funny?" I'll cover your mouth with my hand and you'll bite my fingers hard enough to make me grit my teeth and wince.

I've seen the way you stare into the camera, turned sideways, a vast necklace like a map of guilt hanging past your chest, pulling you down. But you don't need to feel guilty about anything we do together. You'll be Rina, my Rina, and sometimes we'll push aside the blankie and pacifier and lie in your bed together, still, on our backs, holding hands, staring at the mobiles spinning above our heads like the planets in their motions around the sun.

ON FATHERS

WE GET ON THE BUS by the Chevron Jackson station. Take two middle seats. Creature turns to me. "You ever wonder about your dad?"

"My dad? You know I never really knew him. I guess he was one of the guys at the motel, but I don't know which one."

Creature spits on the floor of the bus. "I didn't know my dad either. But do you wonder sometimes?"

I do, but I don't like to admit it. For me, admitting it is somehow letting him win. So I say, "No, not too much."

"But a little bit?"

"Yeah, I guess so."

"Me too. A little."

I say, "We shouldn't waste our time thinking about them."

"So fuck them?"

"Yeah," I say. "Motherfuckers never loved us."

"That's right." Creature smiles. "I got that song right here." He plugs in his earbuds and hands one to me.

ON THE COURT THAT NIGHT

I LIKE WATCHING BASKETBALL, BUT pickup is annoying if I can't play. It makes me feel twitchy, like a meth-head. I get too involved. I see every opportunity I can't exploit, people making the same mistakes over and over.

In the second game, the other team gives up a dunk to Creature on three straight possessions, all three on the same backdoor cut. On the third dunk, Creature does a couple of pull-ups on the rim afterward. Yells, "Feels good up here. I guess the city built me a pull-up bar."

The gangbanger from Portland arrives after that. He warms up across the court, dribbling left and right, crossing through his legs, taking a few shots. I watch the snap of his wrist, how he drops two fingers on his release, arm straight, and I realize that he must've played somewhere real, not just on project courts. He's played a lot of basketball in his lifetime. He's been coached.

He comes over and stands next to a few guys I've never

seen before. I realize that they all came together, maybe rolled down from Portland. Maybe they all played on the same junior college team or something. Three of them are wearing Trail Blazers jerseys, and I laugh to myself when I see that one is a Rudy Fernandez jersey because Fernandez couldn't guard a chair and had no mental game. He earned millions on a spot-up three because he was tall.

The game in front of us ends and Creature goes to get a drink of water. I walk over there. "You're in the flow, man."

"Hoping to dominate all night, baby. 10 more dunks." He winks at me. Picks up his ball and dribbles a crossover with his left shin, back to his right hand. Then he pinches his throw-back jersey and pops it. "Old-school Rip City. Rasheed Wallace."

I smile. Creature dribbles out onto the court and I yell, "Ball don't lie."

The score hits 5-0 fast, four of the baskets to Creature. The gangbanger's guarding him, but there's no point. Creature's fired up, trash-talking, hits two floaters, a reverse layin, and a baseline fade from the right side. As he jogs back up the court, he yells, "Ball don't lie, baby."

The guys on the sideline start chanting, "Creat! Creat! Creat! Creat!"

The gangbanger doesn't have any look on his face. He doesn't seem bothered, and I should notice that something's off but I don't. I'm not paying good enough attention. I'm right there, but I don't see what's about to happen.

Creature inbounds the ball on the opposite sideline and makes a cut up-court around the gangbanger, but the gang-banger holds him up on a pick. Creature trips as he goes by. The gangbanger catches him. Creature pushes forward and trips again, the gangbanger still holding him, Creature's mouth open.

Creature falls down, the wind knocked out of him. He doesn't scream. He doesn't make any sound. We're all watching him doubled over on the ground and a guy near me says, "Hold the ball. Let him get his breath back."

"Yeah, sorry, man."

The game stops. All of us on the sideline take a few steps forward.

"Creature?"

I don't see the gangbanger leave. Later, one of the players on Creature's team tells the police that the gangbanger walked underneath the far basket and kept on walking, over the dirt mound to the gap where the railroad tracks run through the park. The guys who came with the gangbanger went the other way and no one saw where they went either. If they all came together, they must've parked far away because no one saw them get in a car. No one saw much of anything. They all wore Trail Blazers jerseys, and that's what people saw. No one noticed any faces. No one knew any names. And by the time we realized what that guy did to Creature, they were gone.

Creature stays down. The point guard in the game, a kid from Willamette High School named Ray, he walks over and says, "You all right, Creat?"

Creature rolls onto his side, and that's when we all see the blood. Ray says, "Oh shit, man."

Another player yells, "Call 911."

Creature is on his side, holding his stomach with two hands. He says, "He got me three times."

I crouch over him. "What?"

"Three times."

Ray's next to me. Looks at Creature, then me. "I think that bitch stabbed him up."

I can hear someone on a phone behind me. I say, "You're gonna be okay, Creat. The ambulance will be here soon."

Creature's breathing quick little breaths in and out, holding his stomach. He closes his eyes.

"Stay awake, Creat. They'll be here real soon, man. You're gonna be all right."

Ray takes off his Iverson jersey, rolls it up, and puts it under Creature's head. Another player says, "We should probably put pressure on his stomach, huh?"

Someone gets a sweatshirt from the sideline and brings it over. Hands it to me. But I don't know what to do. I'm sort of panicking. The court feels like it's spinning and I'm off balance. I just hold that sweatshirt in my hands and stare at the blood.

Ray takes the sweatshirt from me. Pushes Creature's hands aside. Says, "Let me press here, Creat." He presses the sweatshirt against Creature's stomach, where the bleeding's coming from.

Creature groans.

"You're okay," Ray says. "We've got you, man."

It doesn't take long for the ambulance to get there because we're near the Delta Highway. The ambulance drives over the curb, down the grass, and onto the court. Paramedics jump out. The first one says, "What do we have?"

I say, "He got stabbed in the stomach."

The paramedic slides in next to Ray. "Thanks," he says, and takes the sweatshirt off. The other paramedic crouches down and cuts Creature's jersey up the front with his scissors. They take out gauze pads and start wiping. "Let's see . . ."

Two of the wounds look like thin lines, like the knife went straight in. The third is more jagged, turns at the bottom, a rip sideways, then the flesh torn back.

Ray says, "What the . . ."

"Relax," the paramedic says. "We're fine here. Everything's just fine." And to the other paramedic, "Do you have that Demerol shot?"

"Yes." The second paramedic lays Creature's arm down flat on the cement, puts a rubber strip around his bicep, bringing up the veins in the forearm. He says to Creature, "I'm going to give you something that will help with the pain." Then he pulls out a syringe and pops the cap off the needle. Guides it in with two fingers on his left hand. Pushes on the stopper and checks the level.

Creature doesn't say anything. His eyes are closed and he's breathing shallow.

Two police cars drive down the grass behind the far rim. Three officers and a K-9 hop out of the cars.

I look at Creature. The second paramedic is wrapping his abdomen. New gauze on the wounds. "Okay, let's go," he says.

They're quick. The one who did the pain shot jogs to get the injury board and then he's back and they roll Creature onto his side, then onto the board. "Do you two want to help us lift him and get him on the gurney?"

Ray and I nod.

"Okay, then. One, two, three, lift." We lift Creature, walk him over, and set the board on the gurney. The paramedic says, "Now let's slide this in."

We do, and the paramedics hit the gurney against the back of the ambulance. It folds and slides in. The first paramedic gets in with Creature and the second paramedic puts his hands on the double doors. He says, "Are either of you family?"

"No."

"Would you like to meet us at the hospital, then?"

"Okay," I say.

"We'll be at RiverBend in 15 minutes. He's probably going into surgery immediately. Can you notify the family?"

"Yes."

"Okay. We've got to go." He closes the doors and jogs to the driver's door and gets in. Starts the ambulance, flicks on the siren, and drives off.

"Damn," Ray says.

"I know."

He says, "Do you have a car?"

"No. Creature and I took the bus."

"You want a ride?"

"Yeah, thanks."

I'm sort of freaking out in my head, and I want to go, want to get to the hospital quick, but we aren't allowed to leave right away. The police officers call us over and we have to give statements, describe what we saw, try to describe the gangbanger and his friends. The police officer we're talking to is short and has a mustache, lifts a lot of weights, and I remember him right away. We're not that far from the motels where I used to live, and he had the night beat back then. I remember how he'd put his hands on his hips and smile at people, and I'd watch him sometimes and wonder what he was thinking. And I remember the time he arrested my mom and I hid in the bushes with the apartment key so he wouldn't arrest me too.

While he's talking to Ray, I'm thinking about how I spent three days alone in the apartment after that, eating Ritz crackers and dry ramen, sprinkling the flavor packs over the noodles, waiting for my mom to come back. I never went outside because I didn't know what would happen, and then she did come back after three days, and the first thing she said was "Pack. We've gotta be out of here in 15 minutes, before the manager comes down looking for rent."

I'm thinking about all of that, and the police officer puts his hands on his hips and licks his mustache and he says to me, "Hey. Focus, kid. Are you high?"

"What?"

"We need your help here to figure out what's going on, so focus up. Got it?"

I nod.

"Okay. Can you describe the assailant for me? Did he have any tattoos we might be able to use as personal identification? Did he have any significant scars?"

I try to describe the gangbanger. Try to remember tattoos, but I didn't pay attention to that. I say, "I know he played ball somewhere. His defense is mediocre but he's solid on offense. Actually, he's better than solid. He's good. And I'd say he's six-foot-zero. Maybe an inch shorter than Creature?"

"Creature?" The police officer stops writing on his little pad. Looks up.

"Malik. The guy who stabbed him was an inch shorter than Malik. And he couldn't guard him."

WAITING

RAY GIVES ME A RIDE back to the trailer park because I ask him to take me to Creature's house. I get out of the car and say, "Thanks." Jog up to the front porch and knock on the door. No one answers. I knock again, and Creature's mom comes to the door looking like she's been sleeping for a year. Wearing one of her tight workout outfits.

Her voice is slurred. "What's it going?"

"Creature . . . I mean Malik, he got hurt. They took him to the hospital."

"Gonna be . . . ?"

"We gotta go," I say. "Can you drive us?" But as soon as I ask that, I know she can't drive. She's messed up on something. "What did you take?"

"Xanax," she says. "A little bit of . . ."

"How many?"

She shakes her head. Holds up three fingers, then adds one to make four.

"Four Xanax? Fuck."

Ray rolls down his passenger-side window. "You guys all right?"

I say, "We might need a ride to the hospital."

"No problem." He reaches across and pops the door.

I walk Creature's mom to the car as she leans on me heavy.

Ray takes us to the emergency room entrance, and we get out. I say, "Thanks again," as I walk through the double doors.

A nurse jogs up to us and says, "What are her symptoms?"

I look at Creature's mom, and her head is all the way back. She's walking forward, but she's asleep on her feet and her body's jerking along like a zombie in a movie.

"No," I say, "she's okay. She just needs a chair to sleep in." I sit Creature's mom in a chair and go up to the desk with the nurse. "I need to check on someone who came in an ambulance a little while ago."

"Okay. Last name?" She moves her mouse and clicks.

"Madison," I say. "First name, Malik."

"Okay, let me see . . ." She scrolls with the mouse. "Now, are you family?"

"Yes, ma'am." I'm so worried about Creature that I don't hesitate. I say, "He's my brother."

The woman behind the desk clicks her tongue as her eyes follow the scrolling on her screen. "Madison . . . ," she says. "Oh, here it is. Let's see . . ." She looks up. "He's in surgery right now, sweetie, third floor. Operating room two. The surgical rooms have no public access, of course, but you're welcome to wait on the third floor at the surgery check-in. I'm sure they'll come out and give updates to family members as soon as possible."

"Okay."

I go back to the chair where Creature's mom is sleeping. Shake her shoulder. She doesn't wake up, so I shake her some more. Rougher. "Come on. We have to go to the surgical center to get news."

Creature's mom blinks. Opens her eyes. Starts to close them again.

"Come on, Mrs. M. We have to go down the hall." I shake her hard enough that her head rolls around. "Listen." I take her face in my hands. "You have to wake up now."

A nurse approaches me. She says, "Is this woman okay?"

"Oh yeah," I say. "She took a little Xanax, but she's fine."

"A little Xanax?"

"She's fine. Really." I'm nervous about Creature. I need to know if he's okay, and I can taste bile in the back of my throat. It makes me feel panicky. I say, "She's fine. Leave her alone. She takes it all the time."

The nurse looks unsure.

I shake Creature's mom again. Say, "Malik's in surgery. We've got to go wait at the surgery center."

"Malik," she says. She opens her eyes and puts both hands on her armrests. Pushes herself up.

"That's it," I say. "There you go. Let's walk down and check on him, okay?"

She stands and I support her. The nurse is still next to us, looking back and forth between Creature's mom and me. She says, "Are you sure she's okay?"

"For sure. She's okay. We're just gonna go check on my brother now."

I walk Creature's mom down three different halls to the main elevators.

I'm nervous and I want the elevator to come quicker. It seems like everything's going too slow, that we're waiting too long. I know Creature's in surgery and nothing I do matters at all, but still I want to get there.

The elevator door opens and I shake Creature's mom and walk her into the elevator. We take it up to the third floor and the door opens again. The surgery check-in desk is in front of us and I say, "Come on, now," and walk Creature's mom into the waiting room. There's a male nurse in front of us. His head is down, and he's writing something on a clipboard.

I say, "My brother, Malik Madison, he's in surgery. They told us to come up. Can you tell me how that surgery's going?"

"Let's see . . . ," the nurse says. He turns to his computer. Types in Creature's name and scrolls the page. "Yes, here it is . . . room two . . . and . . . his surgery is scheduled for four more hours." He looks up. "I'm sorry. But we have drinks and vending machines down the hall. A waiting area here." He points. "Family members are more than welcome, and we'll give you updates as they come in."

"Okay."

"Also, I do need to see the family insurance information if you have that."

Creature's mom is leaning against me and her eyes are closed. I say, "Yeah, I don't know about that. I'll see what she's got with her when she wakes up a little bit more."

The man stares at Creature's mom, asleep on her feet, so I walk her away before he asks me anything else. I take her over to a comfortable-looking chair in the corner and let her slump down sideways. Tilt her head against the armrest cushion. Drape her knees over the other side of the chair.

I walk down to the vending area and find the free soda

machine. Pour myself ice in a little plastic cup, some Sprite to go with it, hoping to wash that bad taste out of my mouth. Then I walk back to where Creature's mom is sleeping and sit down next to her.

I drink the Sprite and think about Creature. Try not to be too nervous for him. Look around the room. There are newspapers on the table, magazines in stacks. I pick up a newspaper and open it to the sports section, but it's all baseball. Baseball won't keep my mind off Creature.

I walk back up to the desk. "Sorry to bother you again, but what kind of surgery is my brother having right now?"

"Let's see here . . . Madison, right?" The man types and clicks. "Let's see . . . bowel repair, multiples . . . then vascular surgery. And that will be at least . . . three more hours, minimum. Could be more." He looks up and smiles like he's chewing on something bitter. "I'm sorry," he says.

I go and sit back down. Look at Creature's mom and wish I had some pills to take, some Percocet to numb me. Something to make me sleep. My ribs ache. I check my pockets, but I don't have any loose Vicodin or Percocet on me. I adjust my body in my seat so I'm leaning back against my good side, tilted.

I see the newest *ESPN The Magazine* and two *Sports Illustrated*s on the table next to me. I pick those up. Flip to the table of contents in *ESPN*. I read an article on Chris Paul, but there's nothing in it that I didn't already know.

I put the magazine down and wonder about Creature some more. Think about him with tubes in his mouth. Knocked out. Cut open. I try to pray the way my grandma used to when I was little. I close my eyes and start the way she always started,

Dear Lord, thank you for everything you give us. Thank you for the good things and the bad things. . . .

I don't know what to say after that, so I say, *And help Creature to be okay. Help him to be good. Really good. All the way strong.* Then I open my eyes and look around the room. Say amen out loud. There's no one in there to hear me. The nurse is too far away to hear, and there's no one else in the room with us.

I don't know if that's a good prayer or not, but I feel a little bit better after I do it, so every once in a while I pray again, and I sort of pray the same prayer over and over like I'm practicing free throws.

Creature's mom is sleeping next to me and I wish I could sleep too, but I'm so worried about Creature, and the lights are bright above us, and I close my eyes for a few minutes, but there's no way I'm going to fall asleep. No way at all.

I pick up one of the *Sports Illustrated*s. Read another article about basketball, this one about a Division III college called Haverford and how they were one of the worst teams in college basketball history. They couldn't win a single game even though they worked really hard, and they ended up losing 46 straight games before they finally won a game against a bad school by using a "run-and-jump trap" zone that turned into a two-three zone by the end of the game. The article is pretty good, much better than the Chris Paul article I read in the ESPN magazine, because this article tells a story no one's ever heard and it's all about guys sort of like me, short guards, short forwards, guys who are maybe not as athletic as the average college basketball player, although I hope I'm a little more athletic than these guys since they sound pretty sad.

I read all the way through the article without looking up, and I forget about everything for 20 minutes until it's over. But then I finish, and I look around, and I think about Creature inside, still in surgery, and I don't know what else to do but pray, so I pray for him again even though I'm not really sure if there is a God up there above us at all.

Then I wait.

ICU

A DOCTOR COMES OUT THROUGH the double doors. It's been four hours, and this man in blue scrubs comes through the door with a clipboard and says, "Is the Madison family here?" He looks around like he's searching through a crowd even though it's two in the morning and we're the only people in the waiting room.

I stand up. Turn and shake Creature's mom. "Hey. Wake up."

She's slept the Xanax off by now and she wakes up all the way. Sniffs a little and rubs her eyes, then stands up next to me.

"Are you Malik Madison's family?" He looks at us, confused.

Creature's mom says, "I'm his mother."

He says, "Okay . . ."

Creature's mom is really awake now. She says, "If you're struggling with this concept, I'm white and his father is black. Does that make sense?"

I can tell that the doctor isn't used to people talking to him like that. "Okay," he says. "Well, let me give you an update on the patient." When he says that, something moves in my lower intestines, something heavy.

Creature's mom has her hands on her hips. "Is he okay?"

"He's doing well," the doctor says. "Malik had bowel and vascular surgery tonight. Both went as well as could be expected in these types of cases. The team had to do a small-bowel resection—"

Creature's mom says, "What does that mean?"

"It means that we had to take out a very small piece of the small intestine that was too damaged to repair. Two of the knife wounds were very clean and easily reparable. The third was much more significant. There was internal damage, and that became the major focus of the first surgery: the resection."

"Is he going to be okay, though?"

"We're quite optimistic. The second surgery was successful as well. His vascular system was repaired in the lower abdomen."

"But is he going to be okay?"

"Like I said, we're optimistic. We're hopeful for a full recovery. But that will take some time. He's going to be sedated in the ICU for a few days, under close observation. He has catheters in place and a feeding tube, and we're hopeful—considering his excellent physical shape—that he'll bounce back quite nicely." The doctor smiles.

Creature's mom doesn't smile. "I want to see him."

"Absolutely." The doctor nods. "But again, he's under heavy sedation and being transferred to the ICU as we speak. Family can visit him there as soon as he's set up. He won't be awake, but you're welcome to visit. Please speak to someone at this desk here and they'll give you information and directions to the ICU. Do you have any other questions for me?"

"Yes," I say. "When can he play basketball again?"

The doctor takes a deep breath and shakes his head. "There's no way for me to know that. I'm optimistic, but can't make any promises. I would hope that he could resume all normal activities in a few months."

"A few months?"

"That would be my best guess, but like I said, I can't make any promises." The doctor looks at his watch. "Any other questions?"

Creature's mom is glaring at the doctor. He doesn't seem to notice.

I say, "So we can go to the ICU now and wait?"

"Yes. They'll give you directions at the desk." The doctor looks at his watch again and says, "I'm sorry you had to go through this. This was a serious case, an unfortunate case. Take good care." He turns and hits a button on the wall. The double doors open again and he walks back inside the surgery center.

At the desk, a new nurse asks Creature's mom for insurance information. She gives the nurse her Oregon Health Plan numbers, and I stand behind her and wait. Then the nurse gives her directions to the ICU, and we walk down the hall.

We're not allowed to enter the room where Creature is, but we get to see him from behind glass. He's sleeping, propped up, his head tilted to the side and a tube taped into his mouth. He looks tall and thin in that bed. An IV line is in his arm. Monitors are behind him.

"Oh my God." Creature's mom begins to cry.

I say, "It'll be okay." But I have to take a deep breath

because I feel like I'm watching a person who's about to die. Then, for some reason, Creature is dead, and I picture a coffin built up around him. He's sitting back against a few of those funeral-home pillows with designs sewn on them, bright flowers in vases all around him, and someone's playing the church organ.

A nurse touches my arm and I jump. She says, "Are you here to see Malik Madison?"

I don't say anything.

"Yes," Creature's mom says. "He's my son."

"Well, the report from surgery is that it went well. He'll be sedated for a while according to the chart, but you'll be able to talk to him, hold his hand, and sit with him starting"—she looks at a clipboard and flips the page—"starting tomorrow, it looks like."

"Tomorrow?"

"Yes. So stay here as long as you'd like tonight. Go ahead and look in on him. Then head home and get some sleep. And tomorrow you'll be able to visit. He won't be fully awake, of course, but you'll be able to go right up to his bed then. Hold his hand and all of that."

Creature's mom is shaking her head and crying without making a sound. I put my arm around her, and her whole body is stiff. "It's okay," I say. "We can come back tomorrow."

We stand there for a long time just looking at him. I can't shake that image of Creature in his coffin, but after a while Creature's mom gets tired and I agree to go.

SALTINES AND SPRITE

I WAKE UP LATE AND walk up the hill to the back porch. When I open the sliding glass door, the whole house smells like vomit.

"Grandma?" I run to her room.

She's in a pool of pink, the vomit chunks like wet confetti. Her voice is quiet. "I'm sorry."

"Where's Grandpa?"

"He went to the store."

"Okay," I say. "It's gonna be okay."

I help her into the bathroom. Get her robe off and turn my back. "Hold on to that rail, Grandma."

"I've got it."

"Don't let go. I'll close my eyes and turn on the water. You get your underwear off."

"Thank you, sweetie."

She steps into the bath, and I help her lower herself with my eyes still closed.

I go back to her bedroom. Strip the bed. Carry everything

to the washing machine and start it. Grandpa put a plastic underlay on the bed after the last accident, so the cleanup isn't too bad. I wipe the plastic sheet. Smear bleach mixed with water to the edges. Take all of my rags to the washing machine that's almost full. Click it to warm-hot and close the lid.

After her bath, I get Grandma back in bed and turn on a rerun of *Jeopardy!* Bring her some saltine crackers and a glass of Sprite.

"Thank you, sweetie." She nibbles on the corner of a cracker. Says, "The Kimballs' Chihuahua? The little hairless one, the one they treat like a baby?"

"Yeah?"

"It was eaten last night. Well, last evening, right before dark. Something came up out of the water and dragged it in. It had been barking at the edge of the lake for a little while, and something came up and pulled it into the water. Dragged it under and that was that."

"They didn't find it afterward?"

"Oh no, sweetie. It was gone. And Pearl Kimball was distraught. She kept yelling, 'My Emily! Oh my Emily!' A few of the neighbors sat with her last night, and I had Grandpa take her a note from me saying that I was sorry."

I pat Grandma's arm. This is what I wanted from the caimans, this moment right here, but I can't enjoy it since I keep thinking about Creature, thinking about him sedated, with a tube going down his throat. I say, "Creature had surgery last night."

"Malik? He had what?"

"He got stabbed in a basketball game."

Grandma points at me with her finger and narrows her

eyes, and for a moment I can picture what she was like when she was younger. She says, "Were you playing in this game?"

"No, Grandma, I still can't play."

"Just what do you mean 'he got stabbed'? Does that normally happen in basketball games?"

"No. Never. But this guy tried to kill him. This guy was some kind of gang member or something."

"Oh my goodness." Grandma holds her hand to her mouth. "How is he? Is he okay now?"

"He had surgery and they repaired everything. They said it went well."

Grandma taps her book against her teeth. "Oh, his poor mother."

"I know."

"She must be falling apart." Grandma takes a sip of Sprite and settles her head on her pillow. She closes her eyes.

I say, "Go to sleep now," and touch her forehead. Then I walk out to the living room and see her pill bottle. Open it. Grab a few pills. Count them in my hand: six. I shake my head. Tell myself I don't want them. But I put five in my pocket and one in my mouth.

THESE TIMES ARE EASY

NATALIE COMES TO THE FRONT door. I can't tell if the house smells like bleach or vomit. I say, "Let's go outside. Let's go sit down by the lake."

We sit in the cut-grass. It's thigh height and seeding now.

I tell her about Creature. The stabbing. The surgery.

She says, "I'm really sorry."

I rub my eyes. I'm so tired, and the Percocet makes me feel oddly numb, like I've stuck a syringe into the front of my brain.

Natalie opens her hands and lets the grass stems brush her palms. She says, "I told her to leave him today."

"Your mom?"

Natalie nods.

"How'd that go?"

"They'd just had sex, so she called me a stupid little bitch."

"Just had sex? How'd you know?"

Natalie picks the seed stem off the end of a grass stalk. Separates the seeds with her fingernails. "They were having sex in the kitchen when I came home from my workout. Right there against the counter, and I felt like maybe they should've known that I was coming home too."

I pick up a handful of rocks, round and gray, roll them around in my hands, try to blink myself all the way awake, all the way conscious. I have this feeling like I'm writing a list of everything bad on a piece of notebook paper in my lap. Things keep coming up and I keep adding them to the list, but it's only one sheet of paper and the pen keeps breaking through the paper as I write, and I'm running out of room too.

Natalie says, "Are you okay?"

I look at her. "Do you ever think this is too much?"

"What is?"

"Everything," I say.

Natalie picks up a large rock, six inches across and covered in little holes. She says, "This is the part where you laugh. You just have to. When things are so shitty that there's nothing you can do, there's no other way to react."

She throws her rock up in the air, not out but up, and it barely catches the edge of the water past our feet. Makes a loud clunk as it hits rock and water at the same time. A little bit of water splashes onto our feet.

Natalie giggles, then shakes her head. "Has it ever been easy for you?"

"Once," I say. "For a little while. I guess not easy, but simple."

"Here with your grandparents?"

"No, in juvie. And in the wilderness program."

"In juvie? Really? That was better?"

"Not better. 'Better' isn't the right word. It was just simple, if that makes any sense."

Natalie throws another rock and it plunks. "But you have basketball now, right?"

"Yeah, basketball's good."

"When you're not hurt."

"Right," I say, "when I'm not hurt."

Natalie taps me with her elbow. "And that other thing?"

"What other thing?"

"Well," she says, and looks at me so serious that the scar on her face twitches. "Let's be honest. I'm pretty fuckin' great."

I laugh. "Yeah," I say, "you're pretty great."

But when I look back out at the water, I think about my grandma, think about her being stuck in bed. About cancer. About her not having much time left. Then I think about Creature again, in the ICU, wonder if he's ever going to fully recover, if he'll ever play basketball like he did before.

Natalie says, "I want things to be good, you know?"

"With us?"

"No, in general. But they never are." She puts her head on my shoulder. "Travis, tell me something. Tell me something that I don't know about you."

My face feels hot when she says that. I say, "Something you don't know?"

"Something you don't tell people. Or something you don't usually tell people."

"Well," I say, "my mom . . ." But I don't know where to go with that, don't know what to tell next. Talking about my mom feels like a big thing, like when you see a stick in the river and you pull on it and realize that it's not just a stick but a small branch poking out of the water and there's a whole tree underneath the surface, that a whole tree's stuck down there, one so huge you'll never be able to pull it up.

Natalie says, "What about your mom?"

"Well, she's . . ." But I hesitate again.

Natalie waits. She picks up a quarter-size rock and holds it in front of one eye like she's trying to inspect the date on a coin. She turns it one way, then the other. Lifts it up above her head and flips it out into the water, making a *plunk*.

"Something you don't know . . . ," I say, "is that my mom shoots heroin."

"Oh shit," Natalie says. "I didn't think you were going to say that. I'm sorry." She looks at me, then puts her head back on my shoulder. "I'm really sorry."

"And she's homeless too. She lives down by the river. Sometimes under the bridge. Sometimes other places."

"Wow," Natalie says. "That's really sad."

"Yeah, well, I'm sort of used to it now. It's been like that for a long time. A real long time. I wish it wasn't, but . . ."

Natalie says, "Nobody should have to get used to that."

"I know."

Natalie reaches and breaks a stem of grass. "Is that why you were so weird about the feed-the-homeless event the other day?"

"Yeah, I guess."

"Sorry. I didn't get that. I just thought you were being a dick for some reason."

"Yeah," I say, "I should've told you."

"Or maybe a good girlfriend can tell when something's wrong. You know?"

"So you're my girlfriend now?"

"I think so." She looks up at me. "Am I?"

"I'd be okay with that." I lean down and kiss her.

"You'd be okay with that? Fuck you." She kisses me. "You'd

be ecstatic. You'd be enraptured. You'd die of happiness, all right?"

"All right."

We kiss, sitting like that. Not like we've ever kissed before. Slower.

The water's warm in front of us. There's a gust of wind and the smell of algae and rot comes over us. Natalie giggles. "That smells amazing."

We both sit there and stare at the lake, smell the foul odor. School pops into my head. It's only a few weeks away now. I say, "It's gonna be different in the fall, you know? I hate Taft."

"Well, maybe this year'll be better. Maybe a full season of basketball will distance you a little from last year."

"Maybe," I say. "I hope so."

"And I'm not going anywhere." Natalie leans her head on my shoulder again. "I'm staying right here."

VISITING

CREATURE'S MOM LEFT A MESSAGE on my grandparents' machine saying that Creature is out of the ICU, that he's awake now and can have visitors. I ride the bus to RiverBend.

When I get to Creature's room, the door is propped open. Coach is next to the bed, talking to Creature, and three of our teammates stand at the foot of the bed. All three of them are bigs on the team, two power forwards and the starting center, and they make the room feel too small.

I talk quietly. "What's up, guys?"

One of the bigs, our center, whispers, "Hey, PG. How's your summer been?"

"Good," I say, "good," since we're not close friends. I don't want to explain anything. Then I point at Creature and shake my head.

One of the forwards whispers, "I know. Crazy, huh? Were you there?"

"Yeah," I say. "It was one of the weirdest things I've ever seen."

"No doubt. And it was in the middle of the game, huh?"

"Yeah."

Creature says, "Wait, what's this voice I hear?" He tilts his head so he can see me between two of the bigs. "T, baby. Come over here." His voice is dry and weak, like he's been eating sheets of sandpaper.

I step up next to his bed, opposite Coach. Say, "How you feeling, Creat?"

"Not too bad, considering."

It's good to see that tube out of his mouth.

Coach says, "Listen here, Creature. You take care of yourself. You hear me?"

"Yes, sir."

"You've got a big season coming. It's important. And you'll be strong by then. So rest up as much as you can right now. Now's the time to get healthy and strong, okay?"

"Yes, sir. I will."

Coach grips Creature's forearm and gives it a little squeeze. "Okay, I'll let you two talk now, but then you go back to sleep, all right?" He pats Creature on the shoulder.

"Okay," Creature says.

Coach points at me. "And we need to have another meeting sometime soon, got it?"

"Yes, sir. Got it."

Coach goes to the door. The bigs follow him. One of the bigs says, "Recover quick so we can pound on you in the paint, right?"

Creature says, "Can't pound on something this fast."

The big flips Creature off as they all leave the room.

After they're gone, I sit down in the plastic chair next to his bed. Say, "Creat, I'm sorry this happened to you."

"Don't worry about me. I'm all right."

I shake my head. Look above me at the syringe and needle box on the wall with the red BIOHAZARD sign. "The police are on it. They talked to all of us. Got descriptions, and said they'd be in contact with the Portland police too."

Creature shakes his head. "They won't find him, T."

"You don't think so?"

"As the great poet Chris Rock once said: 'If you wanna get away with murder, shoot somebody in the head and put a demo tape in their pocket.'" Creature smiles at the old joke.

I say, "So you're a rapper now?"

"No, baby. But to cops, black people are black people."

"Never know," I say. "They might find him."

Creature adjusts himself. Looks uncomfortable. "How are your ribs, T?"

"A little better. Still sore, but better."

I point at his stomach. "How does that feel?"

He pulls the gown back, reveals the line of staples, a small clear tube draining something from the bottom of the incision. "It's not the most pleasant thing I've ever felt in my entire life."

We both laugh, but Creature stops short, puts his hand to his bandage and breathes deep. Closes his eyes.

I say, "Hospital rooms make me nervous." I stand up and walk to the table. Pick up the TV card. "They've got ESPN2 here, and it's Summer League week. I saw an ad when I was watching baseball with my grandpa."

"Baseball?" Creature turns his head and pretends to spit on the floor.

"Exactly." I pick up the remote.

"Is basketball on?"

"Games all day. We could see if they're still running." I click the power button, flip to ESPN2, and find a game. "Who is this? Let's see . . . Cleveland and Orlando. At least we can see Kyrie Irving."

Creature says, "The metronome of his left-hand dribbling, the quick beat of his crossover."

The game's at the start of the second half and we sit and watch. Don't talk. A nurse wearing a panda shirt comes in once to check on Creature and do something with his IV, but she doesn't kick me out. Kyrie goes for 23 and 8 before they pull him halfway through the fourth.

Creature says, "He looks good. Controlling the game, and he's a serial killer in the pick-and-roll."

"Tough to guard."

The nurse comes in again. "I'm sorry," she says. "I wanted to let you two watch until the end, but it's time for rest now. Malik, you've had visitors for more than two hours."

"Yes, ma'am."

She says, "I'm going to give you some pain medication now and it'll help you go right to sleep."

Creature smiles at her.

I stand up and get out of the nurse's way. "Take care of yourself. Okay, Creat?"

"Back at you, baby." He lifts his fist off the bedsheet and I lean forward to tap it.

CROCODILE HUNTING

NATALIE AND I PADDLE OUT into the dark. We both have head-lamps, but we keep them turned off.

"You think you know where?"

She points. "I'm pretty sure."

I paddle us in that direction, paddle slowly because my ribs are still sore.

Natalie sees me wince as I follow through on a stroke. "Here," she says. "Give that to me. Let me paddle."

From the bow, she has to paddle back and forth more. She strokes right side, then left. Left again. Then right again. But she keeps us straight. She says, "I noticed this the other day. I was looking for frogs, and I saw the buildup. Look past there." She points with the paddle.

I can't see anything in the dark.

"Use your headlamp," she says.

I flick it on. Shine it across the water. See two eyes on the surface.

"See?"

"Yeah, I think you're right."

As we come closer, the eyes slide under the water, disappear into the black.

Natalie says, "Creepy, huh?"

"Yeah, it'd be scary if we tipped."

"Don't say that," she says, and giggles. "Don't even think that."

I say, "Where's the other one?"

"I don't know. But let's paddle up to that nest."

"You want to paddle up to it?"

"We're in a boat, right?" She guides us to the buildup. It looks like the start of a beaver dam. Less woven and not as thick, but a rounded area with leaves and long grasses, sticks on the edges. "You think they'll have babies?"

I say, "It's too cold here. Or at least I think so."

"Too cold to mate or too cold to live through the winter?"

"Both, maybe. I think. But I don't know."

Neither of the caimans is in the nest. Natalie pokes at it with the end of the paddle and nothing moves. Nothing reacts. "So they'll just die?"

"I don't know. From what I read about them, these caimans are five or six years old, as tough as they're going to be. They're at the right age to have a chance."

"But they're from the tropics, right?"

"Central and South America."

"So come winter, they're dead?"

"I guess we'll see. Everything's got to work for survival. Everything's gotta try."

Natalie paddles us in a circle. Looks out across the water

where I'm shining my headlamp. We don't see any eyes now. Natalie says, "It'll be sad if they die."

"Yeah, I'd feel bad about that."

Natalie turns the boat and starts paddling back across the lake. "Do you want to call Animal Control?"

"No. I've thought about it."

"And you don't think that's best?"

"No."

She paddles a few strokes. The boat carves right and she straightens it out. "Why not?"

"Because I'd rather die in the wild. If I was them, I'd rather not be in a cement pen, even if I got fed regularly."

"So not a wildlife preserve?"

"You mean a zoo?"

Natalie stops paddling for a second. "I guess that's a pretty shitty life, huh?"

"That's the worst."

Natalie paddles again and I turn my headlamp off. Watch the outline of her as she guides the boat across the lake. When we're near the shore, the bank below my tent, she backstrokes and ships the paddle. Steps out and catches the bow. "So you're just gonna let whatever happens happen?"

"That's my plan." I hop out. We pull the boat up on the round rocks together.

"Well," she says, "the neighborhood pets will throw a huge party if those caimans don't make it through the winter. There'll be balloons, drinks, housecats playing spin the bottle, dogs making YouTube videos of themselves shooting off fireworks."

"Yeah, they might be kinda happy about that."

We pull the canoe the rest of the way up the bank, tip it over in the grass. Natalie leans the paddle against the hull. "I have to get home now." She kisses me. Turns and walks a few steps down the path. "Thank you for telling me, Travis. You're insane, but I like that. You put small crocodiles in a city lake?" She shakes her head. "You're a wild card."

NEEDING THE JUICE

GRANDPA'S WATCHING BASEBALL AND I walk past him. Go to Grandma's room to check on her. There's a lamp on next to her, but she's not reading or watching TV. She's staring at the wall.

"Grandma?"

She turns as if she's looking away from a movie screen. She looks at me. Blinks. "Oh hi, sweetie."

"Are you okay?"

Her hands are shaky. Lips quivering, her mouth looks like she's trying to chew something small. She says, "I had to take pain pills."

"You did?"

"Yes," she says. "We should talk."

I'm holding on to the doorjamb. "Can we go out in the canoe and talk there? I can show you something cool out there in the dark."

"No. I'm not strong enough."

"Are you sure? You could just sit in there and I'd paddle. You wouldn't be cold. I'd put a blanket around you."

"No, sweetie. I really can't."

I'm gripping the doorjamb tight, my thumbs and fingers clenching the painted wood. "Do you want to at least go out on the porch together?"

Grandma moves her hands in circles on her bedsheet like she's feeling for sand particles.

"Please?" I say.

Her hands are still shaking a little. She looks up. "Okay."

I support her as we walk through the house. Grandpa doesn't say anything as we pass him. We step out on the porch and I help her sit down in a deck chair. Then I drape a blanket over her lap. I sit down in the chair next to hers.

Grandma sighs. "You know, Travis, I told you that I'm going to die soon. Do you understand that?"

It feels like my mouth is full of dryer lint.

She says, "I just want you to be ready, you know?"

We stare out at the dark. The porch light behind us obscures everything beyond. It's like looking into the mouth of a cave, the illuminated edges, nothing in the middle, black in the middle of that deep.

Grandma says, "I want you to know that you're going to do great things."

I don't know what to say to that.

The picnic table is between us. We're sitting on either side of it, and Grandpa's new pipe is in the center of the table next to Grandma's bottle of prescription marijuana nuggets.

Grandma says, "It's not just that you're talented at things like basketball. You also know how to work hard. And that's rare. You need to go to college and find something that you love."

"Okay, Grandma."

"I mean that. It's important. If you don't go somewhere and do something, you'll get stuck. And you're too good for that. You're too kindhearted."

I can't look her in the eyes when she says that. I think about so many bad things I've done.

She says, "Do you hear me?"

"Yes, Grandma."

"Good," she says, "but you also have to watch out. There's a lot that can trip you up. There are a lot of decisions that you might make, and those decisions could get you off track. Do you know what I mean?"

I nod. "I think so."

"Like these, for example." She taps the top of the orange pill bottle that sits in between us. "What goes in these"—she shakes her head—"is never good."

I keep nodding. The lake is out in front of us, a hidden black space in the bright yellow of the porch light's wash.

"Don't get caught up, okay, Travis?"

"Okay."

"You hear me?" she says.

"Yes. I hear you."

"Good," Grandma says. "Now I'm a little tired. Can we go in?"

I stand and step over to her chair. Say, "I'll help you up." She's not heavy, but my ribs are sore. I suck in breath so I don't groan as I support her. I don't want her to feel bad about anything. "Here, Grandma," I say. "Let me get you to bed now."

NO HYPNOTISM HERE

I'M IN THE CHEVRON JACKSON, with too many things to choose from: Mack's earplugs, Cheddar Bugles, Arizona iced tea, Planters smoked almonds, Chevron brand sunglasses, Double-mint gum, trucker hats that read BEER PONG.

I've got my hoodie. Anything will fit in its loose front pocket or underneath, up against my stomach, tucked into my waistband so it won't fall out as I bail.

But I don't choose anything. Everything swirls around me, seems to hover in the air, mixes, and there's no difference between Cool Ranch Doritos and Children's Chewable Tylenol. Choices, possibilities, splits from the location where I stand.

WHERE'S JOHN STARKS NOW?

CREATURE'S MOM CALLS AND TELLS me that he's been released from the hospital, that he's home now. I go over to his house. He's sitting up in bed—his bare mattress on the floor—reading *ESPN The Magazine.*

I say, "Anything good in there?"

"Some stat comparisons and analysis."

I look over his shoulder. "LeBron vs. Jordan? They're not too imaginative, are they?"

"No, baby. Here's what I want: Durant vs. Dr. J in his prime. Can you imagine that one-on-one? I want a YouTube video of that."

I kick a sweatshirt out of my way. Move a stack of books that's next to Creat's mattress. Sit down on the floor. Lean back against the wall. "How are you?"

"Pretty good."

"Yeah? What've you been up to today?"

"Reading," Creature says. "I finished *The Brief Wondrous*

Life of Oscar Wao this morning. For some reason, I'd never finished that book."

"Is that a good one?"

"It won the Pulitzer Prize," he says. "Díaz is a linguistic genius."

I smile. "Basketball and books, huh?"

"All that's worth anything in this world, baby." Creature flips the page and there's the classic picture of Jordan dunking from the free-throw line. And an inset picture of LeBron dunking in traffic against the Knicks. I think about that John Starks dunk against Jordan's Bulls. They don't have a picture of that one.

Creature points to the laptop that's next to him. "Been writing too."

"More Russian princesses?"

"You know it. Wanna read what I wrote today?"

"Is it as messed up as every other one you've written?"

"Perfectly messed up." Creature winks at me. "And she's got a super hot name too. Wait 'til you hear this." He reaches for the laptop and makes an uncomfortable groaning sound. I stand up to help him, but he says, "Sit back down, baby. What do you think, I'm dying?" He opens it and I wait while he retrieves the file. "Okay," he says. "Here. I'll print. Then you can take it with you." He clicks his mouse and his printer starts up on the table next to the bed. When the pages are finished, he takes and folds them into quarters. Hands the pages to me.

I put them in my pocket. Roll my neck and stretch my shoulders, right then left. "So what's the plan here, Creat? When will you be healed up?"

"It'll be a while," he says. "The staples are out, but I have internal stitches that are fragile, or at least that's what they say. They want me to do nothing for a while, to be careful."

"How long?"

"At least a month. Then I'll have a lot of scar tissue to work through. Rehab after that."

"I guess that makes sense. And when will you be able to play ball?"

Creature laughs. "Nobody wanted to tell me that. Can you imagine?"

I smile.

He says, "Can you play yet?"

"Not really. I'm gonna shoot today, take some shots and dribble. See how that goes."

"Well, don't hurt yourself worse. Not now."

"I know," I say. "I won't."

Creature breathes through his teeth. "Ooh, I might've let my pain medication wear off. Better take some, then crash."

"All right. I'll come back and check on you later. Do you need anything?"

"No, baby. Thanks, though. I've got a water bottle, a laptop, and Demerol tabs. What else could a man need?"

I dribble down to the school and practice on the court. No one else is there. I shoot one-handed each side and work my way out. Take Steve Nash free throws, 10 right-handed, 10 left-handed. Back and forth for five sets. But that's the extent of my shooting range. I don't shoot fades or threes. I'll wait 'til I'm stronger.

After shooting, I dribble home left-handed the whole way, trying to keep my dribble without a turnover, but I lose it five or six times. My handles are sloppy. Even so, I'm happy to be drilling again, happy to have that ball in my hand.

I come in the house, into the cool. Sit down in the big chair and read Creat's pages.

The Pervert's Guide to Russian Princesses
Princess #53 (First Draft)

Malmfred Haraldsdotter of Holmgard, oh Malmfred of Kiev, my Malmfred always. I want to call out your name in the dark, kiss your unclean mouth, your 12th-century teeth, the reek of rot as you breathe down my throat.

I'll be a wandering poet and you'll allow me to enter your castle as a visitor when the king is away at war. I'll stay the winter with you, waiting in the guests' quarters off the banquet hall, waiting for your midnight visits, the smells of snow and wet stone seeping through the walls.

You are the known consort of two kings, and now you'll consort with me. We will writhe under a blanket of bearskin, the pale white of your body, the brown of mine, and the deeper brown of the bear's winter fur, the black of his nose and paws.

Some nights you'll be in my room when I return from dinner, having snuck off while the men were drinking at the table. You know the quickest passageways through the castle, the back way to my room from your quarters, and these are the nights I love you the most, when you've removed your jeweled belt, that royal band on your head, that dress with the long sleeves like triangles, your undershirt and boots and wool socks, all in a pile next to my bed.

You lay facedown under the thick hide of the bear, your arms and legs spread like a star, your

skin bare against the tanned hides and the fur, and
I take off the dress that I've been given, the man's
dress of a royal visitor, I peel it and slide in bed
with you.

I like to swim through the fur over your body,
start at the bottom of the bed. Stop at the backs of
your knees, the creases at the tops of each of your
legs, the half-moon at the small of your back.

You whisper to me in Russian, in Danish, in Nor-
wegian, and I understand none of your words. I've
learned Italian to recite the rhymed verses, son-
nets, epics, poems that pay for my supper and lodg-
ing as I travel, but I don't quote anything, and you
stop talking. You listen to the words as I slide my
fingertips over your forearm, past your elbow, along
your bicep to your shoulder.

I'm traveling in the year that your husband re-
pudiates you, the year 1128 A.D. He leaves you for
Certain Cecilia, a girl that can't be half as interesting as Malmfred, my Uncertain Malmfred, Whis-
pering Malmfred, a woman of changing opinions, of
clothes and no clothes, of giving and withholding,
of evening and morning.

When I am a guest at dinner, I stand and recite
poetry, epic poems, long tales of war and betrayal,
love and loss, while the listeners sip from cups
of mead, eat hunks of meat speared on the ends of
their sheath knives. I look into the eyes of the men
around the table, but the words are sliding from my
brain, emptying, and my head fills with your skin,

your scent against me, your chin tilted back, the
catch in your throat like gasping for air after being held underwater, and you do not whisper anymore,
not in any language, but call out to God with your
moaning.

DO WHAT WE DO

AFTERNOON. GRANDPA'S ON THE COUCH in the living room. The TV off. No baseball. He's crying, his face in his hands and his shoulders shaking.

"Grandpa?"

He wipes his face. Looks up.

"Are you okay?"

He shakes his head. "We went to the doctor's today."

"And?"

"And it's not going to be long, Travis."

"But she's a fighter, Grandpa. They always say this, but did she die two years ago when they talked like that?"

Grandpa takes a handkerchief out of his pocket and blows his nose. Wipes it. Puts the handkerchief back in his pocket. "She won't be able to fight this one much longer. We need to get used to that idea."

"So they said she'll . . ."

"They said it's not long now. Not more than a month or two. Could be sooner."

"But they could be wrong too. It could be longer." I sort of yell that at him.

He waves his hands. "Keep your voice down. She's sleeping right now, and I don't want to wake her."

"They're probably wrong," I say. "Doctors don't know what they're talking about."

I walk through the sliding glass door, out onto the back porch and down to my tent. I stand next to it. Drink warm water from my water bottle. Stare out at the lake, the water flat under the midday heat. I reach in my tent for a T-shirt. Put the shirt on and start walking the lake path, through the blackberries, around the north end to the street cut-through. I get to Natalie's house and knock on the front door.

She opens it. "Oh shit. Travis? Are you all right?"

I shake my head. Start to cry.

"Whoa, what is it?" She hugs me. Pulls me into the house and closes the door behind me. "Come here." She leads me up the stairs, down the hall to her room. I lie on the bed and she lies down behind me, pulling me in. "It's gonna be okay," she says. She hugs me tighter, her body against me, her arm draped over me, her hand on my chest.

We don't say anything for a while. We lie there, the sunlight coming in through the big window, shining across the foot of the bed, our lower legs.

I say, "Do you think things ever work out?"

She puts her hand on my head, rubs my scalp with her fingernails. "Do you mean, Will our problems go away?"

"Maybe."

"Then no," she says. "Probably not. Am I still gonna have Will as a piece-of-shit stepfather?"

I don't say anything.

"And your grandpa," she says. "Will he stop smoking weed? Or is your grandma gonna beat cancer?"

"I just mean . . ."

"But what are we gonna do?" Her fingernails make a scraping sound against my skull. "What can we control?"

"Not much," I say.

"But enough, right? We can control some things. I've thought about it."

I lie there and let her rub my head, my scalp, her fingernails scraping. I close my eyes.

"We keep working," she says. "We keep trying. 'Cause, fuck everyone else, you know? We just do what we do."

I open my eyes. Look at her frog's aquarium. "So we keep trying hard?"

She stops rubbing my scalp. Puts her arm around me again, scooches closer, and I feel her breasts against my back, her kneecaps grooved into the backs of my knees.

"Yes," she says. "I guess that's what I'm saying. All we can do is keep trying hard."

TWO GODS TO ONE

I EAT A BOWL OF cereal over the sink. Mix a cup of Tang and drink it. See Grandma's pill bottle on the counter. Half full. No one else is home.

I open the bottle. Dump the pills out and count them. Twenty-two. Enough for someone else to lose count. I take two. Hold them. Almost pop them in my mouth, then stop myself. Think about Grandma needing them, and drop them back in the bottle. Put the cap back on. Go outside to shoot hoops in the driveway.

While I shoot, I think about that tingly feeling of a Percocet kicking in. I work on set shots and form, extending the shooting arm, but as I work, I think about that pill bottle the whole time. The electric grid of my body coming alive 30 minutes after swallowing.

Creature walks up as I'm shooting. "What's up?"

"Same as always. Working on my left now."

"Every good player on earth, baby."

"Except for left-handers."

Creature laughs. Holds his stomach. "Don't joke around. It hurts to laugh."

"Are you all right? Are you supposed to be out walking?"

"They said I could a little. Not far. Not much. And I'm not feeling so good today."

"Let's take it easy then, Creat. Let's go inside."

Grandpa's on the couch when we go in watching a *Baseball Tonight* rerun. Creature sits down in the big chair, and I go to check on Grandma.

She's leaning back against the headboard, looking thin and tired. She says, "Read me something funny, sweetie."

"What do you want to hear?"

"Anything funny. That's all I ask."

"You mean like—what's that guy, David Sedus or something?"

"Sedaris. David Sedaris."

"Yeah, him," I say. "I've seen you read those and giggle."

Grandma smiles, and I can't imagine her dying for real. Her sickness is real, I know that, I've seen it, but dying is something else. I stare off and picture her in a coffin, wonder if they'll make her face smile or if they'll put her lips straight, like in movies. I've never seen anyone in a real coffin. Never in real life.

I'm staring off.

Grandma says, "Travis?"

"Yeah?"

"I know all of them by heart, but any of them would work."

"What?"

"Any of David Sedaris's stories would work. They're all funny enough."

Then I have an idea. "Actually," I say, "I have some things that Creature's written."

"Really?" Grandma says. "Malik enjoys writing?"

"Oh yeah."

"Really?"

"To be honest, it's hard to tell if he loves basketball or writing more. That's the truth."

"Isn't that something," she says. "Then I need to hear some of his writing, don't I? I am an old English teacher, after all."

"Well, he's here right now. He's out with Grandpa. I could grab him. Tell him to read a few pages to you."

I walk out to the living room. "Hey, Creat, would you read some of your guidebook to my grandma?"

"What?" he says. Then he mouths the words "Hell no."

"No, it's fine, man. She likes funny stuff."

Creature shakes his head. "Not a good idea, baby."

"Trust me, Creat. She's like you. She'll read anything as long as it's well written."

Creature readjusts in the recliner, settles back, and props his feet up. "I would," he says, "but I don't have the pages with me. So I just can't, you know?"

"Oh, don't worry, Creat. I've got a bunch of your pages down in my tent. I'll just run and grab them."

As I open the sliding glass door, Creature yells after me, "You really shouldn't—" But I close the door before he can say anything else, go down to my tent, and retrieve his guidebook. When I bring the pages back inside, Creature says, "Come on, baby. Really?"

"Trust me." I hand him the pages. "She'll like them. Go read to her."

"I guess. . . . It's your grandma." Creature lowers the footrest. Sits forward and stands up. Walks down the hall. Goes in her room, and I hear him say, "Hello, Mrs. Radcliffe."

"Well, hello, Malik. I hear that you've been writing."

"Yes, ma'am."

"That's excellent. Now close that door and read to me a little bit."

"Uh . . . yes, ma'am. But I have to warn you: this is some weird stuff." He closes the door and I go to the kitchen to make food.

MR. TYLER'S PORCH

CREATURE AND I START WALKING to his house.

I say, "How was it, Mr. Author?"

"Super awkward, baby."

"But did she like them?"

"Yeah," he says, "she did. It felt weird to read those pages to her, but then she told me to never change what I write for someone else. She said all of the greatest writers stick to their visions."

"See, Creat? She knows stuff from being an English teacher."

"Yeah, we talked about writing for a while, and she gave me some good ideas too."

"Nice."

"And she said I had to read *Delta of Venus* by Anaïs Nin."

"What's that?"

"Erotica, I guess. Something like old-timey *Fifty Shades of Grey*?" Creature holds his stomach and slows down.

"Are you all right?"

"Not feeling good today. It's hurting."

"We better get you home, then. Come on, man."

It's twilight as we walk down the street past Mr. Tyler's front porch.

"Should we?" Creature says.

"No," I whisper, trying to keep quiet. "We shouldn't."

"Come on, baby. Just a quick piss?"

"Another day," I say. "You better get home and rest. You don't look good."

But Creature's already sneaking up the front walk, looking left and right, his head ducked low. He steps up on the porch, and I follow him. I say, "Let's go. Come on."

"No," Creature says, "I'm pissing. Right here. Right now."

Creature puts up one finger, then two, then three, then pulls down his shorts and I turn my back and pull down my shorts too, start going on the rocking chair again. I make an S pattern back and forth all over that chair, smiling and pissing, 'cause it's always funny to me. I have to press my lips together so I don't laugh out loud, but still I'm shaking with laughter as I finish pissing.

I'm still shaking the drips off when the door opens. It's so fast that I don't even recognize what I'm seeing at first. But Mr. Tyler is there in that open door. He's holding a shotgun, and he says, "Hands up, you little pieces of shit."

Creature yells, "Run, baby!" and jumps off the top step.

I jump off after him, roll in the grass, wait for the sound of the shotgun blast in my ears, but it doesn't come. I hop up and follow Creature as he hurdles the hedge, cuts at the next driveway, and runs down the street. We sprint for a block before we slow up.

Creature stops in front of me. Stumbles against the side of a truck. Holds his stomach. "Oh fuck," he says. He has both of his hands there, down low.

"Creat, are you all right?"

"It hurts." He's leaning against the side of the truck.

We're not too far from his house and I say, "We've gotta get you home. Get some ice on that."

Creature's gritting his teeth, holding his stomach, and breathing hard.

"Come on, Creat. Let's go." I get underneath his armpit to support him. He grips my shoulder with one hand, holds his stomach with the other.

When we get to his front door, Creature pulls his key out of his pocket and hands it to me. I fumble with the lock, get the key to slide in, and open the door. I flip on the hall light and help Creature down to his bedroom. Lower him onto his mattress. He lies there and I get two pillows under his head to prop him up.

"Do you have ice packs in your freezer?"

"Mhmm." Creature nods.

"I'll go grab a couple. Don't move, okay?"

I go up to the kitchen and find the packs. Wrap them in a towel. Bring them back. Creature's on his side, with the pillows under his shoulder and head. His knees are tucked up, both hands on his stomach, his face sweaty.

I feel like I'm trying to breathe through a wet cloth. "Creat?"

"Yep?"

I lean over and slide the ice packs between his hands and his stomach. Adjust them so they're flat. I say, "We shouldn't have pissed on his porch until you were healed up. I should've stopped you."

"Don't worry about it."

"I didn't think about him coming out. I never even considered that possibility."

Creature breathes through his teeth. Grips the ice packs. "My fault. I went up first." He closes his eyes and breathes shallow little breaths.

"How's that feel with the ice on it?"

"Okay."

"Do you think it will help?"

Creature holds the pack against his stomach, his eyes still closed. "I don't know."

"Do you think something bad happened in there? Something real bad?"

"I don't know."

I look at his face. His eyes are shut. His lips are peeled back and his teeth are showing. I can hear his breathing through his teeth. I touch his forehead and feel how wet it is, the sweat running. I say, "Do we need to go to the hospital?"

"No." He keeps his eyes shut. "I'll be okay."

"I don't know, Creat. Maybe we should just go to the hospital. Have someone look at you."

"No," he says. "I'm fine."

There's a chair next to his bed with two stacks of books on it. I move the books to the floor. Sit down. Lean forward and bite my fingernails. Feel the room turning like it's on an axle. Watch Creature's face.

He stays in that hunched-up position. Keeps his eyes closed. Doesn't say anything, just breathes.

"Man, you gotta talk to me. Is it getting any better with the ice on it?"

"No."

"So the ice isn't making it any better?"

"No."

I stand up. "We're going to the hospital. We've got to."

"Okay," Creature says. He's holding the ice with both hands. He's on his side, his knees tucked up.

"Creat, where's your mom?"

"Uh . . ." He breathes in and out. "What day is it?"

"Thursday."

"Uh . . . ," he says. "Bingo."

"That's down at the center, right? Does she walk to it or drive?"

"Drive."

"We gotta call an ambulance, then."

"No," Creature says. "An ambulance is crazy expensive. My mom won't even be able to pay the last bill."

"Okay, let me think. . . . We need to get you there quick. I guess my grandpa could do it."

Creature's sweating a lot now, drizzling like in the fourth quarter of a basketball game.

"I'll run to my grandparents' house and my grandpa can drive us. We'll be right back."

I run down the street, switching to the far side as I pass Mr. Tyler's. When I get to my house, I jump up on the porch and knock. I didn't bring my key and Grandpa keeps the door locked. I bang on the door again.

I hear my grandpa's voice inside. "Take it easy out there. Who is it?"

"It's Travis, Grandpa. Let me in quick."

He opens the door and I push in.

"Hold on," he says. "Hold on." He struggles to get out of my way.

In that small space by the door, he smells like a cloud of marijuana. "Grandpa, what the hell?"

"Whoa, Travis. Don't you cuss at me."

We're face to face, shoulders squared, his marijuana reek heavy in the air. I have an urge to punch my grandpa, to knock him down and kick him against the door. "You're high right now?"

"I don't know what you're—"

"Creature's hurt. He messed up something in his stomach, and it's bad."

"His stomach?" Grandpa puts his hand out. Steadies himself against the wall.

"Yeah, where he had surgery. Like something's torn up inside."

"Hmm . . ." Grandpa nods. Too slow. He smoked too much.

"Grandpa, we need to hurry."

"What?"

"We need to get him to the hospital. Can you drive? How much did you smoke?"

"Okay, okay, okay," Grandpa says. "Okay." He tries to turn around but he walks into the hall table, knocking a vase off and it shatters on the floor, the water splashing our shins. Grandpa looks down at the vase like it's an animal he never knew existed. He says, "Oh my."

"Grandpa . . ." I push past him. Go into the kitchen.

He follows me. "I'm not high, if you think—"

"I'm taking the car. I'm taking Creat to the hospital right now."

Grandpa waves his hands in the air like he's shooing away mosquitos. "I can drive us."

"No. You can't."

I look next to the mail stack where Grandpa usually sets the car keys, but they aren't there. I open the cupboard and check the nail for the spare set, but it isn't hanging there either. "Where the . . . ?" I pull out one of the junk drawers and dump it on the floor. Kick through the staples, pens, business cards, balls of tinfoil, finishing nails, pennies, and rubber bands. "Where are the keys, Grandpa?"

"Travis"—Grandpa's in the kitchen doorway—"now you just listen to me."

I pull out the next junk drawer and dump that on the floor as well. Broken watchbands, staplers, mini-screwdrivers, balls of string, electrical tape, box cutters, pencils, nuts and bolts, matches, lighters, shed keys, and house keys, but no car key sets. I push past Grandpa and walk out into the living room, look on the coffee table, the end tables, and the computer table. "Where are the . . ."

I feel in the crack of the recliner, then go to the couch and flip the cushions. One set of keys is there, under the middle cushion, and I grab that set. "Thank God . . . I gotta go now."

I shove past Grandpa and get to the door. Open it and run out to the car. Get in on the driver's side, turn the key, hear the engine catch, pop the car into reverse, and back up quick. But I don't look in the rearview mirror, and I slam into a car across the street. My seat belt isn't on, and I plant my face on the steering wheel as the car rebounds back into the street.

There's blood on the wheel. I feel my face, a vertical split in my lower lip, my two teeth behind it loose. "Dammit." I look in the mirror, blood running out of the gap, dripping off my chin.

I press my shirt against it, pop the car into drive, and get over to Creature's house. His mom's car still isn't back, so I pull into the driveway, hop out, and run into the house.

Creature's where I left him. He's in the fetal position, curled around the ice packs.

"Creat," I say, "you're okay, man. You're all right. I'm taking you to the hospital now." I lean over and drip blood on him.

He says, "I'm just . . ."

"You're fine, Creat. Come on, man. I gotta get you up." I slide my arms underneath him. Feel the wet of his T-shirt. Struggle to lift him. He doesn't help me at all, and when I pull him to his feet, he screams.

"I'm so sorry, Creat." I've got my arms around him and his head's on my shoulder and I can smell the weird smell, nervous body odor or something else, and I drag his feet as I pull him out of the room, all his weight in my arms, and he mumbles something but I can't tell what he's saying anymore.

My ribs feel like they're twisting inside my back as I drag him down the hall, to the front door, and out onto the porch. "I've got you, man. I've got you."

When I get Creature to my grandpa's Buick, I hold him against the side of the car with my body and my one arm, open the passenger door with the other hand. Then I fold Creature in, his body seeming too tall to force inside that small space, but I have his weight working for me, and I let go and pop the seat back, let it recline, and I hold Creature's head and shoulders as I push him into the car. "We're okay," I say. "We're okay."

I don't go back to the porch to shut the house door. I leave it. I just hop in the car on the driver's side, put the car in reverse, back up hard, and swerve this time to avoid the car behind us. Then I put the Buick in drive and take off.

I drive fast. Talk to Creature as I drive. "We're gonna be there so soon, Creat, so soon, and you're gonna be okay, man." I speed down Green Acres to Crescent, keep driving east, gun it through the red light at Gilham, all the way to Coburg, slow and look both ways so I don't get us crushed from the side, but then I run that red light too, punch it without ever coming close to stopping. I say, "I'm getting us there, man. You're gonna be fine. You're gonna be good. We just gotta get you to the hospital, right?" On the straightaway behind Shopko, I take a quick look at Creature and see his eyes closed, his head tilted forward at an awkward angle. "Wake up, Creat. Come on, man."

I know that driving was a big mistake. I should've called an ambulance first thing, right when he got hurt. We shouldn't have gone to his house. We shouldn't have wasted time with ice. I shouldn't have hesitated at all.

I'm thinking about all of that as lights flash in my mirror and I whip my head around to see a state trooper following me down Crescent. I look at the speedometer and it says 50-something and I keep driving. Rush the wide turn. Push the gas pedal down as I come out of the turn and the Buick goes over 60 into that straight.

The cop stays with me, right behind us, and I don't stop when I get to the end of Crescent, just slow a little, then blow the stop sign turning right onto Game Farm. I say, "I'm getting us there, man. We're gonna get there so quick, and you're gonna be just fine, Creat."

My shoulders are tensed and my arms are tight. I'm over-gripping the steering wheel like I might just turn and rip it off. I take a deep breath and focus on driving fast.

Coming up to Beltline Road, the Oregon State Police head-quarters to my right, I see cars in front of me at the light, five or six deep at each lane, but no one in the huge pull-through at the AMPM, the gas pumps under the lights, so I let off the pedal and swerve left into the parking lot, pull beneath the overhang, past the attendants, and roll to the edge of Beltline.

The lights are still flashing in my rearview mirror, that trooper still behind me, but there are no cars coming on the left side of the six-lane road, so I pull out and drive down the wrong side of the road until I can get my speed up again, then I look over my shoulder and swerve right, dip into the correct lane going east, and drop the gas pedal to the floor on the big, wide straightaway, with the blue HOSPITAL signs on both sides of the road now and the Buick growling as I go over 70 miles an hour. I say, "Almost there, Creat. We're almost there, man. Just hold on."

At the last blue H sign, I let off and slow up, brake a little and turn left, whipping the car through the S-turn, around the outer lots, then gun it to the emergency room, not the parking lot for the emergency room, but the entrance doors up front.

I jump out of the car. See the state trooper pull in sideways behind me. He jumps out of his driver's door and yells some-thing at me as I run around to the other side, but I ignore him. I pop the passenger door open, get my arms in, and start trying to work Creature out of the car. But Creature's body is even heavier than before. He's passed out and so difficult to move. I'm struggling with him, and he's leaning in toward the driver's side, away from me. Then the state trooper's next to me, and he says, "Here, let me help you. Let me get in there too," and I let him wedge into the space at the front of the open door, and he gets his arms under Creature's legs and I reach under Creature's armpit and get ahold of him around his body. Creature is slumped sideways still, but we've got him now and the trooper says, "One, two, three," and we lift, and together we pull him out of the car, turn, and carry him into the hospital.

As soon as we're through the entrance doors, I yell, "Help us! We need help right now!"

The state trooper yells, "We need a doctor!"

A nurse runs up and says, "Let's get him on this gurney right here. What happened to him?"

I say, "He had surgery not too long ago, and I think something tore open."

The nurse waves her arms at the desk for someone to come quick. "Now!" she says.

We lay Creature on the gurney. I say, "You're gonna be okay, Creat. It's gonna be okay, man. We're at the hospital now."

A nurse and an orderly are pushing the gurney down the hall, and the state trooper and I are jogging alongside it. Creature's unconscious and his head looks too loose, his mouth open, his teeth showing. We get to a set of double doors and it opens. A man in a security uniform steps out and stops us, puts a hand on each of us, my chest and the state trooper's. He says, "I'm sorry, but you two will have to wait out here."

I stand there at the double doors and it feels like right after I punched that kid in the basketball game. All three refs were walking toward me, and the kid was on the ground, and the crowd was silent, and I knew that things might never be the same.

WAITING AGAIN

I SIT WITH THE STATE trooper. He doesn't say anything for a long time, then an orderly comes up and takes him over to the front desk. They talk for a minute. The trooper comes back and says, "Can I have your keys? I need to move both of our cars."

I give them to him.

When he returns, he hands me the keys again, and sits back down next to me. He doesn't say anything.

We wait.

I bite my fingernails and worry about Creature. I bite all of my nails too short and when I'm finished with the last one, I bite the skin on my index finger, next to the nail. Work the skin on the next finger. And the next. My stomach isn't good. I feel like I've chugged a bottle of hot sauce. I stand up and walk around, then sit back down.

A nurse walks up to me. "Can I look at your lip?"

I'd forgotten about it. I look down at the blood on the front of my shirt. I look back at the nurse. Say, "No thanks."

"That might need a couple of stitches."

"I think it'll be okay." I go back to my seat and sit down.

The trooper says, "What did your friend need surgery for?"

I shake my head.

We sit and, after a while, the trooper leans forward, pats my knee, and stands up. He walks over to the nurse's station and talks to them for a minute. Then he comes back and sits down next to me. He says, "I'm really sorry about Malik."

I nod.

"What's your name?" he says.

"Travis."

"I'm Ben." He sits back down and leans his head against the wall. We wait some more.

After 30 minutes or so, a tall man in blue scrubs comes through the double doors and walks up to us. He has a paper mask that's pulled down and hanging around his neck. He wears glasses. He looks at us and says, "I'm Dr. Tiller. I'm a surgeon at this hospital, and I was in the room with Malik." He looks at the floor. He says, "I'm sorry. We did all we could."

"What?" I feel like when I have a really high fever and I can't figure out something easy. "Wait, what?"

The doctor is nodding like I asked him a yes-or-no question. He says, "We did all we could, but we couldn't save him. Malik was already gone."

"No." I stand up. I look the doctor in the eye and point at him. "That's a lie and you know it. He was alive in the car, and he's alive now."

The state trooper stands up next to me. "Travis," he says, "I'm so sorry."

"We're all sorry," the doctor says. "There was too much

internal bleeding. He was gone before we had him in the operating room. And unfortunately—"

Before he can finish, I hit him. I want to shut him up, and I do. I punch him in the face, in the left eye, and he goes down, and I step up over him and yell, "You fucking liar!" and that's when someone tackles me and I hit the floor, and I'm facedown and my arms are pulled behind my back and two people kneel on me while someone zip-ties my wrists.

WHEN YOU GONNA WAKE UP?

I'M IN A BED, IN a room with the lights off. I don't know where I am. My brain is wet steel wool. I blink and try to clear my mind. Try to open my eyes all the way, but my eyelids are weighted down and I think of fishhooks pulling the lids closed. I can't keep them open, and I start dreaming, then force my eyes open once again. Take a deep breath. Blink. The corners of the room go gray. The window. The light fixture turned off.

Drugs like syrup drizzling over my brain.

I remember one needle, one needle going into my leg at the hospital, on the floor of the emergency room's waiting area. My hands behind my back, zip-tied. My yelling and yelling. That one needle and that's it. Nothing after.

My eyes close. I'm so tired. I go back to sleep.

CORRECTIONS

IT TAKES ME A MINUTE to realize where I am. The light's on now. There's light coming in the window too. I lie there. Stare at the ceiling. Sit up. Swing my legs off the edge of the bed and put my feet on the floor. I think about standing up, but I don't feel coordinated enough to do it.

My wrists are bruised. Small cuts wrap around each one. My left elbow is sore. My ribs are sore.

A corrections officer opens my door and says, "Lunchtime."

I shuffle down the hallway, still hazy from the drugs. A kid in front of me makes a birdcall and the corrections officer to our right says, "That's enough of that."

We go to the cafeteria, everything shiny, everything stainless steel.

We stay in line. Move forward every five seconds. The kid in front of me turns around and stares at me. A corrections officer says, "Eyes forward, feet forward," and the kid turns back around.

I get my soup and sandwich, orange juice, and walk to a seat on the far side. I don't sit near anyone. I'm not hungry, but I try to eat. Take a bite and chew. Think about Creature. He and I have both been in here. Him for beating the shit out of two white kids who called him "a nigger rapper bitch."

I keep looking for Creature in the lunchroom even as I remember the hospital. I imagine Creature as the tall kid to my right, the one with the long arms, but when he turns toward me his face is all wrong and I look back at my own food.

I look for Creature in the next line, when the second detention pod comes to get its lunch. They're told to wait, and we're finishing up even though I haven't eaten much, and I look along that line for Creature, but he isn't there.

After lunch, they take us back to our rooms and close the doors so they can select who goes out to the common area in the afternoon. I remember this from before. And like before, I'm not let out into the common area.

Later, it gets dark outside. A corrections officer brings me a small paper cup with two white pills in it. Then he hands me a Dixie cup of water.

I put the pills on my tongue and swallow them with the water.

"Open your mouth," he says.

I open it.

"Now lift your tongue," he says. "Left. Okay. And right. Okay."

Fuzziness. Dreaming and awake. My mom sits on the bed next to me. Pulls up her sleeve. Shows me the track marks. I picture leeches sleeping on her arm, her brushing them off, and this is what they left behind.

VISITING HOURS

Sunday, after lunch, we're back in our rooms until 3:00 p.m. visiting hours. A corrections officer comes to my door and says, "You have visitors."

My grandma and grandpa are waiting for me at the table. I look for a third visitor and wonder if Creature will come. Then I blink and try to clear my head. I feel like a grasshopper caught by a fence lizard, feel its teeth against the sides of my skull.

Grandma hugs me and I kiss her head. She's thin. Feels brittle.

Grandpa hugs me too, and I don't think he's ever hugged me before. He says, "I'm so sorry, Travis."

"It's okay."

"No." He taps his chest with his finger. "I'm sorry."

I start to cry then and I sit down, and I can't look at either of them.

"Oh, sweetie." Grandma leans across the table and takes

my hands. Then I'm crying harder, and I put my hands over my face and duck my head, and I'm shaking and crying, and I can't stop.

Grandma says, "I love you, Travis. I really love you."

It takes a long time for me to stop crying.

Grandpa says, "We've talked to your lawyer, and you're lucky. Things look good for you. You have it pretty easy, considering that you've been in here before."

Grandma reaches into her purse and pulls out a manila file folder. Sets it on the table in front of me.

I open it. It's half an inch thick, full of typed forms and letters. I flip through the pages and stop on my mug shot from my first arrest.

Grandpa says, "You're going to have a pretrial hearing. And it looks like the charges will be dropped in exchange for what they call 'concessions.'"

"What does that mean?"

"Well, you're going to have a suspended driver's license until you're 18. That's for the hit-and-run without a driver's license. But that's not the good news. The good news is that the doctor at the hospital, the man you punched, doesn't want to press charges. He said he understands your grief."

"Oh."

Grandma leans across the table and pats my hand.

I feel like I'm going to start crying again.

Grandpa says, "You're really lucky. Everything could be a lot worse . . . legally speaking."

"So is that everything?"

"No," he says, "but the resisting-arrest portion will be paid for by your time in here. The lawyer said that adults at the Lane

County Jail get out after two days on that charge, so we're confident that your time this week will amount to enough time for that."

"Okay."

Grandma says, "You'll have counseling too, once a week for 12 weeks. The meeting with the judge is tomorrow morning, and if you accept the terms, everything will be put in place. You'll get out in two or three days."

I say, "All right."

It's hard to explain, but this all feels like it's happening to someone else. I don't know if it's the drugs they give me, or how tired I am, or everything that's happened, but I don't feel like myself right now.

The corrections officer comes over and says, "That's time."

Grandma pats my hand once more and takes the file folder. She puts it back in her purse and stands up. Then Grandpa and I stand as well.

The corrections officer is standing behind my grandparents, and they both look at him. He points to the door.

My grandma steps around the table and hugs me, her arms feeling so thin, then my grandpa hugs me again too. Grandpa says, "We'll be back to see you soon, okay? If you're not released tomorrow, we'll be back again." He smiles and puts his hands on my shoulders, and I keep myself from crying.

The corrections officer says, "It really is time now."

I watch them leave through the double doors, and I wave to my grandma when she turns and looks back.

I have a phone call later, and they come and get me from my room.

I say, "Hello?"

The person on the other end of the line clears his throat. "Travis?"

"Coach?"

"Yeah, it's me. How are you holding up?"

"I'm okay."

"I just heard about you last night, and I was worried about you."

"You don't have to worry about me, Coach. That's not your job."

"Well," he says, "anyway, I was worried."

I flick my fingertip against the wall a couple of times. Say, "I know this is pretty messed up. Will I even be able to play after all of this?"

"I hope so," Coach says. "To be honest, I don't know, though. You might be able to play this year, and I'll do everything I can to make that happen. I'll be behind you the whole way."

My throat feels thick and scratchy. I don't say anything. Coach waits for me to get my voice back. Finally, he says, "Travis?"

"Yeah?"

"I'm sorry about before, about how hard I was on you. And I'm really sorry about Creature."

I put my hand over my eyes. Take a deep breath. Try not to cry again. I tap my forehead against the wall.

Coach says, "That should never happen. You guys are good kids with rough lives. Or . . . he was a good kid, I guess. And you still are. You've got a lot going for you."

"Yeah, well . . ."

"And I'm going to help you as much as I can, you hear me?"

"Thanks, Coach."

I nod and close my eyes. Feel the cool of the wall against my forehead.

The corrections officer taps me on the shoulder, then points to the sign on the wall next to the phone. It says: THREE-MINUTE CALL LIMIT.

I say, "Sorry, Coach, but I've gotta go. There's a time limit."

"I understand," he says. "We'll talk soon, all right?"

"All right, Coach."

NO MATTER WHAT

THE WOMAN PSYCHIATRIST IS YOUNG and pretty but she doesn't smile. We sit across from each other in a room in the front of the building. She doesn't say anything for a long time. I look around the room. There's a bookshelf with lots of thick books on it, and I wonder if she's read all of them. There's a desk with a lamp. Nothing else on top of the desk. We're sitting on blue plastic chairs in front of the desk.

The psychiatrist crosses her legs. She has thin, strong legs and I wonder what sport she played in high school. She's reading a file. "Tell me about your mother."

I point at the file. "What does it say there?"

"Well, let's start with your living situation. Why don't you live with your mother?"

"She uses heroin."

The psychiatrist closes the file folder. "Have you seen her use heroin?"

"Yes."

"How many times?"

I shake my head.

"A lot?"

"Yes."

The psychiatrist cocks her head sideways. "When you were little too?"

I nod.

She picks up a yellow legal pad and writes a few notes. "And when was the last time you saw her?"

"Last summer."

"You saw her this last summer?" She makes a circular motion with her finger. "So that means roughly a year ago?"

"Yes. Once."

"And how long had it been before that?"

I count on my fingers. "I think maybe three years?"

"And how was she doing when you saw her last summer?"

I shake my head.

"I'm sorry," she says. "This is really sad. We have to collect these facts, though." She doesn't smile, but she says "sorry" like she means it.

I breathe. Look around the room. Try to think about anything other than my mom. Anything other than Creature.

I look back at the psychiatrist and she leans forward. "Now tell me about Malik."

I start to cry. I've cried more this week than in my whole life combined, and now I can't stop myself. I grit my teeth and close my eyes and drop my head. Try to breathe through my nose, the tears leaking out the corners of my eyes.

"It's okay," she says. "It's all right."

I open my eyes and wipe my face with my hands. Take a big, deep breath.

The psychiatrist stands up and walks over to her desk. Opens a drawer and gets out tissues.

I say, "Thanks."

She sits back down. Leans forward. "You've had a tough life in some significant ways, Travis. But the key here is making positive choices going forward. It's my job to determine if you understand that."

I wipe my eyes and nose with a tissue.

"So," she says, "do you understand that?"

I look around for a garbage can and the psychiatrist reaches back for the wastebasket. Holds it out to me.

"Yes," I say.

She hands me another tissue, and now she does smile at me. "I believe that. I think you do."

We sit there and don't talk for a minute. I hold the tissue in my hand because I don't really need it now. I'm not crying anymore.

The psychiatrist picks up the file again. Settles back in her chair. Says, "Is there anything that you want to pursue? Anything that you love?"

"Basketball."

"Basketball?" She flips to a different page in the file and taps something with her finger.

"Yes."

She says, "And what's your goal there?"

"To play D-1 college ball, to get a scholarship."

"And are you playing now? I mean, I know you played on the school team last year until your first assault, but do you still play now? AAU? Or on another summer team?"

I shake my head. "I've been running drills. Working on my game."

"And do you work hard?" She looks up from the file.

"What?"

"Well, most of reaching a long-term goal is doing daily practice. So, do you work hard when it's not basketball season?"

"Yes," I say. "Creature and I worked out every weekday morning this summer when we weren't hurt. 500 shots, dribbling drills, push-ups, and pull-ups."

"Creature?"

"Malik."

"Oh," she says. "I see."

I don't cry then. I don't know why. I picture Creature practicing spin moves, right to left, left to right, and I smile. And that's how it is in here, this week. I can't tell these days whether I'm gonna smile or cry at any moment. It's like I don't even know myself right now.

The psychiatrist leans toward me. "So will you continue to pursue your dream now, even without Malik?"

"Yes."

"No matter what?" she says. She closes the file and looks at me.

"Yes," I say. "No matter what."

FAMILY

I'LL GET OUT TODAY, AND there are too many thoughts in my head, like trying to hold a gallon of water in my bare hands. Someone keeps pouring and I keep trying to make a better cup out of my palms and knitted-together fingers.

The drug's haze wears off and I sit on my bunk in the afternoon and watch the angle of the sunlight slowly move across the floor.

I've spent a lot of time alone in my life and I always wonder at the strange concept of brothers and sisters, of a family that sits down and eats dinner together, of people talking in turn about what happened during their day at school and work. I wonder how many people really have that. I wonder if that exists anymore beyond TV shows and movies, if that's something we're supposed to think is real, something we're supposed to hope for.

This is what I know about brothers:

Creature is dead, and there's no way around that.

FiNDiNG

At home, I unzip the pillow and take out the jar. It's stuffed with money. I don't count it, but it's a lot. $2,000 maybe. I pull twenties out, count and lay them down by hundreds until I have exactly $1,000 on the floor. I'll pay the court-appointed fine with that. I slide the thousand in an envelope, seal it, and slip it underneath my mattress. Then I put the jar with the rest of my money in my backpack. Go to the kitchen.

I make sandwiches. Spread yellow mustard on both pieces of bread. No mayo 'cause she always hated it. Salami, turkey, and cheddar. Slice tomatoes. Add lettuce. I make three sandwiches. Cut them in half and wrap each in foil. Pull Chips Ahoy! out of the cupboard and drop a dozen in a Ziploc. Find two unopened Gatorades and put those in my pack as well.

I look along the river first. Spend an hour on the North Bank trails. Then through Alton Baker. The shelters. The lowlands. Under the two bridges, Ferry and DiFazio.

Then I pedal down to the Washington-Jefferson Bridge

319

and lock up my bike. I don't walk out onto the court because I don't want to see the bloodstain if it's still there. In my head I can see a game going, fives running shirts and skins, but it's daylight and the court's empty.

I walk south under the bridge, past the cleared pylons, no ivy, but two tables, groups of people huddled next to shopping carts. Blankets. Army tarps. Rolled sleeping bags and extra coats. A tent without a stuff sack. They're sitting on the benches, cans of Sparks and Mad Dog 20/20 on the table.

I look at each face to make sure. Then I keep walking. Walk to the sculpture at the end of the park, its iron painted red, a film of green lichen creeping from the corners.

Two men stand at the end of the highway off-ramp. A woman across from them, 60 or 70 years old. I check the west end of the park. See no one. Walk north again, back past the picnic tables to the basketball courts, then up past the construction zone for the skate park. Check underneath the forms, the first one empty, but the second one with two people in it.

I lean in to see past the line of the shadow, the overhang. Blink and open my eyes wide, and there she is, inside the dark, just like that. Her face. Her dirty hair, a little more gray in it than the last time I saw her. She's wearing a different coat. Red. Mud stains on the left arm and a hood pulled halfway up.

"Mom?"

She shifts in her sleep.

"Mom?"

Her eyes open. Lips peel back. Then her lips relax and she moves her mouth like a fish.

"How have you been, Mom?" I lean in, touch her shoulder.

"Hmm?" She exhales and her breath is like a casserole left to rot on the counter for a week.

I say, "I've been looking for you." I sit down next to her, on the line between the shadow and the sunlight.

She shifts and closes her eyes again.

"Things have been good," I say. I take a deep breath. Feel the sunlight on my face. "Actually, that's a lie. I don't know why I said that. Things have been messed up." I drum my fingers on my knees, look out at the construction site, the grass beyond, the benches under the maple trees.

My mom's asleep, and I shake her shoulder. "Wake up."

She shifts. Rubs her face on the concrete, her eyes closed. Her nose rasps against the cement's grit.

I say, "Don't do that." Put my hand under her face. "Mom?"

She doesn't wake up. I shake her again, one hand under her face and one on her shoulder. "Mom?"

She doesn't move. Doesn't shift.

In the dark behind her, there's someone else sleeping. Snoring. A deeper-voiced snore—a man, maybe. I lean in and see a bigger person, thick clothes and a wool ski hat, even in the claustrophobic heat of midday.

I slide my hand out from under my mom's face. Stand up. The daylight is bright on the concrete, August hot and no wind, and I look up at the top half of the bridge pylon above me. Someone's spray-painted YOLO 20 feet above me, in silver paint, and I wonder for a second how a kid could get up there. There aren't any ladders and there's no girder to hang from.

YOLO. I look down at my mom, asleep just inside the shadow.

I set my backpack down next to her. Unzip it. Pull out the food and the Gatorades. Then the jar of money. I hold it in my hands and look at the bills stuffed in, twenties mostly, a few tens and fives.

I put the sandwiches in a stack, all three on top of each other, and the cookies next to them. I place the Gatorades on either end, a foot from her face. Then I put the jar of money in her hands, against her stomach, reach behind her to pull a blanket over the top of her so people won't see the glint of glass and metal that she's holding.

I kneel there, my hand on her shoulder. I say, "Don't get this stolen, okay? Go rent an apartment with it. Use it to get back on your feet, all right?"

I stand back up. Turn around. Look to see if anyone's watching. But I don't see anybody. This doesn't feel good, exactly. It isn't how I planned it. I imagined a long conversation down by the river, my mom and I talking about what we're doing now, how things could have been, how things will change.

THE SERVICE

THE SERVICE IS ON A Sunday, and a lot of people come. Basketball made Creature well-known in the city, a high school cult hero cut down too early.

People get up, one after another, to tell stories, to talk about Creature, to say things they'll miss about him. An old coach. Two of his teachers. A girl he used to hang around with for a while. A man that knew his mom a long time ago. But I don't get up. I sit in my pew at the church. I sit and try to listen to what they say, see if I can clear my head that's full of water-logged computer parts.

I don't cry. I don't know how to describe what I feel. It's like my body is a wind tunnel, not just a hollow, but a moving hollow, as if two weather fronts are sitting on either side of me, and neither one of them can settle the way it wants. I don't really hear anything people have to say. I keep thinking that Creature couldn't play defense once he started trash-talking in a game. Gary Payton could trash-talk and "D-up" just fine, but not Creature. Once Creature's mouth started moving, he'd drop his hands, he wouldn't spin or run around a screen, his butt would be up, his hips out of place. It was like all of the blood that should've been in his mind and in his muscles was stuck in his swollen-up tongue.

I don't know why I keep thinking about this.

After the memorial service, a couple dozen people go up to the graveside. I know some of them: Grandpa pushing Grandma in a wheelchair, Creature's mom, Jill, and Coach. Then I see Natalie trailing behind. I didn't even know she was at the funeral service until this moment. She's walking in the back of the group, and when we get to the top, she steps up and stands behind Creature's mom. Where I'm standing, I can't really see her.

A pastor reads a passage from the Bible, then says a prayer while we all listen and close our eyes. Then we say, "Amen."

Creature's mom doesn't look like herself. She isn't wearing a tight Lycra bodysuit. I don't know why I keep thinking about these little things.

She hands each of us a peach-colored rose. "Malik loved this color, said it was a man's pink." She puts her rose on the coffin. We each place our roses on top after her, so there's a small pile of roses on that big silver casket, too big-seeming even for Creature's long body.

We stand there for a few moments in the shade of the tree behind the grave. There's a little bit of wind but it's still hot— late-summer hot—and everyone is quiet and sweating. No one knows what to say, so we stand and mostly just look at the casket. People nod to each other or keep their heads down.

Grandpa steps over next to me and squeezes my shoulder. He holds it for a minute, then lets go.

After a while, Creature's mom says, "I love you, Malik," and after that, we all say, "I love you," one by one.

Then people are hugging each other, and Creature's mom starts walking down the hill, and everyone follows her. Natalie takes my hand and pulls me off to the side. "Let's stay up here for a minute."

"Why?"

"I have a reason."

We stand next to the casket. Natalie says, "It's August 28th, and you started camping May 21st, right?"

"Yeah."

"So tonight would be 100 nights, right?"

"Yeah," I say, "but I wrecked that streak when I was arrested. Sleeping in juvie is sleeping inside."

Natalie shrugs. "What are you gonna do?"

"I've been sleeping inside since I got out, and I probably will again tonight."

"No," Natalie says. "Breaking the streak doesn't matter, but quitting does. You've got to start over. Treat 100 like 1."

"But breaking the streak matters to me."

"Travis," she says. "I've been wanting to tell you something." She touches the scar on her face. "We were biking."

"Who was biking?"

"My dad and I. We had one of those tag-alongs, a sort of trailer-bike thing behind his bike. That's what I rode."

"What are you talking about?"

"In Portland," she says, "when we lived there. When I was little. My dad turned a corner onto a one-way. He must not've seen the sign. And the truck hit him but not me. The truck was going 40 miles an hour. That's pretty much all I know. I just remember how much white there was in front of me, a huge, white truck. And then I was on the ground and I cut my face on something, we never really knew what, some sort of metal or something, and there was so much blood. Blood everywhere."

"So that's the scar on your cheek?"

"Yeah, kids used to make fun of it in grade school. And I used to punch people in the face when they said something about it. One time I knocked out a boy's two front teeth. I hit him with a metal water bottle."

"I wouldn't feel bad about that."

"No, I don't." Natalie is crying a little and she wipes a tear with the back of her wrist. "No, fuck that kid. Fuck all of those kids. Making fun of a girl with a scar on her face? I mean, he didn't even know about my dad or anything, but fuck him anyways."

"Yeah," I say, and wipe one of her tears away with my thumb.

Natalie laughs. "So I guess I hit people like you do."

"I guess so. I'm sorry about your dad, though. I'm sorry to hear that."

"It was a long time ago. It's been 11 years."

"Still, that's horrible."

"Yeah, it was messed up. I'm not gonna lie." Natalie touches her scar with her index finger, pushes on the pink.

I reach and trace my finger across that scar, feel the ridge of it, the hardened line where the L shape turns down.

Natalie says, "Things get messed up. I think about my dad sometimes, or Creature now. Or my knee injury. Or your ribs. Or you being in juvie."

I say, "I don't know how to feel about any of that."

"That's okay. Who cares? But you should camp tonight no matter what, and I'll camp with you. It'll be a different 100. I'll help you start again, or finish. Whatever."

I close my eyes. I don't want to cry again. I've cried so much in the last week, and suddenly I feel like I could start again.

Natalie says, "We'll do it together." She puts her arms around me. Kisses the side of my face.

I open my eyes and stare over her shoulder at the big silver casket. The loose roses we put on top, the petals quivering in the wind.

Natalie says, "And I wanted to stay up here because I have something to read."

"To read?"

"It's some of Creature's pages." Natalie lets go of me and reaches into her pocket. Takes out two pages all folded up. She unfolds them. "One night I came over to your house, and your grandma read these to me. She said Creature gave them to her. I wish I'd known him better."

"Are those part of his Russian princesses book?"

"Yeah," she says. "Entry number 69."

"Oh no."

"No," she says, "they're really sweet. And your grandma loves them too. She let me borrow them to read to you today, but she wants them back."

I shake my head. Picture Grandma reading Creature's dirty love letters.

Natalie says, "Your grandma called this 'the real Creature,' right here. She said, 'in all his glory.' And you've never heard these pages, Travis. So listen."

The Pervert's Guide to Russian Princesses
Princess #69 (First Draft)

Oh, Anna Anderson, I don't care about DNA tests or the lies that came out of Prince Dimitri's mouth. You will forever be my Princess Anastasia, royal and blue-blooded in America or anywhere.

We'll grow old together. We'll have matching walkers and oxygen tanks. We'll both groan as we struggle to stand up from couches, from bus seats, from restaurant chairs pushed back. I'll stroke the sun-spotted skin of your neck with my arthritic fingers, feel the heft of the gained weight in your hips, feel your thick waist through the sequined dresses that you like to wear. We'll make slow love on our Sealy Posturepedic bed on Sunday afternoons, in your house in Los Angeles, the cricks in our bodies ticking in time with the titanium ball joint of my replaced hip.

You'll beg me to rub your sagging breasts and my hands will shake as I try to undo your enormous bra. We'll be like teenagers again, the expanse of your chest making me light-headed, my tongue thickening.

"I'm sorry about your family's execution," I'll whisper. "I'm sorry that you had to lie still among your family's bodies, that you had to crawl and climb out of that mass grave." I won't know why I bring that up when we're together like this, naked. Something about your nakedness reminds me of that history.

You'll be angry, but I'll settle you with my fingers, my body spooning you until your shaking stops.

Then we'll start slowly again, gaining momentum, the sheets heating with the friction of our bodies.

Your dentures will fall out on your pillow as you cry, "Oh, oh, oh," your mouth open so wide, your Russian accent hidden in those cries like the accents of British rock stars bent around the runs of a lead guitar.

You'll gum your pillow as I finish, your head turned, the images of the Revolution in your mind, each family member shot and thrown in the newly dug ground. You'll speak the names of your relatives as you fall asleep next to me, the last six tsars in order, their names as your daily rosary: Paul, Alexander I, Nicholas I, Alexander II, Alexander III, and Nicholas II.

I'll say, "You are my princess, my last princess, my Anastasia. I believe in you. I believe in your story. You are my Russian girl forever, my Russian royal, my Anna, my Anai, the end of me, the end of this. You are the end of my Russian addiction."

ACKNOWLEDGMENTS

THANK YOU FIRST AND FOREMOST to Adriann Ranta, my super agent, for stopping next to your rental car on that back street in Berkeley the day that we met and telling me that I needed to write something like this. I *guess* you were right. And thank you for the countless little things that you do, too.

To Katherine Harrison, the hardest-working novel editor I've ever met. 447 pages, edited by hand. Thank you for all of the penciled-in ideas, funny little reactions, and personal anecdotes. You made novel revision fun. But more importantly, you made this book better.

Thank you to my mother, the artist Pamela Hoffmeister, for your paintings, your storytelling, your love of history, poetry, and good novels, and for so many great conversations about making art.

To my father, Charlie Hoffmeister, who still models hard work to this day. A writer might have talent, but he better have a work ethic. And you've always inspired me to get up early and finish my work. Plus, baseball games are good, too.

Love to Zeb Rear for musical inspiration and humor. On a Tuesday. At the combination Pizza Hut and Taco Bell.

Thank you to the Joshua Tree National Park Association, particularly Caryn Davidson, for selecting me as writer-in-residence and giving me both the time in the desert and the Lost Horse Ranger Station to finish the revisions of this book.

On the copyediting team, thank you to copy editor Nancy Elgin, proofreader Amy Schroeder, and executive copy editor Artie Bennett. Your precise notes—back and forth, in different-colored ink—were the calculus that this big, messy pile of a book needed.

Thank you also to my managing editor, Dawn Ryan, for keeping things on schedule and running smoothly. The behind-the-scenes people truly make books happen.

On design, thanks so much to my cover designer, Angela Carlino, and interior designer, Kenneth Crossland. The book would be a big white nothing without you two, and big white nothings aren't as cool as they sound.

To Ruth. My Tortuga. Thank you for our wonderful early-morning writing-and-reading sessions. Your poetry. I love seeing your face come around that corner.

And to Rain. My coyote trickster. Thank you for the best bread and cookies ever baked by human hands. Plus circuits. Plus sarcasm.

Finally, as always, to Jennie Pam. You know that the bridge was real. All I wanted was to impress you so that we could be together forever. Is that too much to ask? You're worth a thousand failed backflips.